UNTIL
IT
WAS
GONE

David B. Seaburn

Black Rose Writing | Texas

This is a work of fiction. Names, characters, businesses, places, events, and incidents are either the products of the author's imagination or used in a fictitious manner. Any resemblance to actual persons, living or dead, or actual events is purely coincidental.

ISBN: 978-1-68513-522-5
PUBLISHED BY BLACK ROSE WRITING
www.blackrosewriting.com

Printed in the United States of America
Suggested Retail Price (SRP) $21.95

Until It Was Gone is printed in Calluna

*As a planet-friendly publisher, Black Rose Writing does its best to eliminate unnecessary waste to reduce paper usage and energy costs, while never compromising the reading experience. As a result, the final word count vs. page count may not meet common expectations.

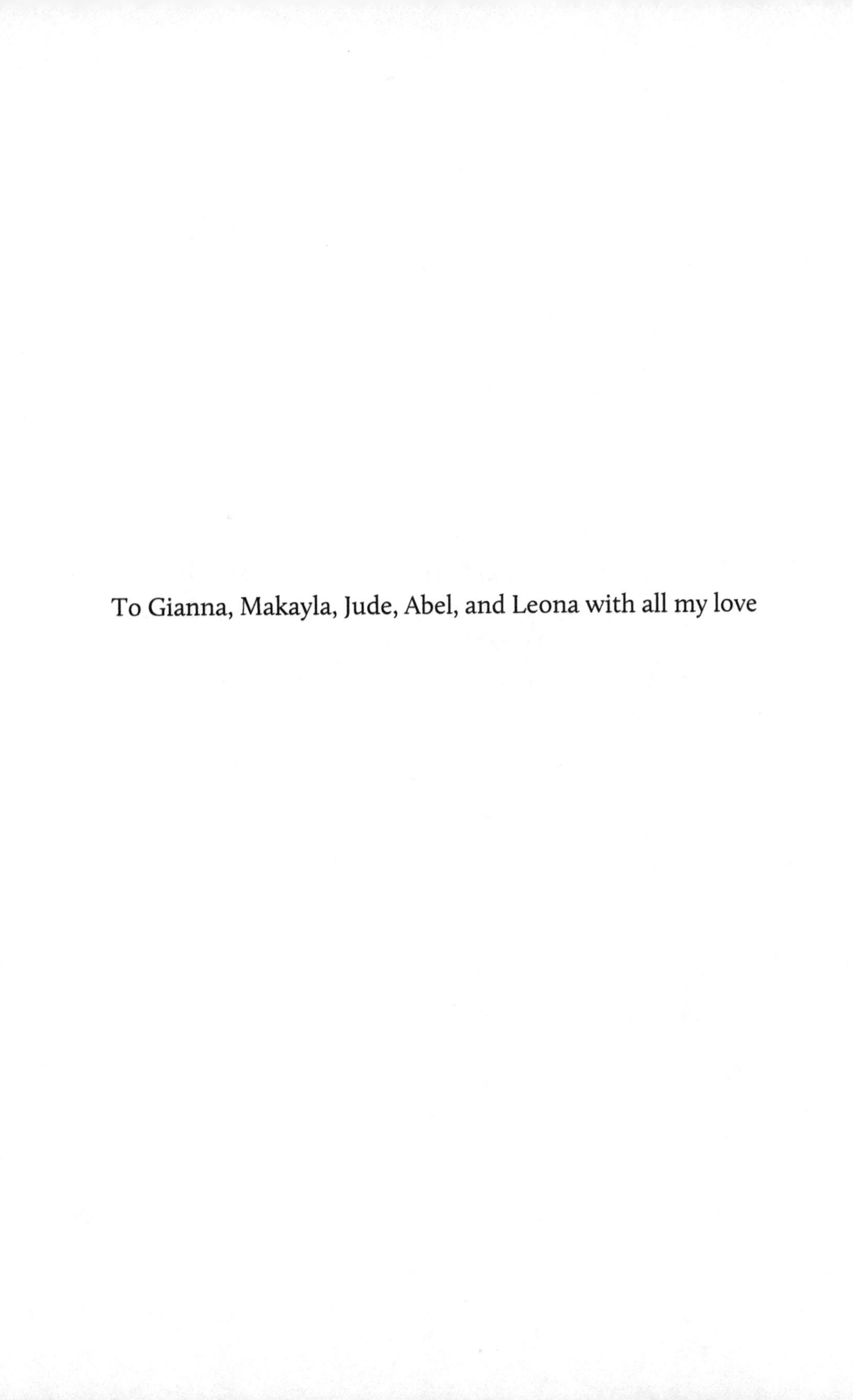

To Gianna, Makayla, Jude, Abel, and Leona with all my love

A big thank you to Reagan Rothe and the team at Black Rose
Writing for the excellent work they do. Thank you to Alan Lorenz.
More than anything,
I am grateful to my wife, Bonnie, who is my heart.

UNTIL
IT
WAS
GONE

CHAPTER 1

Franklin Stafford smiled proudly as he perused the greeting cards he and Laney had received in recent weeks. He hung them from the mahogany mantel and taped them to the hand carved spindles on the staircase. He dangled a few from the chandelier over the kitchen table, and plastered some on their bed posts. "It's not Christmas," Laney would say. "You're right, dear," he'd reply. "This is much bigger." Franklin added three more that day.

"I'm ready," called Laney as she walked briskly down the stairs. "How long will you be?"

Franklin stood in front of the full-length mirror in their dressing room. He'd settled on the grey pin-striped suit because it had always been Laney's favorite. He was sure once upon a time it fit. He frowned at his belly hanging over his waistband, like a cooled lava flow. He ran his fingers through his salt and pepper hair, trying to decide. He returned to his dressing room, removed the suit jacket, then pulled a black, silk dress shirt off a hanger and put it on. He opened his trousers, tucked the shirt in, then put the suit coat on again.

"Soon, I promise!" he called. Laney responded, but he couldn't hear what she said. "Okay, okay," he said.

He stepped back, his eyes closed, and then dared to look. Thank God for the color black, he thought, it hides so much. He sat on the stool and reached for the black wing-tips he hadn't worn in months.

He walked back and forth across the room several times, but kept clunking the tips on the floor. He took them off and tossed them back on the shelf, then put on his New Balance sneakers, black leather, the ones he used to wear to work every day, the ones that helped him keep his balance.

He heard Laney's voice again and replied "Okay!" to whatever she was saying. He looked in the mirror, then unbuttoned three buttons on his shirt, revealing a nest of graying hair. He smiled, visualizing who he once was.

He dug through his bedside table for the gold watch Laney had given him on their tenth anniversary. It had been replaced by his iPhone long ago. He found it in the back corner of the drawer behind a broken reading lamp, three used wallets, and an array of small stones. Nothing exotic; stones he'd pick up on vacations or walks in their nearby park. He would keep them on his dresser until Laney would complain— "Franklin, really?"—and then he'd toss them in their daisy garden or in the drawer.

He pulled one out, a flat stone that fit perfectly along the ridge of his pointer and thumb, making it the quintessential skipping stone. There were thousands of them on the Presque Isle beaches. He remembered the day. He found a different perfect stone, rolled his pants up, waded into the water, then leaned over and threw it flat, like a frisbee, and watched it skip one, two, three, and finally eight times. Pretty damn good, he thought. When he turned around, hoping to see an admiring smile on his wife's face, she had already headed back to their towels. How long ago was that?

He slipped the watch onto his wrist and buffed it with a tissue.

When he came downstairs, Laney was sitting on the platform rocker in the living room tapping its arm with one stiffened finger. She stood and smiled. She looked elegant in her silver duster coat which draped gracefully to her knees. Under it she wore a white V-neck tee accented with a simple silver chain. Her skinny jeans tapered perfectly to a pair of black ballet flats that had a perforated dreamcatcher design. She wore her silver-streaked hair in a short bob with feathery bangs. Franklin couldn't have been happier with his beautiful wife.

He crossed the room and hugged Laney. He leaned in to kiss her, but she turned her cheek. "Lipstick, darling." He kissed one cheek, then the other.

When Franklin pulled his cardinal red Beemer into the Grayson Inn and Restaurant parking lot, an attendant, hands clasped in front of him, pulled down his mask and smiled.

"Hello, Mr. Stafford." The attendant bowed slightly.

"How are you, Christopher?" He reached out to shake Christopher's hand, a twenty nestled in his palm.

"Thank you, sir; special night, I hear." Christopher took Franklin's car keys and then opened the door for Laney.

"The news is out, I suppose," said Laney, as she reached for Christopher's hand.

"Congratulations, both of you."

"Thank you, Chris," said Laney.

Alexander Grayson, a massive man with a striking black toupee and clunky rings on every finger, met them at the door. "Come'ere, the both of you." He took them in his arms and shook them hard. "I love you! What a night, what a night!" They stood for a moment before entering the dining room. Several tables had been removed to comply with the governor's Covid rules for spacing. He led them to their favorite corner table where a bottle of Dom Perignon and two crystal flutes awaited them.

"You shouldn't have," said Franklin.

"How many pairs of shoes have you given me over the years, Italian leather, no less?" said Alexander as he poked Franklin's belly. "This is a special night for my two favorite people in the world."

As their server seated them, Alexander struggled with the champagne, his face like a tomato about to split. After more strenuous grunting, the cork popped, and then he poured. "Enjoy!" he said, retreating to the kitchen.

"Hard to believe," said Franklin.

"What's that, darling?"

"Forty years. I mean, do we know any couple who've lasted that long?"

Laney removed her mask.

"Husbands die early."

"What?"

"Husbands tend not to make it to the fortieth anniversary."

"Okay, well...a toast."

Franklin, beaming now, raised his glass and reached across the table to clink Laney's.

"To lasting love; may the next forty years be as wonderful as the first."

They both sipped their champagne. Franklin put his glass back on the table while Laney took another sip and then another.

"When I met you, Jesus, I thought, 'Is she gorgeous, or what?' I mean, even now when you enter a room, any room, all eyes turn to you." Franklin breathed out a prideful sigh.

"Aw, that's sweet," she said, and sipped more champagne.

It was true. Franklin had just opened his second shoe store when she arrived at his office door unannounced, a little breathless, pink cheeks, arms swinging at her side. Those eyes, that hair, the only word he could think of was aura, a certain undefinable something. He closed his mouth. She stuck out her hand. "I'm Laney Marcus, Mr. Stafford, and I would like a job." She raised her chin as she said this, then laughed and patted his arm.

Laney didn't come with a resume, but she left with a job.

"We don't really need someone, do we?" said Wilson, his business manager.

"Not really."

"So, what's she going to do here?"

"I'll think of something. Maybe her job will be to fall in love with me."

"I'll see if I can work up a job description."

"I'm serious, Wilson."

"Tall order, Franklin. She's what, a generation younger than you?"

"Say what you want, but I'm going to marry that girl."

At first, they had bag lunches together in the back room. Then they graduated to the corner coffee shop for BLTs. One night when they both worked late on inventory, he suggested they have a bite at the only place in town that was still open—the Copper Kettle, an actual sit-down-and-be-waited-on restaurant. He didn't know what she thought, but in *his* book, this was an official date. When their waitress referred to them as a "couple," it was clear to Franklin that the die had been cast.

She was polite on the way home. "I just loved that place. I was starving. Thanks," she said, cocking her head. He offered to walk her to her apartment door, but she said, "No need, my roommate's home." She stuck her hand out, much as she had the day they met. He took it and held it an extra beat, the extended handshake substituting for the kiss he'd hoped for. As far as he could tell, no die had been cast in Laney's heart.

"I was thinking back to our courtship," he said.

"Oh?" Laney studied her menu as if preparing for a test.

"Did you ever feel like our courtship and marriage happened too fast?" What he wanted her to say was, 'Absolutely not!' Instead, she said:

"We went as fast as we went."

At the time, he worried their ten-month courtship was brief, maybe too brief. It wasn't until the fourth date that he kissed her and touched her. She breathed deep and pressed herself against his searching hand. A week later, her roommate was away for the weekend so she invited him to stay over. When he eventually asked her to marry him, pulling his grandmother's engagement ring from his pocket as he kneeled, she said, without hesitation or enthusiasm, "Sure."

He'd beaten the deadline. He'd promised himself to settle down before turning thirty. He had made it with a month to spare. A

Justice of the Peace officiated the ceremony, and they honeymooned in Hawaii. Then they returned to the life they'd live for the next forty years.

"I'll have the salmon, thanks."

"Eggplant parm, for me." Franklin looked up, surprise on his face. "Salmon. I don't think I've ever seen you eat salmon."

"Branching out, spreading my wings." She looked up from the plate, a bite of French bread in her mouth, then raised her eyebrows.

"Never too late, I guess," said Franklin.

"No, never." She wiped her mouth with the linen napkin, folded it, and placed it carefully beside her plate. She cleared her throat and leaned forward. "It's easy, though."

"What's easy?" Franklin raised the Champagne, Laney nodded, and he poured.

"It's easy to believe it's too late. When you've been walking up and down, back and forth on the same path for so long, you forget there might be other paths to follow. You just accept the one you're on, you know?"

"I know exactly what you mean. I'm so happy that we found a good path, the right path for our lives together. Till death do we part." Franklin raised his glass again, and downed the remainder of his bubbly. "That's how you stay married for forty years."

Laney topped off her glass and gulped the pink elixir.

"I mean forty years! Who stays married forty years?" he asked.

"The Campbells. The Campbells have been married fifty-two years. And the Arensons, forty-two years, and—"

"You know what I mean. It's rare. Couples stray, divorce, die. They lose the will to stay on the path they've created for themselves. And when they do...well (he shrugged), disaster follows." Franklin leaned forward to put another slice of eggplant in his mouth.

Laney gouged her salmon with her fork. "I think lots of people, even people who've been married forty years, I think they stay on the same path because it's a habit; it's just the thing they've always done.

They're not cruising along, they're plodding, like they've given up but don't realize it."

"Given up?" Franklin picked a roll from the basket and waved to their server for more butter.

"Yeah. Take Brad and Felicity, they're not too many years behind us. Would you believe she cooks the same meals every week? Monday, meatloaf; Tuesday, hot meatloaf sandwiches; Wednesday, pasta of some sort; Thursday, ham; Friday, chicken; Saturday, pizza takeout; Sunday, roast beef."

"What's wrong with that? Wouldn't you love to know what you're going to cook each week. It'd make grocery shopping easier. It's planful, dependable."

"They've given up. Their tastebuds, and their lives, have atrophied. What would happen if they had mac and cheese on Sunday?"

"I like mac and cheese."

Laney's face was sour as she laughed. She looked at her plate and then forked another piece of salmon.

A couple entered the restaurant without masks on. Franklin watched them, hoping Laney wouldn't notice.

"Look at these two," she whispered. Laney put her fork down, sat back, her arms folded, and glared at the couple as they walked by. "Imbeciles." Franklin wasn't convinced that "government mandated bullshit" would work, but Laney was. Out of respect for her, he wore a mask (not an N95) when she was around but never over his nose, a personal statement.

Their Covid Cold War had been like 2016 all over again. When the election results were finalized, she burst into tears and glared at Franklin, as if he was responsible for electing "that moronic liar."

"America has spoken," he had said, shrugging and trying to suppress a grin.

They didn't watch the news for four years, at least not together. Avoidance, by any other name.

Franklin dove deep into his apple pie a la mode, ice cream dripping from the corner of his mouth. Laney sipped yet another glass of champagne and shook her head at the spectacle unfolding across the table.

Franklin, crust sticking to his teeth, shifted a mouthful of pie into one bulging cheek. "My God, this is good."

"Would you like me to ask for a trough?" She sat motionless, except for her thumb and pointer gliding up and down the wine glass stem.

"You okay?"

"Couldn't be better." She smiled again, and this time it looked real to Franklin.

He finished the pie and scooped the pool of melted ice cream and bits of soggy crust left behind. "Delicious." He asked his wife if she wanted coffee and she nodded no. He waved to the server. "Coffee, black, nothing for the lady."

Laney put all her utensils and her napkin on her plate and pushed them aside. She finished her fourth glass of champagne and put the glass beside the plate, along with her half empty glass of water. She swept a few remaining crumbs onto the floor. Her palms were on the table top now, as if she was going to do some push-ups.

"Franklin, thank you so much for this lovely dinner."

"You're very—"

"And thank you for everything."

"Well—"

"I think we've done a good job."

Franklin sat up straight and put his coffee cup on the saucer.

"What good job?"

"Forty years is quite an accomplishment. I mean, it's half a lifetime. Actually, it's been two thirds of my life. By any measure, that's a long time."

"What are you saying?"

Laney was standing now, clutch in hand. Her skin wasn't as smooth as it once was, there were lines across her forehead, some extra flesh dangling from her arms, but dammit, thought Franklin, she's still a beautiful woman.

"I'm saying—enough. Forty years is enough. I think it's time we put a period at the end of this sentence."

"A period at what?"

"I'm leaving you, Franklin."

"What do you mean?"

"Just what I said. If I wasn't clear, I can say it again."

"Absolutely not." He looked at the surrounding tables to see if anyone was watching. "What's going on? Is this some kind of joke?

"Do I look like I'm joking?"

Laney didn't blink, her mouth didn't move, her nose didn't twitch.

"This is...surely we can talk about whatever is bothering you."

"You think so?"

"Come on, really. Every marriage hits some bumps in the road. We could see that therapist again, what was her name, always wore Birkenstocks, didn't like me."

"Dr. Rothman."

"We could see her again. I could be more friendly."

"You are the way you are, Franklin. And it works admirably well for you. But not for me."

Chairs at other tables were turning.

"But I can change."

"It's not about you. At least not completely. It's also about me. I need to do this for myself. Call it my Declaration of Independence. Life, liberty and, more to the point, the pursuit of happiness."

"Happiness?"

"Yes."

"Who said marriage was about happiness?"

"And here we go."

"After forty years, who thinks about happiness? You're just thankful every night that you have someone beside you, someone to pick up the yoke of life with you each morning so you can keep going. Otherwise, what's the point? You can't live a decent life all by yourself."

"Franklin, did you know that over one third of adults in this country never marry? Did you?"

"That makes total sense to me. I mean, who's kidding who? Have you ever looked at people? When I used to walk to work, every third person I saw was ugly, or unreasonably fat, or clearly stupid. Who would marry them? They don't even want to marry each other? But the rest of us should be married and stay married."

"My God."

"What? I'm being honest."

"I'm going to leave now, Franklin." Laney put on her mask, the one that said, "I Don't Want to Die Because of You."

"Is it because I'm older than you? I can tighten things up, hit the gym, you know, ten thousand steps a day, the whole deal." A confident smile curled the corners of his mouth, as if he'd stumbled onto an irresistibly tantalizing solution.

"You were ten years older than me when we married. I didn't forget that for forty years and then suddenly remember today. Age was never a problem, Franklin."

Franklin's shoulders tightened and his toes curled. What's going on? Maybe it's menopause. He knew that could make a woman episodically crazy, but Laney didn't look crazy, at all. She looked calm, focused, reasonable. She had a faint Mona Lisa smile on her face. Maybe it's another man, he thought. A younger, more viral type (Of course age was an issue! When he had leg cramps during sex and they had to stop, she'd say, "It's just an age thing, I'm sure.").

"Is there someone else?"

"What?" said Laney, her brow furrowed.

"Another guy, a younger guy."

"God, no."

This is worse than being left for another man. Laney is leaving *him*, because he is *him*. His friend Randy's wife left him. She said it was because she couldn't bear the sight of him for one more minute.

This left Randy in a terrible way. Two months later, he found out that Carol, his ex, had been sleeping with another guy for six months. The relief on his face was palpable. It's better to be left because of someone else than because of yourself.

"Then why?"

"Like I said, forty years is enough."

Franklin chewed what was left in his mouth, swallowed, cleared his throat, and coughed into his fist. He smiled at Laney, but she wasn't looking. His neck pulsed like a snare drum, as he placed a hand on his chest.

"Laney, don't you love me anymore?"

Laney had hoped she'd get away without hearing those words. She steadied her gaze and wished she felt sad.

"No, Franklin, I don't."

"Jesus, God." Franklin stared at Laney, his mouth wide. "Did you ever love me?"

"Of course, I loved you." She nestled the clutch under one arm. "Until it was gone." With that, she headed for the door.

Franklin watched her walk away, now fully aware of what was happening.

"Wait, you need a ride," he called.

"Uber," she said over her shoulder. "Remember to mask up, Franklin, it's dangerous out there." Then she walked out the door.

All eyes were on him. He said, "Show's over folks. Move it along; nothing to see here." He used the British accent that Laney never liked. Everyone laughed and turned back to their meals while Frank Sinatra sang "My Way" in the background.

Franklin slumped in his chair, balancing his coffee cup on one leg. It had been a long time, maybe twelve or thirteen years, since Laney's last departure. She had also left shortly after their twentieth wedding anniversary. And after their honeymoon. He wasn't sure the first time counted, because she was gone for only two days, and Laney was very convincing when she said, "I'm just so overwhelmed. This is a whole new life, a different one than..." They made love that night. Twice. Laney did things she'd refused to do in the past. It wasn't make-up sex, more like guilt sex, but it was good, very good.

This time felt different to Franklin. In the past, she'd leave without a word. Then she'd call from some motel saying she was okay, just needed space, and so on. Always the same script. She felt hemmed in, stifled, smothered, muffled, and her favorite descriptor, suffocated. She'd stay away for a week or so, checking in each day, but never letting him know where she was.

He stared at the muddy water in his coffee cup as a server approached.

"Would you like me to box the rest so you can eat it later?"

Franklin bristled and glared at him like he was an idiot.

"Of course, box it up."

When Franklin turned onto Oak Leaf Lane, he saw Laney getting into her Mercedes. He sped up but was too late. He waved and beeped as the car passed.

Declaration of Independence, my ass.

Once home, Franklin sat on the back patio in his favorite lounge chair listening to the high-pitched chirping of katydids and crickets, all those desperate males trying to attract a mate. Attracting them had nothing to do with keeping them, thought Franklin. He hadn't learned the right chirp for that.

He didn't worry excessively for the first five days, but when he reached seven and eight, his sleep waned, his appetite soared and even ibuprofen, taken liberally, couldn't touch his persistent, thumping headache. He called her cell multiple times a day and only got her sing-songy message: "I'm on an adventure. Don't expect me to reply. That means you, Franklin."

He texted: "Where are you?" "Why are you doing this?" "Are you safe?" "Are you staying with someone? What's his name?" "Come on, Laney, this is ridiculous!" "Okay, okay, suit yourself; two can play this game." He went two whole days without trying to reach her. That would show her. Then: "At least let me know you're alive!" "I've decided to paint the house black." "I met one of those street walker ladies, and she's moving in." "Where do you hide the plunger? Toilet emergency." "Goddammit, Goddammit, Goddammit! How could you do this!"

Soon thereafter, he gathered all the Covid masks together, piled them on the back patio, burned them, and toasted a marshmallow over the embers. *His* Declaration of Independence. No longer would they dangle from one ear like a strand of spaghetti when he tried to make a phone call. No longer would his glasses steam up in the checkout line. No longer would he have to scratch his nose every five minutes because of those fucking little fibers. He could take deep breaths. He could take deep breaths everywhere he went without a certain someone pointing at him, scolding him, shaking her head in disgust.

A week later, when he opened his eyes in the pre-dawn darkness, he could barely breathe. The quilt he had pulled up to his chin felt like a lead blanket. He struggled to move his arms. His mouth and throat were parched and sweat ran in rivulets across his shoulders and down his back. With great effort, he rolled over and slid onto the floor. But there was no use trying to stand, his legs laid lifeless in front of him.

He was exhausted and lay still for a few minutes. He woke up twelve hours later, wondering why it was so dark. Then fell asleep for twelve more.

CHAPTER 2

When Laney walked out of the Grayson House, she felt years of chainmail fall from her shoulders. She was free. She took her mask off. She stretched her neck, arched her back, took a deep breath, and let it out slowly through flared nostrils. She took her wedding ring off and put it in her purse. She looked up and down the street, waiting for her Uber. She smiled and held back laughter. She shifted her weight from one hip to the other and back again. She checked the time and answered one text: "I will be away for the foreseeable future."

It started raining; she snuck under an awning that sheltered everything except her brand-new ballet flats. She sighed as patrons, all witnesses of her declaration, filed out and nodded at her. She heard whispers as they disappeared into the parking lot. Her shoulders tensed again and the rain felt colder on her toes. She looked at her cell. The feeling of freedom had lasted five minutes.

What had she expected? When she entered the restaurant, she had no idea that she would come out alone.

The Uber arrived and she tiptoed, bag over head, to the back door. She slid across the seat, leaving room for...who?

"Oak Leaf Lane, 405, right?"

"Yes," said Laney.

It stopped raining and the driver turned off the wipers. He looked in the rear-view mirror.

"You're all dressed up. Big night?"

"I guess you could say that."

"Lemme guess."

"No need for that. It was my fortieth wedding anniversary."

"Forty? Jesus. That's up there. Me and my wife been married fifteen years and it already feels like forty, you know what I mean?"

Laney smiled at the mirror, then looked out the window.

"So, where is he?"

"My husband?"

"Yeah."

"He's…well, I can't be sure, but I think he's still at the restaurant."

The driver grimaced.

"Why's he at the restaurant and you're in my car?"

Laney tried to laugh but coughed instead. He'd asked the right question. What was the right answer?

Shadows of doubt had loitered around the edges of their relationship from the beginning. It's just cold feet, her mother said as the wedding approached. You'll be fine. But standing in front of a church full of people, making promises no one could keep, looking into the eyes of a man she was supposed to love forever, my God, really? Having cold feet wasn't an adequate explanation. But it was all she had, so she held her breath and jumped into the water, hoping they could keep each other afloat. Forever.

She liked Franklin from the very first time they met at his shoe store. He was so attentive, so kind, so warm that she immediately felt comfortable, the way one might feel comfortable with a TV game show host or news anchor. The first time he kissed her, she wasn't surprised. By then she knew he loved her; she could tell by his moony eyes and frozen smile. She had never felt like she was the center of anyone's world before, not even at home. This man, a decade older, mature, stable, successful, wanted only her. She loved how he loved her.

Laney'd had sex before with boys who acted like they were conquering her rather than making love to her. Franklin was a man, a man with experience, a man who could have had any woman he wanted, a man who worshipped her, who was so appreciative, so grateful to sleep with her. He didn't roll off and slink away. He held her, caressed her, kissed her gently, whispered things to her, things that made her feel good.

She wasn't surprised when he proposed to her. She agreed without giving it a single thought.

It wasn't until they were standing at the altar, and she looked at him with discerning eyes, that doubt entered her mind. Who was this man with a receding hairline, bags under his eyes, and a fatherly smell? Until death do us part, what exactly did that mean? Do-over, please! She looked at the smiling guests, some wiping tears from their eyes. She looked at the minister who was going on and on, love is this…love is that. She looked at the flowers and the white lanterns and the rose petals on the satin runner. This was real. When she began to cry, a soft, collective "Aww" rose from the sanctuary.

When the "I do's" were done and they kissed, she fell into his arms. They seemed strong and safe and sure. She was overcome, not with love or affection but with relief that she was married, and that she wouldn't have to think about it ever again.

Soon thereafter, she bolted, ending up at a Best Western in a neighboring town. She called him a day later. He was upset at first, but she convinced him it was her, not him; she was just overwhelmed. When she came back, her doubts and her lukewarm feelings for Franklin had receded. She was confident those feelings had retreated to a far corner of her heart. Her doubts lay dormant for years, but eventually they reawakened, demanding to be heard. Tonight, without warning, they walked onto the stage, grabbed the mic, and declared her independence.

"Yes, I'm sure he's still at the restaurant drinking coffee, maybe ordering another dessert."

The driver looked into the mirror to see if she was serious.

"Oh, and he's got the car. Mine's at home."

"I don't get it."

"What don't you get?"

"I mean, well, you been married forever, but on the most important night of your marriage, here you are and there he is."

Laney looked out the passenger window. She took a deep breath and answered.

"It *is* the most important night of my life. But not for the reason you'd think."

"Like I said, I don't get it."

"I told him we were done, I'd had enough, that after forty years it was time to call it quits, time to move on, time to figure out what I should do next."

"Ouch."

It was quiet in the car for the next few miles as the driver, Rudy, chewed on this news. He studied her through the mirror. He'd taken break-ups home before. They sobbed and wailed and their smeared makeup made them look like Alice Cooper. They cursed; they heaved; they moaned. And these were the ones who'd broken up with their boyfriends, *boyfriends*, not husbands. They'd been together maybe forty days or forty weeks. A drop in the relational bucket. But she did none of this. She didn't look the least bit upset. Her makeup and hair were perfect. No shadowy guilt on her face and no second guesses in her eyes.

"So, this is for real."

"As real as it gets."

"It's your life. You can do what you want with it." Rudy shrugged and frowned.

For a moment, Laney wanted to reach around the headrest and strangle Rudy to death. Who's he to judge? Where does he get the gall to shrug and frown, and, what was that? A sigh? Her face was burning. She pursed her lips and clenched her jaw. Why did she give a shit what this guy thought? I know exactly what I'm doing.

But a goddam still small voice whispered: "Are you sure about this? Are you sure you want to give it all up so late in the game? Maybe a trip to Europe would ease the pain? Or two weeks at that yoga center in Santa Fe? Are things so bad that a juicy affair with a younger man, say Rudy, wouldn't snap you out of it? Take a good look at Rudy. What the hell?"

"Shut up!" she said.

"What?"

"Nothing, sorry...just thinking."

She was breathing quick and shallow; her palms were sweating; she cracked the window, the breeze feeling like pure oxygen.

Laney remembered her mother on the morning of the wedding: "If he doesn't hit you; if he doesn't go out on you; if he's not a drunk; if he makes a good living; if he does all these things, count yourself lucky. You've found a keeper." At the time, Laney, still a teenager, didn't know what to say. She gave her mother a hug. She thought, That's the saddest recipe for a marriage I've ever heard. I'd never settle for that.

Frank drank socially but seldom problematically. As far as she knew, he never cheated. They were financially flush. (Once he franchised his stores, she bought two of them and no longer depended on his money.) He never hit her, but he had his moods. Some days he didn't talk. He had spells of fear so strong that he couldn't go to work. He would call the office, pretending he was on the road checking on his stores, when he was actually in bed. She would pamper him, bring him coffee and chocolate, but he would barely acknowledge her.

The following day, he might be fine and come home with a bouquet of roses. If she asked him what had been wrong, he would look at her like she was crazy.

When she confided this to her mother, she said, "That's all! Ha! Come back when you have a real problem." When Laney said her husband never listened to her, she said, "I don't remember that being in the vows."

Even though her husband met her mother's criteria for a "keeper," she couldn't escape a nagging truth—she had settled. She had wanted love and had settled for what her mother got, a man who'd never leave.

She cringed when she thought—forty years. She had unwittingly volunteered for a three-legged race with a man who could have been her uncle, a race with trips and falls and awkward lurches, a race with no point and no end.

She packed two suitcases with enough clothing and et ceteras to last two months, maybe more. She glanced around the bedroom. Franklin's work suit and shirt and tie and socks were still on the floor, like he'd vanished—Poof! How many times had she picked up his goddam clothes?

She rolled her suitcases to the stairs. Too heavy to haul, she slid the first one down and watched it crash into the wall beside the front door, leaving a crisp divot. Then she let the other one go. A wheel flew off, cracking one of the side windows. She clapped her hands once, loudly. "Okay, then."

She leveraged one, then the other suitcase into the trunk of her shimmering lavender AMG GT Mercedes coupe. She checked her purse for cash, credit cards, keys, and iPhone. As she eased down the brick driveway under rows of poplars, she wondered for the first time, Where am I going?

She stopped at the bottom of driveway and entered an Oklahoma address into her GPS. Fourteen-hundred and thirty-five miles. If she didn't stop, she could make it in twenty-one hours and thirty-five minutes. She hoped the address she had for Roz was still correct. Then she rolled down all the windows, turned Sirius on to a light jazz station and headed into the wind.

CHAPTER 3

Gretchen Hennefer rapped on the door five times, and yet her brother didn't answer. When she scrunched her face against the window pane, she could see him sitting in his lounge chair in front of the fireplace. She watched as he tried to get up. When he fell back for the third time, he gave up.

She pounded the door with both fists. She waved frantically, hoping to stir him. He stared at her for a moment, then raised his hand and waved. He tried again to get up, but couldn't.

"What the fuck." She placed one hand on the door and pushed. It had been unlocked all along. She stood in the foyer, catching her breath. The (ridiculously expensive) paintings that Franklin had hung at Laney's behest were covered with dust. The wall that Laney had gouged with her (goddam) suitcase was unrepaired. Mail was stacked on an ornate glass table under the oak and ebony spiral staircase. Everything about the house smelled lifeless.

"You told me you never leave the front door unlocked. You told me there were, what was the word, yes, 'nefarious,' nefarious people all around who would break in when you least expected it."

"I'm sorry, I'm sorry. You came at the wrong time." Franklin Stafford yawned. "This is nap o'clock."

"Jesus Christ."

"When my body wants to sleep, it sleeps."

Franklin fell limp into his leather lounge chair and snored softly.

"No, please, don't get up. Really. I can handle the luggage."

The steamer trunk was so heavy she could barely lift it with a two-fisted grip. A scowl crossed her face as she yanked and grunted, grunted and yanked, one step, then another, and another. "Shit," she said. Pain, like lightning, shot through her elbow and shoulder.

She leaned against the front door, huffing, and puffing. Her glasses slid down her nose and her upper lip felt dewy. If Griswald were here, she wouldn't be in this predicament.

Once inside the door, she let the suitcase fall with a loud clunk. Franklin's arms and legs shot up like a startled cat. "What, what?"

"You're up?"

Franklin rocked forward trying to make his footrest go down. Gretchen watched, arms folded. Finally, she kicked the footrest back into place.

"Thank you." Franklin looked like he had run a mile in a minute. He exhaled in short spirts, like he was in labor and about to drop a newborn. He puckered his lips and tried to deepen each breath until, at last, he was breathing normally, almost.

"Are you always like this?"

"No," Franklin said. "This is a good day." He started hacking again, this time folding over like a jackknife.

"Christ on a bike," she murmured. She knew he wasn't well, but she couldn't believe how much worse he was in person. "What do the doctors say?"

"New normal." Franklin was on his feet now, breathing evenly. "Sorry Gretchen, I meant to have the place in order by the time you arrived."

Gretchen scanned the living room, pillows about, newspapers under the couch, dust bunnies huddled in the corners, the kitchen sink piled high. "Well, it could be worse."

"How?" Franklin forced a smile. "I'm glad you're here. I'm glad you've come." A full foot taller than his sister, he leaned over and wrapped his spidery arms around her.

He smells like something you might find under the refrigerator, thought Gretchen. "Well, you're helping me out as much as I'm helping you. Don't know where I would have gone."

"The dynamic duo, together again," he said, his voice sad.

Franklin smiled his lopsided smile. His shaggy hair, more salt than pepper now, was an inch or more too long; his face was stubbled and creased; his shoulders, saggy; yet, she could still see a much younger brother in his sky-blue eyes, a brother who was always there for her. How odd it was to be standing together, arm in arm, now more for balance than affection.

Franklin felt a modest surge of energy and strode to the kitchen where Gretchen had cracked some hard-boiled eggs, mixed them vigorously in a bowl with mayo, and then added sweet pickle relish and chopped celery. Franklin filled two glasses with water. He added ice cubes since it was a special occasion. He talked to his sister often but seldom saw her in person. He was surprised that she had gained weight. Her neck and upper arms had a Michelin quality to them. Her eyes were sunken and tired. Her hair, always a source of pride, looked like a pile of straw.

Gretchen stacked the sandwiches with mounds of golden delicious egg salad. She snitched one lone potato chip and then put handfuls on their plates. She took the bowl of red grapes from the refrigerator and put it on the table between them.

They sat opposite each other, Franklin smiling, his palms resting in his lap.

"Welcome. Welcome to my home, Sister."

"Thank you, Brother."

They both took bites of their sandwiches, their eyes scurrying to find something neutral to stare at.

"Yummy," said Franklin, his mouth still full.

"Mom's recipe."

"I didn't know you needed a recipe for egg salad."

Another bite and a slurp of water. One chip, two chips.

Franklin reached for his glass with both hands. Gretchen stopped chewing until the water-to-mouth transfer was completed.

"Who bought the house?" said Franklin.

"The Smedlings from up the street. Now, how stupid is that, moving ten houses to live on the same old street in the same old neighborhood?"

"Huh."

"Clara told me she and Fred had 'coveted,' that's the word she used, 'coveted' our house for years. Sounded sexual to me, the way she said it, 'coveted'."

"Never thought of it that way."

"You remember them, don't you? Clara is short, hefty, pretty face. And Fred, you golfed with him. Remember?"

"Oh." Sometimes the fog rolled in just as he thought the sun was rising. And when he was surrounded by the mist, Franklin was amazed at what he would lose. The other day he couldn't find his shoes. They were on his feet.

He washed the dishes, and she dried and then stacked them in the cupboard. He handed each dish to her with both hands. He couldn't remember when he first noticed the tingling and then the numbness, which had now reached his toes. Franklin leaned against the sink and folded his arms. Gretchen wiped her hands dry and tossed the dish towel into the drainer.

"You haven't asked me the question, but I'll answer it, anyway. I don't know how long I'll be staying with you. Sorry about that. I know it's an inconvenience, but—"

"Don't be foolish. You're my sister, for chrissakes. I'm the one who should be apologizing. You didn't sign on for this mess." He shook his head apologetically. "Consider this your home."

"Well, thank you, Brother."

"You're going through just as hard a time as me."

After dinner, they played War, the only card game Franklin could manage.

"You got three Queens in a row."

"I guess so," said Franklin, as his pile of cards increased.

"And you dealt them."

"What are you saying, Sister?"

"Nothing, just wanted you to know I know."

Gretchen never liked to lose, especially to her brother. He was older and bigger; there was no way she could compete in games or sports that involved, speed, strength, or doing something with a ball. Their mother suggested cards. They played poker, bridge, hearts, gin, just about any card game you could think of. And most of the time she won. It leveled their playing field. At least a little.

After dinner, Gretchen pestered her brother into going for a walk, even though the thought of going out in the evening frightened him. Once it was dark, he seldom ventured out. The pain in his wrists and elbows spiked when the sun went down, and his head pounded. When the nightly news was over, he sat and rested before going to bed.

But Gretchen believed fresh air was always beneficial. "It'll do us good. Especially going out together."

Franklin held the railing and stepped gingerly onto the front walkway. He stopped to catch his breath. Gretchen watched, concerned with how weak he was, yet determined that she could make him feel better. She put her arm through his. "Hold me up," she said. Franklin didn't respond. He was concentrating on putting one foot in front of the other. He coughed hard and Gretchen clapped his back with her hand. "How's your headache?" she said, as they stood motionless under an elm. Franklin's eyes hurt to blink.

"Still got it."

Two boys on Schwinn's zoomed past. "Get off the goddam sidewalk!" Gretchen advised. "What are they thinking?" Franklin forced a deep breath. She looped her arm inside his again. "Keep going?" Franklin shook his head.

As they passed in front of his house, Gretchen studied its pillared front, its curlicue lattice work, its three chimneys, its massive side porch, and the brick driveway that snaked back to the three-car garage. So different from the modest house where they grew up.

Franklin walked with great care, searching for each crack in the cement, each tree root that had burst through the sidewalk, threatening to topple him. He had fallen twice at home. The first time he woke up on the bathroom floor, shower still running, a knot on his forehead. He had no idea how he got there, and it frightened him so much he pretended it hadn't happened. He remembered the second time. He had gone to Wegman's to pick up a few things. He was in a buoyant mood, stopping to talk to acquaintances, even strangers, enjoying the early fall display of pumpkins and gourds, apple cider and corn stalks. He felt alive, alive enough to stop by the old shoe store, his first and favorite one, to see how things were going. He was greeted warmly and felt remembered, even appreciated.

He listened to his favorite oldies station on the way home, rolling the window down, despite the frosty air, and singing along. When he got out of the car, he felt odd. He faltered on his first step but caught himself. It was dark and he felt like he was in the middle of a race track, everything circling round him at hyper speed, the trees, the houses, the star-studded sky. He took deep breath after deep breath and felt steady enough to walk up the back steps. He stopped and reached into his pocket for the house key.

Then everything came undone. It was like someone had snapped their fingers and his inner gyroscope had stopped. This time it wasn't the world that was spinning, it was him. He wavered, unable to maintain his footing, and hit the porch floor solidly, a jar of peanut butter from the grocery bag leaving a bloody gash on his cheek. Had he passed out? He couldn't tell.

He had asked the doctor about the symptoms of long haul Covid. The doctor had leaned back in his chair and chuckled softly. "You name it. Just about everything." He ran through a long list, fainting being nearer the bottom. But it was there. Franklin felt like he was playing *Wheel of Misfortune*, and each stop resulted in a new symptom.

Street lights, headlights, anything that glared was disorienting. He decided keeping his head down was the best strategy. He felt Gretchen tugging his arm. He looked at her.

"Hey, anyone home? Did you hear what I said?"

"I don't think so."

"I said your freaking mansion sure is different than the house we grew up in."

"Yeah, I suppose it is."

"What do you think Dad would have said about it? Having such a big deal house."

"He would have found something wrong with it. And with me for buying it."

"Hm."

"He never thought much of me..."

Franklin sniffed once and wiped his nose on his sleeve.

"The day he died was like a fresh start, a new birthday for me."

They walked a little further until they were safely under a street light. She looked at her brother. His face was blank, his mouth hung open as he sucked air.

"Are you okay?"

He didn't answer.

"Mom would have liked the house. She would have liked it plenty," said Gretchen.

"Too bad she didn't live to see it."

Gretchen side-glanced him, concern in her eyes. She thought of their childhood, and how she often felt uncomfortable, like something was going on right in front of her eyes, but she couldn't see it. Something was going on, something that wasn't right. As the family sat quietly watching television, a strange feeling would come over her, a numbness inside. "Is something wrong?" she would say to no one in particular. Her mother would look at her, puzzled. Her father would pick up the newspaper and start reading. Her brother would go upstairs to do homework. "Whatever do you mean?" her mother would say. Gretchen would answer, "I don't know." Her mother would reply, "Then there must not be anything wrong." But Gretchen's numbness would linger.

Gretchen slid her arm around Franklin. "C'mon, let's head back. It's starting to sprinkle."

"I'm so tired."

"I'll get us back fine. Then you can lie down."

Franklin looked at her, then looked down the sidewalk, hoping she was right.

CHAPTER 4

Roz Stafford stood on the roadside staring across the field of limp sorghum that stretched far beyond what her eye could see. Who said the world wasn't flat? she thought. The sky was blue in every direction, the sun already beating her back. She knelt and scooped a handful of dry red dirt, the wind blowing it away in a dusty cloud. If every farmer in the county spat on the ground at the same time, it would be a more productive rainfall than they'd had in years.

A passing semi blew her hair wild. She turned and listened to the whir of its wheels until it was a dot on the horizon.

Is that Horace or Emma? she wondered. She shielded her eyes and squinted. Her nearest neighbors, the Turners, lived three quarters of a mile down the road. When she first bought her house, it seemed like quite a distance. But over the years, it felt closer and closer. She raised her arm high and waved broadly. Horace, or maybe it was Emma, waved back. Three miles beyond the Turner's was Righteous, where Roz managed the local Save-a-Lot.

Once a haven for moonshiners and ladies of the night, Righteous, Oklahoma, dangling on the tip of the state's panhandle, had been redeeming its reputation ever since prohibition had been repealed. Brothels were replaced by wood framed churches with spires you could see for miles. There were a few bars but none of the excitement that accompanied the moonshine era. Most of the young people in town knew nothing of this history and no one dared tell them. Towns folk were reserved, friendly, private, suspicious of outsiders, and willing to do anything for you when you were in need. It took time, but Roz warmed to Righteous and, eventually, thought of it as the only home she'd ever had.

Roz looked back across the road at her humble dwelling. She hoped she would see signs of activity inside but didn't. When she got to the porch, she called to her daughter through the screen door. "Maggie, are you going to work today or not?" There was a groan but not a word.

Roz felt certain her daughter was the laziest person to have ever graced God's good earth. Been that way from the beginning. She was two weeks late. When they induced her, Maggie still wouldn't budge. Thought they'd have to send a search party in to get her out. She took forever to walk and talk. Maggie never liked school and avoided going as often as possible. She made cheerleader but wouldn't go to practice. She was whip smart but wouldn't do the work. The guidance counselor said, "Well, Maggie is Maggie; I'da thought by now you'd realize that."

"Girl! Get your ass up right now...Please!"

The only thing Roz felt for Maggie that was stronger than anger was love. She loved that girl more than life itself.

"Maggie!"

"Ma! I'm up!" Maggie was sitting on her bed, which counted as being up. "I don't have to be there for an hour."

"It's gonna take you an hour and a half to get ready."

"So, I'll be a half hour late. It doesn't matter to Sandman. He won't say a thing."

Maggie was right. Her midnight eyes, waist long auburn hair, and porcelain skin were her free pass to almost everything. Roz shook her head, dismayed. When she was nineteen, Maggie was already three. Roz had had four jobs and lost them all. Her youthful optimism was on the wane. She got a job at the Save-a-Lot and figured she could make do until she had enough money to get out of town. But she stayed and made a life. Finding the road into

Righteous had been a blessing, but she hoped Maggie's blessing would be to find the road out.

Maggie put her feet on the floor. Her face was puffy with sleep. She yawned and stretched her arms and back. Her mother came to the bedroom door, arms folded, the corner of her mouth pinched in disapproval.

"What?"

"Nothin'."

"You're looking at me like I robbed a bank or something."

"You'd never rob a bank."

"Well, thank you."

"It would take too much gumption."

"Go to hell, Ma."

The words came easily, as if she'd been saying them her whole life. Sometimes Maggie meant what she said, sometimes she didn't. Roz had stopped trying to figure out which was which.

The wind blew the screen door open and then slammed it closed again.

Maggie took a long, leisurely shower, the steam clouding the room and creeping under the door into the hall. She loved the feel of hot water on her face, sluicing down her spine. She turned around and tilted her head back, letting the water refresh her hair.

She wrapped her hair in a towel and drip dried herself on the bathroom floor. She squeegeed the mirror, her face appearing as if in a rainforest. She sighed. She pulled her mouth one way, then the other, testing the suppleness of her skin. Brushed her hair slowly with a boar-bristled brush she'd bought on a rare trip to Austin. She pinched her cheeks and rubbed her eyes, then brushed her hair again and shook it out. She admired her neck, so long and sleek. Maggie inspected a zit on her forehead, then frowned and dabbed on some Clearasil.

She stepped back from the mirror, her bottom lip sucked into her mouth. She drew air through her front teeth and examined what she saw. She was always disappointed her mother's nose, her mother's ears, and her mother's mouth were right there on *her* face. Nothing of her own. Except that hair. "I don't know where that dark ginger came from. Not my side. Must have come from the other."

Maggie headed to her room. "Dry the floor!" called her mother. She turned back to the bathroom, dropped a towel onto the floor, and, without looking, swished it back and forth with one foot, then tossed it into the wicker basket behind the door. "Done!" she called back.

Maggie opened the dresser drawer, hoping to find something new, something different. Instead, she found what was always there—well-worn hoodies and pairs of jeans, all ragged at the knees. She pulled the jeans over her rounded hips and the extra-large sweatshirt over her head. She stepped back, held a mirror out from her body and checked. She had achieved the desired degree of bagginess.

She flared her fingers and ran them through her hair, messing it exactly the way she wanted. Then she tucked her iPhone into her back pocket and stuffed a few dollars into her front.

When she took one final look in the mirror, her face was ghostly white. It had been a long night and a lot of beer. She felt light-headed and thought she might faint. She sat on the floor to catch her breath. Then leaned over the toilet and threw up.

"Maggie!"

"Yeah, yeah, I'm leaving."

As Maggie pulled away, a lavender Mercedes approached from the opposite direction.

CHAPTER 5

"Where the hell are you?" said Roz.

"I love you, too," said Laney, her voice calm.

Driving to Oklahoma had been more daunting than Laney expected. She almost fell asleep in Ohio. Who knew it was so flat, so rural, so boring. She pulled into a rest area, put her seat back and slept until the middle of the afternoon. A security guard knocked on her window. "Thought you were dead," he'd said. "Guess you're not," he had deduced.

Her mouth tasted like the inside of an old sock. She squinted into the sun. The sign said Indian Meadow Rest Stop. She stood in the parking lot watching the semis roll by. In the distance was a water tower, a herd of Holsteins, and a barn with two flags. One said "TRUMP 2024" and the other said "Let's Go Brandon." She shook her head and scowled. No one else seemed to notice. She shook her head again.

Laney pulled her N95 up over her nose. She bought wipes in the convenience store, headed to the ladies' room, and cleaned herself as best she could. She ordered a double espresso at Starbucks—Jump start yourself, she thought—and an iced coffee for later. Also, an everything bagel with double cream cheese.

Laney pulled her mask under her chin and hit the double espresso hard, downing it before she left the plaza. Soon her hands were shaking like a hummingbird's wings. Too unsteady to open the car door, she hoisted herself onto the hood and waited, her heart pounding.

Once her shakes subsided, the remaining adrenaline was intoxicating. She breezed through Indiana before she realized it wasn't Ohio. Reached St. Louis late in the evening. Found the Sunset Motel adjacent to the Arch. There was a brochure on the bed and a rattling air conditioner in the window. She sat and read—630 feet tall, ten-minute tram ride, 1076 steps, sways eighteen inches in a one hundred-fifty mile per hour wind, thirty-mile view in every direction. It was built to honor Thomas Jefferson's role in opening the west. Sally Hemmings and their kids would have been proud, thought Laney.

Finally asleep, she dreamed she was standing on top of the Arch in a one-hundred-fifty mile per hour wind storm. The Arch had swayed nineteen, then twenty inches. An alarm sounded as it started toppling into the Mississippi.

She awoke with a start. She tossed, she turned, but sleep eluded her, so she honored Jefferson's mandate and headed west.

Laney stopped at a gas station about fifty miles short of the Oklahoma line. A boy filled her tank while she dialed Roz.

"I said, where the hell are you?"

"Thought I'd come for a visit."

"Why would you do that?"

Laney called her daughter twice a year, Christmas and Roz's birthday. They didn't talk on Laney's birthday because it was only three weeks before Christmas. 'Talk' suggested the exchange of words, many words, actually, and even laughter or tears or whatever emotion the words evoked. Their talks took roughly forty-five seconds, a minute, tops:

"Hi."

Pause

"Hi."

Pause.

"How are you?"

"Fine, you?"

Sigh.

"I don't know...Okay I guess."

"Sure is hot (cold) here. What's it like there."

They were flexible here, answers varying depending on the season.

More pauses and sighs.

"Okay, well, happy birthday (or Merry Christmas)."

"Yeah, good bye."

It hadn't always been that way. Just the last twenty years. Before that, they were as close as a mother and daughter could be, maybe closer. They shopped together, went out for dinner, saw movies on nights that Franklin worked late. Laney let Roz drink a juice glass of wine now and then, smoke a joint on occasion, try on her clothes.

Despite their closeness, having a mother like Laney was often difficult. Her mother was gorgeous and knew it, which made Roz feel like a dish rag. Roz's friends worshipped Laney, and called her by her first name. She gave great makeup advice, clothing advice, and boy advice. Sometimes it felt like they came to the house to visit her instead of Roz. Her mom told her she was being "silly." So did her friends.

Roz rested on one leg and parked a fist on her hip.

"So, where are you?"

"The guy says about fifty miles to the state line."

"What guy?"

"The gas station guy."

"You drove?"

"Nice guy, helpful."

"You drove." Roz let her arm and cell phone drop to her side. "You can't stay here."

Laney knew this would be hard. She knew her daughter would balk, that she would try to dissuade her or at least make it torturous.

"Okay. Is there a motel?"

"Sort of," said Roz.

"How's my granddaughter?"

"Find out for yourself. She cleans rooms at the Sunrise Motel out on 66."

And so, the family reunion began.

"Hello," said Laney in a whisper, a smile on her face.

Maggie sloshed her mop in the bucket and looked over her shoulder. Immediately, her attention was drawn to the Mercedes. She dropped her mop, wiped her hands on her jeans, and strode past the lady wearing the mask. Laney watched her granddaughter, admiring the swagger in her walk.

"This yours?"

"As a matter of fact, it is." Laney smiled broadly.

"Jesus. Well, now *you're* the one and only."

"One and only what?"

"The one and only super-hot set of wheels in Righteous. Claude Delacorte's Beamer was The Big Deal around here until he went on a drunk and totaled it." Maggie looked at the car again. "So now yours is the biggest deal in town. Congrats to you, whoever you are."

Laney pulled her mask off and smiled, as if that would give Maggie a hint.

"Do you know who I am?" she asked.

Maggie checked out the stranger, her high heels, her paisley skirt, and cream-colored blouse cut low at the neck, her gold chains, her rings, her row of earrings on both ears. Who was this masked lady come out of nowhere driving a lavender Mercedes Benz automobile? She'd heard about a woman over in Claymore who moved in with a family, claiming she was a long-lost cousin twice removed. She stayed for a week and then left in the middle of the night with everything she could fit in her trunk. But this lady didn't look like she needed to steal anything from anybody. It was more likely Maggie would steal from her.

"Nope." Maggie picked up her wash bucket, mop, and sponges.

"Your mother's name is Roz, right?"

Maggie put the bucket down and wiped her hands on her jeans.

"Rosalyn Kathleen." Laney smiled. "That's your mom, isn't it?"

"How'd you know my mother's name?"

Laney took two steps forward while Maggie leaned back.

"Because I'm her mother."

Maggie pursed her lips and looked hard at this lady. Can't be, she thought. But the high cheekbones and cleft chin, the same as her mother, the same as herself, were clear evidence. She relaxed her shoulders and took a deep breath.

Her voice was small. "I got your birthday cards. All of them. Thanks." This is the person my mother had taught me to despise, thought Maggie. This is my one and only grandmother, come the whole way from who-knows-where to meet me. She seems nice.

How could that be?

"You did?"

"Yes, and the money, too. Five dollars for every year. Fifty dollars when I turned ten."

Laney shifted her weight and breathed a laugh.

"Helped me buy my first iPod," said Maggie, her voice controlled.

"That's wonderful." She smiled at Maggie, who was looking at her feet. "I'm so happy to finally—"

"Does Mom know you are here?"

"Yes, I spoke with her."

"Did she tell you to go back to where you came from?" Maggie forced a smile and squinted into the sun.

"Not in so many words, but—"

"She doesn't much care for you, I'm afraid." Maggie looked her grandmother up and down, the Mercedes, as well. How could we be in the same family? she thought.

"Yes. Yes, I know." Laney looked down. There were holes in her granddaughter's Nikes.

"She wouldn't let you stay there, would she?"

"No. No she wouldn't. She said to come here." Laney folded her hands and waited.

"There's room for you here if you want." She pointed toward the office. "Just look for Sandman. He'll take care of you." Then she picked up her bucket and sponges and walked away.

"Thank you," called Laney. She wanted to hug her granddaughter, to hold her so close they would become one.

CHAPTER 6

Of course, Laney was gone. How could he have forgotten? "Easily," Gretchen had said. "Your memory is asleep most of the time." They had this conversation every other day. Franklin would be alarmed at Gretchen's angry confirmation. "Oh," he'd say, mouth open, confusion on his face.

When Laney walked out, Gretchen wasn't surprised. Gretchen had pegged Laney as a "user" from the beginning. "She may look cute and innocent, but that girl knows exactly what she's doing, from the goddam coyness of her fresh scrubbed face to the goddam plunging neckline of her sweaters."

Gretchen had told Franklin what she thought, but he wouldn't listen. It didn't matter that she was so young, that she was inexperienced, that she was little more than eye-candy. He didn't care about any of that. The most beautiful girl in the whole county did not oppose marrying him. That was all that mattered. The rest was noise.

Gretchen was jealous, plain and simple, Franklin had thought. Laney was everything Gretchen hated in a girl—bright eyes, silky smooth skin, dazzling from top to bottom, striking clothes, hair that shone, even in the dark. Fake, all of it, she'd say.

Gretchen was a "handsome woman." Back in the day, that's what they called a woman who was average in every way but not unappealing if you looked closely. Franklin understood her frustrations, her disappointments. He loved her. He would do anything for her. Except indulge her jealousies.

Was it Laney's fault that everything came to her effortlessly, as if the world was a metal ball and she was a magnet. No, he would not entertain his sister's twisted viewpoint, her warnings about a "wolf in sheep's clothing."

Gretchen had gone to Griswald Hennefer's apartment to blow off steam a few days before Franklin and Laney got married. Gris had been a classmate and long-time friend. It would be overstating things to suggest Gris was handsome. He was plain looking but nice, considerate, and attentive. She was pissed to beat the band over Laney and her manipulative ways. He listened to her tirade but said little. Gris knew who Laney was. Who wouldn't be jealous of perfection? he thought.

The night Gretchen came to Gris's to complain about Laney was memorable in other ways. Namely, they made love for the first time. Right on his couch. With most of their clothing still on. When it was over, they both looked surprised, dumbfounded. Gretchen left without a word. They carried on as friends until it happened again, just as unexpectedly, three weeks after Franklin and Laney's wedding. Only then did they admit that "friends" no longer defined their relationship.

Two years later they married. By then Gris had finished his apprenticeship and had been accepted into the electricians' union. A month later, they married at the county courthouse. She didn't tell Franklin, because she knew he'd want to come, and if he came, Laney would come, too.

For six months he worked for a building contractor on a new housing development. Around the time that job ended, Gris got a call from an old friend, Artie Mok, who lived in Pennsylvania. Gretchen had vague recollections of Artie from high school. He was part of the group that languished on the periphery of the social universe, like Pluto. Gris, though, was good friends with Artie. They built transistor radios together and fixed automobile engines they stole from a local junk yard. When he graduated high school, Artie moved with his family to western Pa.

Just shy of his nineteenth birthday, Artie became the youngest person in western Pa. to garner a real estate license. He was an overnight success. The money that was flowing into his coffers ignited greater ambitions. He started buying commercial property, which he renovated and flipped with surprising success. He told Gris that money was "falling from his pockets." Gris said, "If you get too much money to handle, feel free to send some my way."

Artie didn't forget. When his Chief Electrician broke his back and became permanently disabled, he called Gris, inviting him to move to Pennsylvania and join his team.

They had been married little more than eighteen months when they moved to Ellwood City. Artie had lined up a house and within a week of their arrival, Gris was working for his friend and loving it.

Gretchen was crestfallen about leaving her brother but also eager to move out of his shadow and start a new life.

Gretchen watched Franklin drink his coffee and eat his oatmeal. What kind of day would it be? she wondered. She thought that moving in with Franklin would give her some companionship, some comfort, but Franklin was not the brother she had known and loved since childhood. And his spacious house felt more like a mausoleum than a home.

But staying in her own home without Gris had been a nightmare. It had also become financially untenable on her salary as an advertising copywriter for the local newspaper.

"I'm so sorry." That's what Gris would have said about her current circumstance. Unlike many men, apologies came easy for him. He always took responsibility for things that went awry, even if he wasn't to blame.

"Come on, you're going to the store with me," said Gretchen.

Somedays, Franklin was like a puppy willing to follow her anywhere.

"I don't want to go to the goddam store."

Other days he wasn't. He needed a little encouragement.

"Don't argue with me. The doctor said normal daily activities would help, getting out would help, doing anything other than sitting on your ass and watching TV all day would help."

Franklin insisted on driving, which set Gretchen's teeth on edge. She could see the headline: "Idiot Sister Lets Incompetent Brother Drive Car Into Tree."

At Wegman's, Franklin told Gretchen he'd catch up with her after he got a cup of coffee at the café. A half hour later, when she came down the last aisle, her cart so full that she had to crane her neck to see where she was going, Franklin was sitting alone at a table, head hanging over his coffee. At least he came with me, she thought.

Shopping with Gris had been different. By the time they were done, he'd put smile on her face with his general lightheartedness and wry wit ("I wish there were ten, maybe twenty, more aisles.")

"Can you push this or do you want me to?" Gretchen huffed. Franklin frowned.

He wrapped his hands around the handle bar and leaned into it like Sisyphus pushing that damn boulder up that damn mountain again. Gretchen watched, making sure he headed straight to their car and didn't wander into parking lot traffic. Franklin was oblivious to the horns blowing at him. Gretchen was offended on his behalf. Who were they to blow their horns at my brother? Don't they know who he was, is? she'd think as she raised her middle finger to them all.

It was her favorite gesture, one she used liberally, much to Griswald's embarrassment.

"Can't you find another way to show your frustration?" he'd ask.

"This works fine. You should try it. It'll make you feel good."

Once he did, but at the last moment hoisted his pointer instead. Gretchen laughed and laughed. "Maybe you should just shake a fist and say 'doggone you!'."

Memories of his last day crept into her mind more often than she would admit. They'd had eggs and bacon for breakfast that morning.

When she offered to pour him a second cup of coffee, he declined, saying he had to stop at a local store, Busy Beaver, to buy some wiring, and didn't want to be late for work. She went to the basement to get clothes out of the dryer and heard him call to her.

"What?" she'd said, but the back door had already closed.

An hour later, a bulletin flashed on the news. The reporter was standing across the road from the Busy Beaver. There were police cars everywhere, sirens screaming, lights flashing. "At this point, the police are not saying very much about what happened, but it appears that several people have been injured...."

At first, she stared at the screen, confused, but as she listened further, she backed out of the room, trying to get as far away as possible from what the reporter was saying. She breathed in quick, short spurts, her mouth puckered, and her teeth clenched.

"Okay, okay," she said, shaking her head, her eyes closed. "Okay, it's okay." How long had Gris been in the store. Not long, she thought. He wouldn't shop around, he'd go in, get what he needed, and leave. Five minutes, ten minutes. Back to work, back to work. She was convinced he'd have left before all the commotion, whatever it was.

She called his cell. It rang five times and when it went to voice mail, she didn't know what to think. Was he at work, just not answering? She could see the TV in the other room and the reporter talking and pointing while the camera zoomed in, and panned out. Her insides tangled into a knot.

"I'll just go," she said, calmly, softly. "I'll just go to make sure he's okay. He'll think I'm crazy but that's okay. I'll just go."

She caught up with Gris in the emergency room just after he'd been pronounced.

It didn't look like him at all. Maybe it wasn't him, she thought. Is this someone else's husband? Does some other wife need to be notified? Maybe Gris was home, wondering where she was. She reached for her phone, then remembered it was on the kitchen table. She looked at him again, lying on the gurney. His right hand, there it was. The onyx ring she'd bought him for their fifteenth anniversary.

What happened to his face? Why was there so much blood? His eyes and mouth, both open wide, gave witness to some horror.

"I'm so sorry," said a nurse. She placed her hand gently on Gretchen's arm and patted three times. She smiled sadly and then walked away.

Gretchen sat down, folded her hands in her lap, and stared at the pale green wall. Her husband of thirty-four years would not be coming home to eat the roast she was planning for dinner. She'd never see his smile or hear his voice or laugh at his humorous take on things again.

It all came and went too fast. After he died, her life was full of leftover time, so many days full of promise that never arrived, replaced by a clock with no hands, a calendar with no dates, a tomorrow with no point.

Franklin didn't turn into his driveway, he veered into it, as if it was not his intended destination. The driver's side front tire screeched as it hit the curb. But he gained control and eased up the dark driveway into the garage, dangerously close to the rakes and shovels hanging on the wall. Without saying a word, he backed up and tried again, making sure he was lined up correctly.

"There," he said triumphantly. He smiled at his sister, but she was looking out her window. He got out of the car and headed toward the kitchen door, two bags in his arms. When Gretchen didn't follow him, he returned to the car.

"So? You coming?"

Gretchen did not move. She did not look at him.

"My foot's asleep. Let me give it a minute to wake up, then I'll be in."

"Suit yourself."

Franklin closed the door and left her there. The headlights dimmed, and soon she was in complete darkness. She sighed, then took a tissue from her purse, wiped her eyes, got out of the car, and went in the house.

CHAPTER 7

Franklin sat alone in front of the TV trying to watch *Ellen*. Today she had...who was it? He sputtered and frowned. "Shit." He clicked on the guide. "Jennifer Aniston." He tried to remember the sit-com she'd been in. He bowed his head for a minute until the light came on. "*Friends*," he said triumphantly.

He tried to focus on Ellen's short hair, her glimmering smile, her jeans and sneakers, her leather vest, her happy, over-exuberant, fawning audience.

But his eyes drifted away, settling on the mantle where a bell jar sat, white tapers in gold candlesticks beside it. His eyes roamed. Crown molding, track lighting, mahogany shelving in the corner, the books gray with dust.

He reached out and touched the wallpaper, Laney's choice. Light gray with tiny flowers (maybe Violets?) in clusters. His eyes defocused. The flowers melted together. He saw nothing now.

When he finally looked up, his father was standing in the corner by a lamp, a shrill grin on his face. He wore a T-shirt with yellow stained armpits, boxer shorts, and black calf-high socks. His thinning hair was slicked back. His face, stubbled. His belly like a beach ball. He smelled like sweat and Old Spice.

The first time this happened, Franklin was so frightened that he ran into his bedroom, turned out the light, and pulled the covers up over his head. The next day, he searched the whole house but found nothing. Then his father came again, and again, always in the early evening twilight, always that same Riddler grin on his face.

The third time he appeared, he wore a black suit, gray tie, and white shirt. Franklin's mother had bought them for his funeral. Franklin had stood in a corner of the funeral parlor. He was pulsing with happiness he couldn't share with anyone.

The fifth time his father appeared, he held a finger in front of his lips, shushing Franklin. Franklin screamed, then stormed at his father, only to blacken one eye against the mahogany shelving.

At his next visit with his doctor, Franklin asked if "seeing things" was common in long Covid. "Do you mean hallucinations?" his doctor had said. He leaned forward, elbows on his knees and said, "Well...there are rare instances of Covid induced psychosis. But I want to emphasize the word rare, very rare." He asked Franklin if he'd had any hallucinations. Franklin paused before saying, no, he'd read about it somewhere. His doctor assured him he didn't need to be concerned.

His father's visitations continued, although, thankfully, he never showed up when Gretchen was around. It was as if Gretchen was their father's kryptonite.

Franklin glared at his father, then closed his eyes for a long time. When he opened them, his father was gone. Slowly, slowly he came back to himself. He looked at the TV. "There's Ellen. I love her show."

Each day, the fog rolled in, making bits and pieces of memory fall away like shingles off a weather worn roof. Sometimes he stood still, afraid to move, unsure where he was or why. When his father came out of the fog, Franklin felt anger, like lightning, followed by a heavy blanket of depression.

Rumor around town was that Franklin had Alzheimer's. As this fake news got legs, friends and former customers added a prefix to his name—'Poor.' "Poor Franklin," they said, followed by head shakes and sighs. "Poor, poor Franklin." Thoughts and prayers came his way, although he never felt them.

"Franklin!" someone called. It came from the kitchen. It had to be his sister. He was sure he knew her name, but where had it gone?

"What is it?"

Gretchen came into the living room, a dish towel in her wet hands.

"You were gonna help me, remember?"

"Of course, I remember. You think I'm stupid? I'm not."

"Point taken," she said, the dull sound of resignation in her voice. She turned and walked back to the kitchen. Franklin followed, hoping for clues about what to do next.

Gretchen blamed Laney for Franklin's predicament. He hadn't been sick a day in his life. He had good genes, exercised regularly at the Y, ate reasonably well, except for an occasional sweet or drink. Nothing in excess. His weight was the same as it was in high school. It was just arranged differently.

But Laney couldn't leave well enough alone. She got on him about the vaccine and the mask and the handwashing. Nearly drove him crazy, her constant preaching at him like he was an ignorant little boy.

She bought him umpty-dump N95s, leaving them around the house, in his car, on his desk. Telling him he'd die if he didn't "wise up." She baited him and baited him, and he couldn't resist the fight.

Gretchen knew her brother would have worn the mask if Laney hadn't made such a big deal out of it. But Laney couldn't take her foot off the gas, so, of course, he couldn't ease up on the brakes. He started bragging about it. How he wasn't vaccinated and never wore a mask, "except on Halloween." And she'd bristle every time he suggested the virus was a hoax. "My God," she'd say, "how could you be so smart about everything and yet so stupid about this?" He'd smile and remind her he was healthy as a horse. "Go ahead, cough on me."

And then, in the middle of everything, she left. For no reason at all. "Forty years is enough." Who says that? Who spends forty years married to someone who has given her a life she could never have imagined and then, completely out of the blue, says b'bye? Gretchen's teeth would grind every time she thought of that woman.

She got in her Mercedes and disappeared. Half her clothes were still in the closet. Twenty-seven pairs of Jimmy Choo's were scattered on the dressing room floor. Not even a note to explain herself. It was cruel, thought Gretchen, just plain cruel. "If there is a God in heaven, she'll get hers...maybe even if there's not."

Franklin had battled through the Covid tsunami that hit him right after Laney left. After a couple of weeks, he was better.

At least until the cough began. He barely noticed it at first, but soon he was hacking so hard it took his breath away. Aches and pains followed and then, for the first time, he woke up in a fog. He gave up going anywhere and spent his days in bed.

The fog wouldn't lift, the pain wouldn't subside.

He saw doctor after doctor. One said it was stress, another said it was a brain tumor, and a third suggested he was grieving the loss of his wife. The fourth said, "I think this is Covid." Franklin said he'd already had Covid and was over it. Had to be something else.

"No, I feel certain it's Covid. We've seen this a lot."

"Can't be."

"Can be. Covid is devious. It hides. It hangs on."

"It hangs on?"

"Yeah."

"What can you do about it? How do you cure it?"

"Well—"

"How long will it last?"

When it came to this question, all the doctors' answers were the same. "I don't know, really. Get enough sleep. Eat healthy. Stay active. Maybe get a hobby that keeps your mind going...spend time with family and friends." Then they'd tilt their heads to one side, as if to say, "Who knows?"

Before she came to visit Franklin, Gretchen had noticed that her brother was preoccupied and distant when she talked to him on the phone. Figured this was due to Laney's departure. Then he stopped responding to her texts. But it wasn't until she was standing on the porch and saw piles of mail and newspapers, that she knew something was very wrong.

Franklin came into the kitchen and took a seat. He leaned on the table and rubbed his face with both hands, then looked at the clock.

"Is that time right?"

"Yeah. Why?"

Franklin squirmed and looked at the clock again.

"She's late."

"Who's late?"

"She's always home by four-thirty."

"I don't know what you're talking about, Brother. Why don't you come over here and help me make these meatballs." The best way to counter her brother's confusion was to distract him, much like you would a toddler. "You know, this is our mother's recipe. And she got it from her mother. Who knows when it started? But I like it because—"

"Do you know when Laney's coming home?"

And sometimes distraction didn't work.

There were minutes, even hours, when he was himself, quick, funny, lively, boisterous. They'd go out to dinner and everyone would stop by his table to see how he was doing. He'd remember every single name, as well as, their spouses, their children, their pets, even their shoe sizes. His hands would be steady and he'd eat like a horse. He wouldn't slump or yawn. He wouldn't ask when Laney was coming home. In fact, he wouldn't mention her, at all.

She appreciated these lucid interludes. They provided respite from a burden she hadn't anticipated and didn't want.

The fog receded over the next few days, so Gretchen thought it was time to go out again. This time, they tried Vinnie's. When they arrived, the place was crowded, more crowded than Gretchen thought it would be, but Franklin seemed fine. They sat at the corner table she'd reserved. They ordered drinks, some starters, then a main course.

As they were waiting, Franklin recognized someone at the bar, a former customer. He got up, walked over to the man, and clapped him on the back. The man gave Franklin a hug and offered to buy him a drink. Franklin parked one cheek on the stool, and his friend waved for the bartender to bring him a gin and tonic. Soon they were gesturing and smiling and tossing their heads back in gales of laughter.

Then she watched Franklin's expression change. She could tell he wasn't sure who he was talking to. His friend was telling what seemed like a hilarious story, but Franklin didn't laugh or respond much at all. He kept his stiff smile, though, and looked around for context clues.

Gretchen stood and watched, hoping something would click and Franklin would be himself again.

He glanced this way and that, his eyes frantic, then got up and made a beeline for the emergency exit. His friend looked puzzled. Franklin stood in front of the door but didn't move. His friend smiled and spoke. Franklin stared, as if he hoped he was invisible.

Gretchen took a deep breath, got up from her seat, and strode to the bar.

"There you are. I was looking all over." She took his arm. "He is such a gadfly," she said to the friend. Then she leaned forward and whispered, "I think my brother may have had one too many drinks, maybe even two or three too many." She poked the man in the arm, laughed, and quickly guided Franklin back to the table.

"What was that all about?" said Franklin.

"Nothing."

"I don't understand what's going on."

"Time for us to go home," said Gretchen. She left cash on the table, took Franklin by the arm, and headed for the door.

He was quiet in the car. She talked about mundane things, the traffic, favorite TV shows, local news, but he didn't respond. He sat still, his hands in his lap, his face forward, his shoulders hunched, like a stranger on a bus. When they got home, Franklin collapsed into his easy chair with a heavy sigh. She asked if he wanted to watch TV, and when he didn't answer, she clicked on *Entertainment Tonight.*

Gretchen stood behind his chair watching the young, stylish hosts chatter on, wondering all the while if this was it, if, from now on, this was life as she would know it, just two people riding a roller coaster that would never stop.

CHAPTER 8

Roz poured cooking oil into the cast-iron skillet. Beside her were two dinner plates. One was heaped with flour seasoned with cayenne pepper, garlic powder, onion powder, and white pepper. Four cuts of beefsteak laid in another plate. She stirred bubbling, creamy, white gravy on a separate burner.

At the opposite counter, Maggie mashed the potatoes over and over, until they were almost lump-less. Then she added heavy cream, garlic powder, pepper, two sticks of butter and chopped green onions. She wiped her hands on her apron, scratched her nose, grabbed the mixer, and started again, this time whipping the potatoes until they were smooth as a baby's behind.

The oil was sizzling now. Roz took the steaks, dropped them onto the plate of flour, then flipped them until both sides were snowy white. Next, she held them over the skillet and eased each one in as carefully as she could.

"Everything smells so...fried," said Laney.

This was the first time Laney had been invited to the house for a meal. The invitation came through Maggie. Laney suspected her mother knew nothing about it.

"Take your mask off," said Roz, "unless you came here to rob me."

"Mom!" Maggie shot her mother a disapproving look.

Laney complied.

"Is there anything I can do to help?" said Laney.

Roz turned a deaf ear.

"Maybe set the table?" said Maggie. She pointed to the cabinet and the silverware drawer.

"Gladly." Laney forced a smile.

Laney purchased her dinnerware and flatware on a weekend spending spree at Neiman Marcus in New York. The dinner plates had lavender lilacs with gold accents adorning the fluted edges. They were quiet but elegant. She couldn't remember the cost, but she remembered the look on Franklin's face when she told him. The flatware was Georg Jensen. She fell in love with the forks and their sleek, long tines.

She held her breath when she opened the cabinet. She put on her mask again. There wasn't a single matching set of plates. In fact, every plate was a different size and color. Some were glass, some were plastic, and there was a stack of Styrofoam plates leaning against the back of the cupboard, just in case. There was an array of jelly jars, Disney cups, and Marvel glasses, each a different superhero.

She studied the aggregation of misfit dinnerware, unsure what to choose. Who drank Goofy or the Hulk? Glass or plastic plates? What color? What about the plaid one? She sought Roz's guidance.

"Do you have a preference?"

"Preference for what?"

"The plates and glasses?"

"Yeah, we'll need both."

Laney grabbed whatever she could reach, same with the silverware. She tore paper towels off the roll and arranged everything on the table; neat, if not so nice.

When the time was right, Maggie gathered the plates and filled them. A hunk of chicken fried steak, a glob of mashed potatoes, slippery stir-fried green beans, a slice of corn bread, plus glasses of Mountain Dew. Everything but the Dew had a thick layer of gelatinous gravy.

"I thought I asked you to take off that mask. Or are you planning to eat through your ears," said Roz, the first bite of steak already in her mouth.

Laney took it off and laid it on the table beside her. "I didn't even realize it was on. I get so used to wearing it, that I don't even know it's there." She looked at Roz and Maggie, an apologetic smile on her face.

"I figured you thought we had the China disease."

"Mom, c'mon." Maggie glared at her mother.

Laney looked at her plate. The gravy was starting to congeal. She wanted to be polite and eat, but she weighed that option against the not-so-polite consequence—a long, unpleasant ride on the porcelain bus. The cornbread looked fine. She cut hers in half and took a bite.

"My goodness, this is delicious!" Laney said as she took another bite and hummed in appreciation.

Roz had forgotten that her mother hummed when she ate something she liked. Roz used to hum along but an octave higher or lower. Her father would laugh and her mother would swat at her playfully.

Roz blinked twice and look a deep breath.

"You don't have to sound surprised."

"I didn't mean it that way, it's just so—"

"Don't let her bother you, Laney. She says the same kind of stuff to me." Maggie didn't look up from her plate when she said this. She knew her mother would be upset, like Maggie was turning on her, switching sides.

She glanced at her mom again. There were clouds under her eyes. A hint of fuzz on her upper lip. Her skin looked like rough terrain. Everything about her sagged like Horace and Emma's hound dog, Ronald.

Laney's face was smooth and tight. A bucket of Botox? wondered Maggie. There was no excess hair anywhere. Her skin was white as a pearl. Not a cultured pearl but a real one. It was also clear to Maggie that nothing on Laney would ever sag.

Jesus, thought Maggie, my mother looks old enough to be my...grandmother.

"What's the matter? You not hungry? My food not good enough for you?" Roz said this while pointing her fork at Laney.

Laney's cheeks glowed like two pink roses.

"No, no, that's not it at all." She wiped her mouth with the napkin. "It's just all this humidity. Takes my appetite away."

Maggie noticed there wasn't any sign of moisture on Laney's face. The room grew quiet. Without thinking, she spoke.

"Mom, why do you hate my grandmother?"

"Eat your supper," said Roz, waving her fork again.

"Why won't you tell me?" said Maggie. She looked at Laney. She didn't know that skin could turn magenta.

That's Roz, thought Laney. Never talk about the important things.

Her *grandmother*? thought Roz. Maggie doesn't know a damn thing about that woman. She's my mother in name only; how could she be anyone's grandmother?

"I know your mother has her reasons," said Laney.

The room went quiet again. Wind blew the porch swing against the house and the late afternoon sun cut a dividing line across the kitchen table. Faces down, all three women looked like archeologists examining their plates for traces of lost relationships.

"Excuse me," said Maggie, and retreated to her bedroom.

Laney and Roz didn't move, their fists clenched on the table top.

"Well...thanks for dinner," said Laney. "It's been...real."

"Who do you think you are, crashing into our lives, turning things upside down, expecting who-knows-what from us? Did you see Maggie? Her face was white as a sheet? Been like that ever since you pulled into town driving that ridiculous goddam car."

For the first time since Laney had arrived, Roz looked at her. She could still see the mother she'd loved once upon a time. There was that spark in her eyes. Her face looked perfect, not a blemish, barely a line anywhere. Even sitting, her posture was straight as a fashion model. "Don't slump," she'd always said. "People will think you don't care about yourself. You're a pretty girl, Rosalyn." She'd frown at her mother when she'd say this, but secretly she was excited to hear that word—pretty—even though she knew she wasn't.

"Stand up and let me take a good look at you." It was Roz's eighth grade dance. Her mother had bought her a cocktail dress with spaghetti straps. "Tuck your tummy in just a little." Roz learned to take shallow breaths so no one would notice her paunch. "Here, let me do just one thing." She added a hint of lipstick and stood back. "Okay, I have an idea." The idea was a large satin bow that her mother clipped to the top of her head. "Makes you look taller."

Roz never made it to the eighth-grade dance. She walked to the Dairy Queen, ordered a chocolate milkshake, went behind the building, and drank it slowly while leaning against the wall. She waited until the dance had started and then went to the Manos Theater, climbed the stairs to the balcony, and watched *Indiana Jones and the Kingdom of the Crystal Skull* twice.

If she was going to be alone, anyway, she preferred being alone at the theater rather than the dance. When she got home, she told her mother she enjoyed herself, which was true and false at the same time. Her mother asked if she had danced with any boys. "I'll never tell," said Roz. Another well-crafted dodge.

"I never intended on crashing your lives," said Laney. "I am sorry if I am 'ridiculous' to you. Just wanted to come visit you and finally meet my granddaughter. Life is very short, Rosalyn."

Roz was stumped by the moisture in her mother's eyes. She never cried, not when Roz broke her leg, not when her dog, Boogy, got hit by a truck, not when anything happened. Once, she told Roz her "tear valve" had been turned off permanently. But there she was, blinking away.

"Maggie told me you left your husband."

"You mean your *father*," said Laney. "He is still your father. And yes, I left him."

"Why?"

"Forty years was enough. They really should make you renew your marriage license every ten years. I would have renewed it once, because you were still so young, and I didn't have the courage after ten years. But I knew I had to leave after twenty."

"Why did it take you twenty more years to leave?"

Laney wondered the same thing.

"I don't know for sure. Maybe because I didn't have my own money yet. Maybe that was it...I didn't know what I'd do if I left. Maybe that was it...Marriage had become a habit that was hard to break. That could have been it. Maybe it took me that long to get strong, you know, strong enough to leave. Not sure."

"I never figured you'd leave him. I always thought you two were tight. He absolutely loved you. I could see it."

"Not sure I ever loved him. Maybe I loved the idea of him, a man you could lean on, a strong man, a man who could give you everything you wanted."

"And that wasn't enough."

Laney shook her head. "No, turns out it wasn't." She patted the top of the gravy with her fork.

Roz swallowed several times before speaking.

"You going back to him?"

"No, I don't think I will. I am trying to move forward."

"So, you can do what?"

Laney shrugged. "I'm not sure. Make a new beginning of some sort."

"Little late for that, isn't it?" Roz counted eight age spots on her mother's hand.

Laney put her fork down. "Roz, it's never too late."

"That's for Hallmark movies and children's books. It doesn't work that way in life." She glared at her mother. Laney looked away.

When it came to her mother, love and hate were always vying for Roz's heart. She teetered back and forth between them, never able to stay put in either place. Seeing her mother after so many years didn't help. She felt dizzy with confusion. Why had she come here? What does she want from me? What do I want from her? She hadn't had any contact with her father in forever. But a year or so after she'd left, her mother started calling now and then. There was so much they needed to say to each other that they barely said anything at all. And now she was right there, standing in front of her, begging for a new start.

Maggie, her face still pale, but her smile broad, appeared in the doorway. In her hands was a pecan pie.

"Room for dessert?"

No one replied.

"I guess I'll get us started."

She cut a wedge and slid it onto her plate. Then she got the vanilla ice cream from the fridge and plopped two scoops on top. She took a large bite. "Mmmmm, that sure is good. I don't know if I can eat the whole pie, though."

She put a piece on her mother's plate, then one on her grandmother's. Then scooped ice cream on both.

"Lemme show you how this works. You put your fork on its edge, like this, so you can cut through the crust, and you make sure you've got a little of the ice cream, too." Her fork was heaping. "There, look at that." She opened her mouth wide and deposited the mound of pie and ice cream. "My God, that's good."

Both women looked at her. She raised her eyebrows and pointed at their plates with her fork. Her grandmother smiled and took a bite. Her mother got up from the table.

"I'm going to my room."

She walked out of the kitchen. A minute later, she returned, picked up her pie, her fork, and her napkin, and retreated once more.

"Hard to stop hating, I guess," said Maggie.

CHAPTER 9

Rumor had it that a superhighway, to be completed in 1968, would be built near Righteous. In a moment of foresight, the Sunrise Motel was built in 1966 to capture as many weary travelers as possible. Turned out the superhighway never progressed beyond the rumor stage. Everyone in Righteous assumed that was the death knell for their twenty-four-room getaway.

To their surprise, the motel went great guns for about seven years. Young people ("them goddam hippies") came from around the country searching for small, soft, spineless blue-green cacti. Native Americans had used peyote in religious ceremonies for centuries. When the mescalin took hold, they could see God.

Most of the long-hairs came from back east. They weren't searching for God. They were hot on the trail of recreational magic. To them, peyote was sport. They wanted to see what the world sounded like, they wanted to feel its colors, and disappear into its hallucinogenic timelessness.

The official stance of Righteous was that the easterners were a godless hoard who valued nothing. They sneered at them, and protected their children from their evil ways.

But hippies ate, bought things, and needed a place to stay when their psychedelic escapades wore off. Enter the Sunrise Motel or the 'button palace,' as the hippies called it. Jimmy Joe Grantham, the original owner, let them do whatever they liked if they had money enough to pay.

When the hippies finally grew up and got jobs, truckers took their place. Even today, under the management of Jimmy Joe's son, Sanford, known to everyone as Sandman, truckers were his top-drawer customers, followed by lost vacationers, characters on the lam, and gals and guys who needed a private place for their indiscretions.

When his father was alive, Sandman scrubbed toilets, ran errands, filled the soda machine and the ice box. He made enough money to enroll in the Oklahoma Panhandle State University.

As luck would have it, Jimmy Joe died, God rest his soul, and left the place to Sandman. Sandman grudgingly dropped out of college and came home to run the business at the tender age of twenty. Since he made little money at first, he moved into room number 24, so he wouldn't have to pay rent somewhere else. He added a full-size refrigerator, a bigger TV, and a better mattress. Soon enough, it felt like home. That's where he drank, that's where he sobered up, that's where he drank some more, that's where he brought his women, and that's where he bolted the lock whenever boyfriends and husbands came calling, guns loaded. And that's where he's lived to this day.

Sandman stood outside his room. He wore a tattered nightshirt and nothing else. He stretched and yawned and shielded his eyes against the eastern sun. A buzzard circled above. A mourning dove cooed. He smiled and yawned again as a gaggle of turkeys gobbled their way across 66. He straightened his back, ran his fingers through his knotted hair, and watched a ramshackle car cough and sputter its way onto the lot.

"Good morning, Miss Maggie."

"Sandman."

He scratched his beard and smiled.

"What's with the get up?" she said.

"It's a new look. You like?"

"I'll have to get back to you on that."

There were two cars in the lot, one in front of 8 and the other in front of 15. The brochure said "Complementary Breakfast," one of Maggie's innovations.

Maggie opened the office door. She poured water into the coffee maker, added scoops of dark roast, and clicked the button. She tore open the Entenmann's, separated the cinnamon rolls, and arranged them on a paper plate. She went into the backroom for a stack of Styrofoam cups. She opened the Coffee Mate, filled a bowl with Sweet and Lo, and placed it beside the sugar.

"Fancy." Sandman leaned against the door.

"Desperate is a better word."

Sandman guffawed, grabbed a tissue, blew his nose, and studied it for a moment before tossing it into the trash can.

"That's special."

He chuckled. "Think I'll go get officially dressed."

When Sandman first learned that Maggie was nineteen, he was disheartened. At forty-one he knew he didn't have a chance with a woman so young, so beautiful, so everything he wasn't. But, still. She arrived at the motel looking lost. She asked for the owner and when he said, "That's me," she looked at him, her eyes uncertain. "I think I know what you're going to say, but I'll ask, anyway. Any chance you're hiring?"

No, he wasn't. "Yes, I am. Do you have any experience in the motel business?"

"Does staying in a motel count?"

"That's more experience than most."

"So?" she said.

"Sure."

They didn't talk much. She was busy with bedsheets, soap, towels, plugged toilets, broken TVs, plugged toilets, and plugged toilets.

"First rule about any electrical stuff, and TVs, all that kind of thing. Same with toilets. Never call a repair man. I'm telling you, money flies out of your pocket before they even get here. Anyway, I can fix most anything. What I can't, can wait."

When the toilet in 18 gushed a steady flow of human detritus, Maggie came running to the office, a tissue over her nose. She pointed down the walkway to the offending room. Sandman shot out the office door, Maggie close behind. Once he reached the room, he opened the door and was hit by a wall of stench so strong that he gasped, stepped back, and gagged up his lunch in the parking lot.

"Lemme call someone," said Maggie.

"What did I say about fixing things around here?"

"You said you could do it, no matter what." She looked at the room and then at Sandman.

"Okay then, stand back, I'm going in."

Sandman buried his face in the crook of his arm and was about to take a deep dive into 18, when Maggie said, "Tools?"

Sandman ran to the office, then back to the room with a metal tool box. He dropped it on the pavement outside 18, pried it open, and searched the trays for just the right implement. He settled on a hammer and a screw driver. And a wrench. And another hammer, this one smaller than the first. And a tape measure. And duct tape.

Maggie leaned against the doorjamb, watching. "Need some help?"

"Naw, I can handle this."

He took two cautious steps forward as if sneaking up on an enemy. But the smell hit him hard again and down he went to his knees. Maggie reached to help him, but he shrugged her off. He stood again, took a deep breath, and held it. His cheeks looked like balloons about to burst.

"Go get 'em, cowboy," said Maggie.

He looked at her and nodded, his face a ripe tomato. He dashed into the room and took a hard right toward the bathroom. He glared at the offending toilet, took another step on the slippery floor, and both feet went out from under him.

Maggie stood on her tiptoes trying to see him.

He stood, his arms dripping with guck.

Maggie leaned against the post again. "Need a towel?"

"Maybe three...make that four."

"Okay." She turned to walk away.

"Maggie, maybe call a plumber."

"I did."

"When?"

"Twenty minutes ago."

After the plumber had fixed the toilet, after Sandman had cleaned the room, after he'd taken a long shower and changed his clothes, he returned to the office. Maggie was sitting in his chair, feet on the desk.

"My hero," she said.

"Jesus God," he said, shaking his head.

Only then did either of them laugh. "Need a towel," became their catch phrase for anything that went wrong—bitchy guests, dead animals in the pool, leaky roofs, whatever. It was something that linked them, made them a part of each other. At least, that's how Sandman saw it.

Sandman was the only friend Maggie had. Righteous didn't have many residents in their late teens or twenties. It was a decade without representation. After high school graduation, all the boys headed to the nearest oil field; the girls got pregnant and, eventually, married the boys who'd left for the nearest oil field.

For a young woman, the options were bleak.

When she first started working at the motel, she tried to avoid Sandman. He was just another guy who stared at her, a dumb smile on his hungry face. The last thing she needed was a guy in his forties following her around like a puppy. They had a monosyllabic relationship: "Hi," "Bye," "Nice weather," "Uh-huh." But as the weeks passed, Sandman calmed down and she felt more comfortable engaging him. She would come to work early some days to have coffee and listen to Sandman's stories. They started eating lunch together. Once or twice a week. A few times, they had a draft together at Cooney's Bar.

Sandman screwed up his courage and asked her to the latest superhero movie showing at the Majestic in Flatland. She considered this for several days. Finally, she said 'Yes,' but made it clear they would drive separately and she'd pay for her ticket and her popcorn.

"Can I sit in the same row with you?" Sandman had said. Maggie didn't even crack a smile. She didn't want to do anything to encourage him or give him the wrong idea.

He then asked her to another movie and she declined. He asked her to go out to eat at Stella's Diner and she said 'No' to that, as well. By then, he'd gotten the message.

They settled into a passable friendship, which was fine.

Until it wasn't.

CHAPTER 10

Franklin sat back in the deep, cushioned lounger in his home movie theater. He coughed and coughed, like a dog barking at a passing truck. Once it stopped, he took several deep breaths, leaned back, and stared at the empty screen. He couldn't remember the last time they'd used this room. He clenched and unclenched his hands, trying to rid himself of the tingling. He coughed, he scratched, he ached, he forgot the simplest things. He rubbed his sore wrists. Sometimes he felt like Gulliver, always under attack by myriad Lilliputians.

Gretchen tiptoed into the room and watched Franklin as he sank ever deeper into his reverie. She knew he was thinking about "that woman."

Franklin startled when she tapped his shoulder.

"Here," said Gretchen, placing a peanut butter and jelly sandwich in his lap and a can of Guinness in the cup holder beside him. "You gotta eat."

"Thank you." Franklin raised the sandwich for Gretchen to see and took a bite.

"I shouldn't have to remind you."

"Then don't."

As she stood beside him, he could feel her heat.

"Sorry. Just a bad day."

"What's wrong?"

"Nothing."

"Whatever 'nothing' is, it sure is bothering the shit out of you." With that, Gretchen turned and walked out of the room.

Gretchen had always been prickly. Her edginess drove Gris mad.

"I love her, I do, but Jesus, sometimes she's...so...difficult."

"Just who she is," Franklin would say. He wanted to say, She's a little nutty, get used to it. But in time, Gris would figure that out.

Gretchen stood at the door again. She cleared her throat.

"Get up," she said. "We're leaving the mausoleum today."

"What?"

"You heard me. We're going out."

"We've already done that."

"Wonder of wonders, we're going to do it again."

"Where?"

"Does it matter? Go to your room. Take off your robe. Put some clothes on."

She was gone before he could protest.

There was no doubt his world had shrunk. It was no larger than his kitchen, living room, movie room, and bathroom. Most nights he slept in his recliner. Gretchen would fetch his clothes if he decided to get dressed. Often, he started the day and ended the day in his silk pajamas, black terry cloth robe, and slippers, the moccasin kind. He rarely went upstairs and when he did, he was wiped out for the rest of the day, sometimes the next, as well.

He held onto the ebony banister and studied the sweeping staircase. It wound its way to the balcony which overlooked both the foyer and the massive, crystal chandelier Laney had bought for their tenth anniversary. It came all the way from the Venetian island of Murano, a substitute for the trip to Italy he had promised.

He counted the steps. Twenty in all. He decided he could make it to the top, if he rested along the way. Four steps, then sit. Four more and sit. And so on. He was perspiring when he reached the top, perspiring and panting.

"How 'bout that? You made it," said Gretchen as she left her bedroom, ready to go. Franklin erupted into a hacking cough as he tried to speak. She sat beside him on the top step and pounded his back until he caught his breath.

"I don't know about this—"

"Get dressed," she said, then disappeared down the steps.

Like every other day, the fine dust of Covid brain-fog had hijacked his mind. When that happened, he only felt safe sitting or lying down. Gretchen struggled to understand. She'd ask him if he was in the fog and if he said he was, she'd ask if he was faint, lightheaded, wobbly, unstable, or weak in the knees. Today she tried dizziness— "Are you dizzy?" He could see she was trying. But, try as he would, he couldn't explain what was happening. No words captured the feeling, at least not entirely. Yes, it made thinking difficult. Yes, he was forgetful, confused. Yes, he was fuzzy headed, spaced out, gone.

But there was something more to it, something that none of these words touched. It was as if dark matter had enveloped his brain, and consequently, everything else. If, as scientists theorized, the universe was composed of 83% dark matter, then his brain was at least 90% Covid dark matter. And like the dark matter of the universe, Franklin's didn't emit or reflect light; it was, in essence, invisible to the most discerning eye.

When they reached Wegman's, the parking lot was packed. Gretchen cruised round and round until she found a spot. To reach the store, Franklin would have to walk about a city block.

Franklin sized up the situation. "I'll stay here."

"No, you won't." Gretchen's jaw was set. She slammed the driver side door, opened Franklin's, and stood with her fist on her hip.

Franklin slowly turned and dangled his legs out the door.

"You're enjoying this, aren't you?" he said, as she stood over him, jaws still locked.

When he stood, the cool night air startled him, and he gasped. Gretchen grabbed his arm with both hands, steadying him. Franklin groaned with every step.

"You're being a baby."

"What did you say?" Franklin stopped.

"You. Are. Being. A. Baby."

"What's that supposed to mean?"

"It means what it means."

Gretchen said this a lot. Every time something went awry, she said some version of "it is what it is." Franklin hated it. He took a deep breath. "Is anything *not* what it is?"

"You."

Gretchen won the battle over mask wearing. But he refused to walk the grocery store aisles with her. She acted annoyed but felt relieved. She escorted him to the café, bought him a cappuccino, and a chocolate chip cookie. Franklin smiled and fluttered his fingers at her as she left. Then he took his mask off.

She disappeared into the produce section just as he started coughing again. The cough was a wild card symptom of long haul Covid, at least for him. He could go a week or more without coughing once, and then out of the blue, he'd be doubled over, unable to breathe. This was one of those days.

The first few shoppers stared at him as they walked by, whispering their concerns to each other, pulling their masks up, and then heading to the bakery for muffins or fresh baked bread. After five, then ten minutes, though, the manager was called.

"Stand back. Let's give this gentleman room to breathe."

Even with additional room, Franklin still hacked away.

"Are you choking, sir?" said the manager. Franklin tried to help by shaking his head. "Is your throat dry?" Another shake of the head. "You sure you didn't get something stuck in your throat, like a piece of that cookie."

"Best cookies in the world," said the man at the next table.

"Thank you," said the manager, straightening his back with pride.

"I could eat a dozen a day, if my wife would let me."

Both men laughed.

Franklin cupped his knee caps with his hands, and continued honking and hacking. He wanted to give the finger to the man who could eat cookies all day.

"Is this a medical thing, a medical condition?" said the manager.

Franklin turned his head, his eyes wide, and nodded.

There were sighs of relief among the eight to ten shoppers who surrounded him, all of them subscribing to the cover-your-mouth-but-under-no-circumstances-cover-your-nose mask wearing strategy.

Could it be pneumonia? or COPD? or throat cancer? A newcomer to the group asked if it could be a psychosomatic problem.

From the periphery of the circle, a man called out: "I have a brother-in-law who coughs like that! It might be a Covid thing!"

Everyone took one step back.

By then, Franklin was getting control of the cough.

"Oh, no," said the manager, as he, too, stepped back. "Are you contagious?"

He choked out a "No."

The group's sigh was so deep Franklin could feel their collective breath on his face.

Gretchen saw a huddle of people in the café. She abandoned her cart just feet from an open checkout line and pushed her way through the crowd. "What's going on here? Franklin!"

"Just coughing," he said.

The crowd quickly lost interest and dispersed, a few wishing him good luck as they walked away.

"Sure you're okay?" asked the manager.

Franklin nodded and the manager went back to work.

What's with this? thought Gretchen. Why the hell is my brother still such a mess? Just as she reached for his arm, Franklin stood up and hustled through the bakery then into the produce section. There was a woman fondling the honeydew melons. Her height was right. The color of her hair was right. Her half-profile fit the bill. It had to be Laney.

Gretchen scampered after her brother, but before she could stop him, he'd tapped the woman's shoulder.

"Oh, I'm sorry. I thought you were my wife." he said. The woman's stone-cold face turned into a forgiving smile. "You look so much like her. You might know her. Laney Franklin?" The woman took one step back. "She left me. It was on our fortieth anniversary. We were out for dinner at Grayson's, Grayson's Inn. Do you know the place? It was the most important night of our life together. Except for our wedding. And the birth of our daughter. Even so, she up and left me." He snapped his fingers. "Just like that. She did."

"I'm so—"

Gretchen reached for Franklin's arm. "That's okay," she said. "I've got it."

The woman smiled. "Good luck."

Franklin watched her walk away, and for a moment he thought again that she was Laney.

"C'mon," said Gretchen.

"Laney's gotta be somewhere, doesn't she? I mean, everyone's gotta be somewhere."

Now Gretchen felt free to hate Laney again. Without guilt.

"You've got to help me find her." Franklin grabbed her jacket sleeve.

"What?"

"You heard me."

CHAPTER 11

It rained hard all morning the day of Griswald's funeral, so hard that when Gretchen finally got up, the whole world seemed blanketed in a dull, gray shroud. She looked back at the bed, one side still perfectly made. She rested her forehead against the window pane.

Twice since Griswald's death, she'd awakened with no memory of what had happened. The first time, she collapsed on the floor and lay there for a half hour. The second time, she held on to the fantasy all morning that he was still alive.

"Til death do us part." Gretchen had spoken the words but hadn't listened to them. She'd heard them, she'd repeated them, and then she had moved on to her new life, a life of endless tomorrows. Together, they luxuriated in the thought of growing old together, of steadfastly marching arm-in-arm into a bright and lasting future. They would beget children who would beget grandchildren who would beget great-grandchildren, on and on, forever.

It would be their dazzling dream come to life. But after the fourth and final miscarriage, they understood that not all dreams come true.

"We will be our own little family," Gris had said. Gretchen had agreed as she lay in bed recovering. She never spoke of the losses again. She never let go of the guilt, though, the last link she had to lives unrealized.

Gris had brought up adoption. But she didn't want someone else's child, she wanted her own. She wanted to see Gris's face looking back at her when she nursed the baby.

How foolish.

The funeral director had questioned the wisdom of showing Gris in an open casket, given what had happened. But standing beside a closed casket seemed unbearably cruel, as if she was embarrassed by him.

Franklin had been at Gretchen's side as hundreds of mourners passed. There were his co-workers, friends, acquaintances, and then there were all the strangers. They came, borrowing her grief for their own reasons. She resented them and appreciated them. She had no time, though, for the demonstrators. No matter their well-intentioned banners and chants, she wished they'd all go to hell.

Franklin stood beside Gretchen for hours, a stone wall of support that she could lean on when needed.

Gretchen had awakened in tears that morning, not because she had forgotten what had happened, but because she had forgotten how many years it had been.

"Four," she said. In her mind, in her heart, there was no time between then and now. He could just as easily have died this morning, and the tears would be as warm, as salty, as they were on the day it happened. "Miss you."

She stood in the shower, water as hot as she could stand, for twice as long as usual. She toweled her hair and let it hang dry. She threw on a track suit and a hoodie and went downstairs. She could smell coffee and the kitchen light was on. There sat Franklin hunched over scattered papers, mumbling to himself.

"Coffee's ready," he said without looking.

Gretchen grabbed a mug, poured, and sat down opposite her brother.

"So, you're up," she said.

"Been up."

"Good for you. Like I told you."

"Like you told me what?"

"To get the eff up and do something every goddam day. I don't care what it is. You could walk to the corner and back. Take out the garbage. Cross the street and go down the block to the drug store. Doesn't matter what. Just do something."

"Oh. Yeah. I think I remember you saying something like that."

His head was still down. He shuffled through the papers. There were maps and printouts from Amazon and Google. There were hazy pictures of women of a certain age.

"We're getting nowhere as fast as we can. Know that?" said Franklin.

"That's because there's nowhere to go."

"There has to be."

"Okay, so, let's say, just for argument's sake, that you find her. Right? Okay, once you find her, then what?"

"What do you mean, 'then what'?"

"You walk up to her at, let's say, a Subway. And there she is, close enough to touch. What would you say?"

"C'mon."

"No, really, what would you say?"

Franklin hesitated, then said, "I still love you, honey. Come home, please."

"I'll be her, 'Excuse me, who are you?'"

"What?"

"'Are you just some old man come to harass me?'"

"Gretchen."

"Make your case, Franklin. Let's try again. This time she doesn't respond like a total ass monkey. 'My God, it's you'."

Franklin stammered. "Look, Gretchen—"

"Make your case!"

Franklin cleared his throat. "Look, Laney, I'm sorry if I've done something wrong. When I find out what it is, I'll never do it again. Truly." He shook his head and curled his lips. "But I never stopped loving you. Never. And I never will. We've been together for forty years. That says something doesn't it?"

"'I'll have the tuna salad, Sun Chips, and a soda. Oh, and a chocolate chip cookie.'"

Franklin made his what-the-fuck face.

"Maybe she's not interested. Get to the point."

Franklin took a deep breath. "I know we can work this out."

"'No, we can't! Excuse me, young man, may I have a few extra napkins?'"

Franklin's eyebrows crashed in the middle of his forehead.

"That's what's gonna happen, Brother. It's been a while, you know, and she's never contacted you. She's moved on. Plain and simple. I think you can call off the dogs."

Franklin sat and looked through his papers for a particular photograph. When he found it, he laid it down in front of his sister.

"What's this?" she said.

"Look familiar?"

"It's a car."

"Not just any car. Lavender Mercedes. New York license."

"Let me see that." The caption read: "Even New Yorkers Want to Be Sooners."

CHAPTER 12

It had been a long day, made longer by "that impossible woman," Maggie's new name for her mother.

Their relationship had always been a wrestling match. Roz won every battle until Maggie was about thirteen, then they usually fought to a draw. By sixteen, seventeen, Maggie was winning consistently. Yes, I will pierce my nipples. Yes, I will get a tattoo sleeve. Yes, I will fuck anyone I want. It wasn't that her mother was getting weaker; Maggie was getting stronger, something that Roz both regretted and admired.

When Roz was young, she never fought back. She ran away, instead. That seemed like the best option. Only later, struggling as a single mom, had she wished she'd stayed to fight, had she wished she'd stayed connected. Even though Maggie didn't understand it yet, Roz believed that fighting was the glue that kept them close. Things end only when you walk away.

Maggie hated fighting. But if she didn't push back, she would suffocate under the dead weight of her mother's demands and criticisms.

"Who are you to judge me? Look at you! Look at your life! I don't see anything that suggests you know anything about anything!"

"You'll see, Miss Hot Shit. Wait until you're on your own and you fall flat on that pretty face. Wait until you're out there not knowing what to do or where to go. Just wait. When no one's there, when no one cares a lick, let's see who you turn to."

This set Maggie's teeth on edge. She feared her mother might be right. The only world she knew was Righteous, Oklahoma, which wasn't much of a world at all. What would she do out there in the wide world, trying to find her way? Sometimes the thought filled her with breathless excitement; other times it filled her with breathless dread.

Lately, dread had the upper hand. She unclogged toilets at a nowhere motel; she took out other people's garbage; she changed their sheets and made their beds, scraped the scum off their shower stalls, and swept filth off their floors. This can't be it, she thought. She was desperate to leave, to go. But where? Anywhere. It didn't matter.

Sometimes she stood on the berm of 66, looking one direction, then the other, wondering which way to go. In the end, she'd stay. And resent it.

She wished she had someone to confide in, someone who would listen to her. But all she had was her mother. Was she someone Maggie could 'turn to'? Not really. Her mother was waging war with her own mother. Nothing else seemed to matter. Worse, Maggie had become the battleground for this decades old conflict. At breakfast that morning:

"You been late getting home most days. What's going on?"

Roz beat some eggs and poured them into a sizzling fry pan beside the bacon.

"Nothing's going on. Nothing's ever going on."

Maggie slumped into her chair and sipped her coffee. Roz scrambled the eggs to death.

"You been staying with *her* after work, haven't you?"

"With who?"

"That grandmother."

My God, thought Maggie.

"What do you care?"

"Have you? Have you been hanging around with her when you should come home?"

"What is it with you and your mother? If I treated you the way you—"

"Just answer me!"

"After work I hang out with whoever I want. I'm nineteen. I'm a grown ass woman, in case you hadn't noticed."

"You're a child."

"You wish."

"Ever since *she* showed up in that goddam car, you been treating me like I'm a second-class piece of shit." Roz took off her apron and threw it on the counter. The eggs were dry as dust now, the bacon black.

"How does that saying go? Something about 'if the shoe fits...'"

"You are a little smart ass."

"Jesus Christ, what do you want from me?" Maggie stood, knocking her chair over in the process. "Seriously, what do you want?"

"A little respect."

"I'm giving you as little respect as I can." She glared at her mother.

Simply put, talking to her mother didn't work. Whatever made talking and listening possible was broken and couldn't be fixed.

Maggie left early for work. When she got there, her grandmother was sitting on the bumper of her car. She waved as Maggie pulled in.

"Morning, Granddaughter."

"I guess."

"What's wrong?"

"Nothing's right, that's what's wrong. I can't do anything right for that woman."

"Your mother."

"If I'm breathing in, I should be breathing out; if I reach with my left hand, I should have used my right. I'm sick of it."

Laney wrapped her arms around Maggie. "Oh, honey." She patted her back. "She's a tough one. I should know." She hesitated to say more.

"Always been tough on me. Always. I don't get it." Maggie pulled a handkerchief from her back pocket, wiped her nose, and walked slowly to the office.

Laney wanted to grab her again. She wanted to hold her, to comfort her, to reassure her. By the time Roz was nineteen, she'd been gone three years. She was fifteen, about to turn sixteen, the last time Laney held her, comforted her, reassured her. She wanted her arms to be full like that again.

There were five guests, all asking for late checkout, which meant Maggie would get into their rooms late, which meant she'd leave work later still. At 5:00pm Sandman left for his favorite watering hole. Maggie was in charge. She sat in his torn leather swivel chair and rocked to a squeaky beat. Her grandmother had stopped by earlier to check on her. She was so thoughtful, it was hard to believe what her mother said about her.

Maggie had never taken an interest in her mother's early life. She knew she'd grown up back east somewhere. She knew her mother was an only child, like her. She knew that her mother had dropped out of school. After that, it seemed her mother's life was a slow but steady tumble down, down, down, until she hit bottom in Righteous. Her mother didn't talk about Maggie's grandmother. They exchanged phone calls twice a year. After these calls, her mother would be out of sorts for days. Either angry or sad or both.

Out the office window, Maggie saw miles upon miles of flatness. An armada of gray, purple clouds rose over the horizon. They always faded away, crossing the plains. The land had little experience with rain. If you were to survive, you'd have to make it on nothing. It was five minutes before a vehicle passed by. She blinked.

She opened the soda machine and pulled out a bottle of Mountain Dew, then gulped half of it in one swallow. She wiped her mouth on her arm and belched.

She was expecting a guest from Missouri. It was past 6:00pm now. They were an hour late and unlikely to come. For every reservation that arrived as planned, there were seven that blew right by without stopping. Righteous was that kind of place. It was a place to pass through. Not a place to stay.

When Maggie was a little girl, she loved the wide-open spaces. She could run as far as she could see and still have further to go. She could teach her dolls on the front porch and lay them down for naps on the cool dirt. She could go to the Save-a-Lot where her mom worked; her mother would give her little jobs to do, taking out the garbage, getting the mail, greeting customers, and asking if they needed help. "You *are* a big girl, aren't you," some of them would say, tousling her long, wind-blown hair.

She was doing precisely the same thing when she became a teenager, small chores, once so fun, became an embarrassment, especially when boys from school would drop by. "Hey, miss, could you fetch me a quart of milk?" They'd snicker behind her back, because she was an Okie, poor and dirty and hopeless.

Roz hoped Maggie would eventually take over the Save-a-Lot so Roz could slow down. Maggie could take care of them both, if she worked hard enough.

"Why in the world would I want your job?"

"Your best option," her mother said, casually.

And she was right. Nevertheless, she went behind her mother's back and took a job at the motel, working for Sandman. Her mother didn't speak to her for a week. Heaven.

Maggie had progressed exactly two hundred yards down the road from the convenience store to the motel. And there, life stopped. She did take a weeklong trip to Austin, hoping to discover herself and find a good job. But Austin was like going from a row boat to a yacht. The energy was too intense. The boys were too cool. Everyone seemed to look down on her even though they never noticed her. She called her mother in tears. "Come home," she said. "I warned you."

Maggie could feel a hole opening inside her, a hole so deep that she could fall in and never be found. She would be gone. Her voice, a distant echo. Would anyone remember she had ever been here in this dusty, sweaty world?

Another hour passed. Finally, the folks from Missouri pulled in. Maggie was in no mood to welcome them. Why hadn't they called? What the hell were they thinking? Like she had nothing better to do than wait for the likes of them?

Maggie met the spindly husband and weary wife before they opened the door.

"Sorry, we're full."

The man took off his ballcap and looked at the empty parking lot.

"You're kidding."

"Everyone's off to the multiplex tonight. One of those Marvel movies just came to town."

The man looked at his wife and then at Maggie. "She's awful tired, miss. I'm sure you got a room, right?"

"Nope." And she closed the door.

The man pounded on the door so hard the walls rattled, and Maggie cowered in the corner.

"Open this goddam door and give us a goddam room!"

Maggie stood in the middle of the office. "Go fuck yourselves!"

There was a standoff for another ten minutes, but then the couple walked slowly to their car. Maggie could see they were arguing. The engine turned over and they headed down 66.

Maggie, who was sure she hadn't taken a breath the whole time, started crying and couldn't stop. She lay on the floor, curled into a ball and wept. Then fell asleep. When she woke up, there was a crick in her neck and one leg was numb. She rubbed her neck and shook her leg. It was dark now. And quiet as death.

"Jesus God, what am I going to do?"

She stood under the awning in the clammy night air and locked the office door. She walked toward her car but then she heard honky-tonk music calling to her from Cooney's Bar. She turned on her heels and trotted to Cooney's, eager to be around someone, anyone. When she opened the door, *Stand by Your Man* was howling from the juke box. The Righteous Dart League was in full swing in one corner while the ax throwers were heaving in the other. In the middle was a pool table, serious faces all around, cash on the felt. And at the bar were four teachers from the high school, two men gawking at them, and, at the far end, another man, his head bent over a beer that was surrounded by empty glasses streaked with dry foam. Sandman.

It was a moment or so before Sandman noticed someone sitting beside him. Maggie laughed quietly to herself. He looked up, his eyes droopy.

"What's wrong," he said. "Did that toilet blow again?"

"No, all the toilets are in working condition."

"Good." He waved to the bartender. "Another. And for the lady?"

"Bourbon neat. Make that a double."

Sandman's eyebrows shot up. "Really?"

•   •   •

The morning sun, already hellishly hot, baked Maggie's face. She held up her arm to block it, and then buried her face in the pillow. The curtain flapped and the door creaked in the stifling wind. Maggie turned over, her face resting on the wrinkled sheet. She sniffed the air. What is that smell? she thought. Her eyes were still closed, she took another sniff. Dust, and pine scented air freshener, and a recently flushed toilet, and sweat, and the empty smell of sheets washed a thousand times or more.

Maggie rubbed her eyes and opened them a crack. She sat bolt upright. She covered her mouth as she looked around. Old bottles of English Leather on the dresser. Dirty underwear and T-shirts in the corner. Empty MacDonald's bags overflowing the trash can. And beer bottles crowding the TV.

On the floor at her feet were her jeans, top, bra and panties. She looked at herself. She was wearing a man's T-shirt.

Her memory was returning. "Shit." She held her head in her hands. "This is twenty-four," she whispered. Sandman's room. "No," she said, her voice tight.

CHAPTER 13

Sandford Grantham peed while looking at himself in the full-length mirror hanging on the door. He looked eight months pregnant. He sucked in his gut, which only made his chest look unnaturally large and his face unnaturally red.

He decided not to flush, fearing he would awaken his guest.

Studying his face in the mirror, he was surprised how grizzled, unkempt, nasty it looked. His beard was patchy and his mustache looked like the bristly end of a worn-out broom.

"You don't have the face for a fucking beard." His father was never burdened with sensitivity. "Maybe sideburns but nothing else...and don't let your hair grow too long. You sweat too much. You'll always look like you just came in from a rain storm."

His father would be dead a week later. Looking back, Sandman wondered if his father knew, if he'd had a premonition or something that his bill was due, because he gave Sandman a lot of advice in those final days.

"You're not cut out for college. Not enough upstairs. I don't mean that as a criticism. I'm just stating a fact. You'll be wasting all that money you've saved. Learn a trade. Plumber, electrician, carpenter. We always need those guys. You'll never be short on work."

"Dabble in women but don't invest in them." Sandman's mother, Gladiola, had stayed on the scene for exactly one year before she "vamoosed," as his father would say. She was found in a Tijuana alley, dead from years of steady drinking. "I've gone the investment route a few times, and I can tell you, you'll always get bamboozled."

"Don't waste your time reading books. Watch television. You learn more and you learn it fast." When Sandman's father was a boy, no one knew about dyslexia. He didn't read because he couldn't. He was too "lazy," "dumb," "delinquent" to learn. These diagnoses came from his parents.

Sandman rubbed his cheeks and chin. He ran hot water into the bowl, got his straight razor and Gillette Foamy from the cabinet, and went to work. One, two, three shaves later, he surveyed the damage. He never realized how much space there was between his nose and his upper lip. It looked like a landing strip. And, where did his chin go? And the dangling turkey wattle, what was that about? He leaned over the sink and rinsed his face a second time. He looked up again, hoping his original assessment had been unnecessarily harsh. But it hadn't. "Goddammit," he whispered to himself. He picked up his jeans, jersey, and socks from the floor and sniffed them. Good enough, he thought, as he put them on.

He turned on the water, cupped some in his hands and drizzled it on his head. He ran his comb through it multiple times, hoping he'd create a clean look. But when he checked the mirror, 'greaser' was the only word that came to mind. "Shit," he said a little too loudly. He held his breath and stood still as a dead man, hoping his guest would not wake up, hoping he could leave before having to face her.

He tiptoed out of the bathroom and picked up his Keds. He reached for the door but heard moaning coming from his bed. She rolled over and pulled the covers up to her chin. Her hair was piled high in tangles. She wiggled her nose, then brushed a single lock of curled hair from her face. She sighed and then fell asleep again.

Sandman leaned against the door and watched. Her eyes rolled and twitched. Must be a dream, he thought. Her lips parted, like she was about to speak. Then her breathing turned heavy.

She had the face of a child, he thought. Her skin looked brand new, like she had just arrived on earth.

When she laughed, though, she had a woman's laugh. He'd heard it for several hours the previous night. It started low and coarse, like a rocket on the launch pad, and then in the blink of an eye, it was aloft, reaching high C, punctuated with a snort.

Last night he was the funniest person the world had ever seen. There were moments when she couldn't find her breath, he was so hysterical. And he was convinced her laugh was true. He believed he was on the world's biggest stage and everyone adored him. It felt like he was floating, light as a feather, unencumbered, free.

Maggie passed gas. He smiled, opened the door, and trotted down the walkway to the office. Two couples wearing masks and pumping tiny bottles of hand sanitizer were waiting.

"Good mornin' folks!" His voice was warm, welcoming, enthusiastic, even charming.

"You don't have any hand sanitizer," said the tall thin man with the bushy gray hair.

Sandman looked at him but didn't speak. Jesus, he thought.

"We wanted to get on the road an hour ago," said one of the wives. "Where's that guy?"

"Excuse me, what guy?"

"The owner. Starts with an S...Sandy maybe."

"Oh, he's off today," said Sandman, not wanting to explain his new look.

After they settled their bill, he gave them each a Snickers and sent them on their way.

It was only 9:00am. It felt like high noon. Eighteen wheelers sped past the Sunrise Hotel, dust billowing in their wake. He walked out to the mailbox and fetched the *Weekly Gazette*. He opened it. Then closed it. He walked back to the office. A trucker blared his air horn, and Sandman waved without looking. He stopped at the office door and glanced down the walkway. He wondered what was going on in 24.

Last night was long gone. In the merciless light of day, he didn't feel so funny anymore.

CHAPTER 14

For the first time in weeks, Franklin was outside on his own. Gretchen had insisted.

"I'm not going with you. You want to go somewhere, feel free."

Franklin noticed a difference. It felt like his internal seasons were changing, winter was giving way to spring, and summer was on the horizon. While his cough persisted, he felt less exhausted and foggy. In the evenings, he was at his worst. But during the day, he was sixty percent himself.

Even Gretchen had noticed.

"What's with you, Brother? If I didn't know better, I'd think you were turning a corner and heading towards 'normal' again."

"Thank you, Sister. Sixty percent of me is better than one hundred percent of most people."

They laughed together more often. It harkened back to earlier days, when they hadn't yet been battered by life, when they were hopeful and confident.

"Life has a way of kicking you in the ass." Gretchen had said this to Franklin when he was feeling hopeless. She wasn't complaining. She was telling the truth. She shrugged when she said it like she might have shrugged at the grocery store if they were out of toilet paper. "Life has upsides and downsides; sometimes the downsides last longer; sometimes you wait and wait for an upside to bail you out, to smooth and straighten the road ahead, but your waiting goes unrewarded; that's when you grit your teeth and keep going, you make your own road."

She came up with these aphorisms shortly after Gris's death. She had been casting about, trying to attribute meaning to something that seemed to diminish the meaning of everything. It was the best she could do.

Franklin clutched the photograph as he opened the car door. He slid into place. Gretchen had driven the car last, so he had to adjust everything. He tilted the steering wheel down a few inches. Lowered the seat. Tilted it back. Angled the mirrors. He changed the channel from Gretchen's country music to twenty-four-hour news. He took the picture out of his jacket pocket and looked at it again.

"What? You think there's only one Mercedes with a New York license in all of Oklahoma?" Gretchen had said.

"Lavender?"

"It was nighttime, for God's sake. You can't tell if it's lavender. You're seeing what you want to see, not what's there."

"And you can't see what's there, because you don't want to."

They had argued to a draw.

Gretchen worried that just as Franklin was returning from one fog, he might be getting lost in another.

"How many times do you have to hear it? She. Does. Not. Love. You. And to tell you the truth, I don't—"

"Think she ever did."

"Yes."

"But I love her."

"So."

"I think that should count for something."

When Gretchen fell silent, Franklin thought he'd won. But Gretchen was silent because she was dumbfounded by his reasoning. If you love someone, but they don't love you...that was it, game, set, match.

Franklin was convinced, though, that if he could only find Laney, the power of his love would win the day. Just as it had in the very beginning. It wasn't clear to him, at the time, whether she wanted to marry him. She was young and gorgeous and sought after by every young man in the county and beyond. Why would she marry someone who was a decade, or more, older than her? What might convince her?

His love, that's what. His calling-all-the-time-sending-flowers-every-day-buying-her-anything-she-wanted-taking-her-on-exotic-vacations-and-ceaselessly-declaring-his-love for her. For a time, she successfully swatted away the mosquitos of his affection.

"I don't think she wants to marry you," Gris had said. "If she did, she would have caved in by now." Gretchen stood by, shaking her head in agreement.

Franklin had smiled. "I think that's her game. She wants me to try harder."

Love sure was blind, but who knew it was so stupid?

And so, on and on it went, until Laney said, "Sure." Like, 'Sure, you can change the channel', or 'Sure, you can have another piece of pie', or 'Sure, I've got nothing better to do'.

What Franklin heard was, "Oh my God, yes, yes! I love you! You've made me the happiest girl in the world!" Everything she said went through a filter and came out exactly as he wanted.

"You don't have a clue how to listen, do you?" Laney's spot-on assessment in the first year of their marriage.

"What?" Franklin had replied.

"I don't think the words that leave my mouth ever reach your ears."

Instead of listening, he bought her fur coats, diamond necklaces, extravagant cars, Gucci everything. Every time she said, "Listen to me!" he would order her a dozen roses. Or schedule a vacation in Hawaii. When he did this, she would calm down for several weeks, sometimes longer.

When she'd go away, heading out for points unknown, he'd try harder. "What more do you want from me?" he'd say when she'd return.

"You don't know how to give me what I want," she'd say, her voice listless.

Sounds like she needs a new pearl necklace, he'd think.

And so it went. For forty years.

Franklin put the photograph on the dashboard and sighed. He rubbed his hands together to warm them. He started the Lexus and eased out of the garage and into the street. He smiled when he put it in drive and sped away. It was his first time behind the wheel since being diagnosed. Maybe this "thing" was finally going away.

He never used the word "Covid" when talking about his illness, especially since he wasn't positive for the virus any longer. It was too hard to explain what was going on—"Okay, so, I had Covid, and it went away, but not really, and then it came back but with different symptoms, and, no, I'm not testing positive anymore" — so he preferred saying, "I have that flu that's going around."

Whether he wanted to use the word or not, Covid tromped through his body like it owned the place. It did whatever it wanted to do whenever it wanted to do it. Sometimes it convinced him that Laney was in the house. He'd hobble to the spiral staircase, clutch the hand-carved spindles, and call up to the balcony, "Laney! Laney, goddammit!" He'd wonder why she didn't come out of the bedroom. Had he given her Covid? Had she died?

To that, Gretchen would say, "Well, in a manner of speaking..."

He found it impossible to concentrate or remember, impossible to imagine, or bend over, or dress himself, or even make a sandwich. He was helpless, something he hadn't felt since he was a boy.

He breathed a sigh of relief when he pulled into the Walgreen's parking lot. He had driven through one stop sign and one red light. He white knuckled it the rest of the way.

There was a girl, maybe sixteen, standing inside the door with a bundle of masks in her arms. And a rainbow mask on her face.

Please don't ask me, thought Franklin. Please.

"Welcome to Walgreens!" she said, perkiness in her voice. She reached out with a mask in her hand. "Would you like a—"

"No!" said Franklin, more stridently than he'd intended.

"Asshole," whispered the girl as Franklin headed to the photography section.

Franklin stood in front of the machine trying to read the directions for enlarging photographs. He couldn't. He squinted, but that didn't make a difference. Neither did rubbing his eyes. He took a pair of reading glasses from a nearby display and put them on.

"There we go," he said.

"What was that, sir?" said another teenager behind a nearby counter.

"Nothing." The world is being run by children, thought Franklin.

"Can I help you with something?"

Jesus, thought Franklin. "No, but thanks." He put the reading glasses on, the price tag dangling over his nose.

"Would you like those?" said the towheaded boy wearing horn-rimmed specs.

"Just need them for a minute." Why do people need to be helpful?

"Okay then. I'll be right here, if you need me." He pulled his mask down and smiled, revealing a set of silver train tracks.

Why does every kid in the world have braces? thought Franklin.

As he entered his eighth decade, he became more critical of the generations following close on his heels, the generations that would escort him from this world. They didn't know how to do anything. They stared at their phones all day and all night, playing games, getting their shorts in a knot when someone said something that hurt their feelings, believing every stupid thing that any lunatic posted.

He looked at the cashier again and shook his head. He's probably vaccinated, too. The government said, Get vaccinated, so that's what he did. No one thinks for themselves anymore.

Franklin took off the reading glasses, dropped them on the counter, and headed for the exit when the cashier called, "Excuse me, sir, but I think you left something behind."

"What?" Franklin glared.

"Right there behind you. I think that's yours, isn't it."

"Oh...yes, it is."

My God, old people! thought the boy cashier.

Franklin shuffled down the aisle, picked up the picture, stared at it, took another pair of reading glasses from the display, and leaned over the copier. He read the directions again, lifted the cover again, put the picture in place again, pushed the button and waited. Out came a copy. Same size as the one he had. He rolled it up and tossed it on the floor. Tried again. Same result. Rolled and tossed.

"Excuse me, sir, do you need some help?"

"No!"

My God, old people! thought the boy cashier.

Franklin decided a third pair of readers were called for. He reread the directions for enlarging photos. Placed the photo on the glass, smoothed it out, shut the lid, pushed the button. This time he got a miniature version of the picture, one he could carry in his wallet. He punched the copier as hard as he could.

"Sir? Sir, please don't hit the copier. Is something the matter?"

Even with a mask on, Franklin could tell the boy was laughing, his head bobbed so much.

Sonofabitch, he thought. "Yes, something's the matter! This damn copier is broken!"

My God, old people! thought the boy cashier.

"Let me take a look," he said.

When he came closer, Franklin could see his name tag—Rusty, Assistant Manager. He was taller than Franklin by an inch, maybe two. Franklin straightened his back and stretched his neck. Probably seventeen, maybe eighteen, thought Franklin. Almost the same age as Laney when I hired her. He shook his head to think that, while she had looked like a woman, she'd been just a girl. He'd been a man and she'd been just a girl.

"So," said Rusty, his hands on his hips. "What's up?"

Franklin explained he wanted to enlarge the picture, but the copier wasn't working right. Rusty picked up the picture, put it on the screen, pushed a button, and out came the picture, twice the size of the original.

"There you go," said Rusty, handing the copy to Franklin. "Need another one?"

"No," he said softly. "What do I owe you?"

Rusty put his hand on Franklin's shoulder and squeezed. "Nothing, old timer. It's on me."

Old timer? Franklin wanted to take Rusty's head and crush it against the copier.

Rusty sauntered back to his place behind the cash register.

As Franklin was leaving, he dropped a ten-dollar bill on the counter in front of Rusty.

"There you go. Keep the change."

Franklin sat in the car and switched the dashboard lights on. He examined the enlarged photo of the license plate. It was hazy at best. He compared it to the original. He held the enlargement close to his face, trying to decipher even one letter, one number. At the end of the plate, was that an eight or a 'B'? Maybe a nine? He held the picture at arm's length and then close to his face again. A three? And there, in the middle, was that a 'C' or a zero? He was sure the first letter was 'M.' Or maybe an 'N.'

He sighed and dropped the picture into his lap, then lay his head on the steering wheel. I've been doing this since the very first time I saw her, he thought. Chasing after her. Trying to catch her love.

He sat up. Shook his head. He stared out the window for a moment, then opened the door, got out, and dropped the picture in the nearest trash receptacle.

He got back in the car, sat for several more minutes. Started the engine. Let it idle. Opened the door and put one foot on the pavement, then stopped. Turned off the engine, got out of the car, and walked over to the trash receptacle. Pulled his cell phone from his pocket and turned on the light. He removed the lid and leaned in. It took a minute, but he found the picture. He pulled it out, put the lid back on, and went back to his car.

Franklin turned on the dashboard lights, and examined the photo. Again. It's got to be an eight, he thought. It's got to. With that, he backed out of his space and headed home.

Rusty had been watching this from the window. He raised his eyebrows and crinkled his forehead. My God, old people, he thought.

CHAPTER 15

To keep her hands warm, Laney wrapped them both around her coffee mug as she stepped out the door. It wasn't necessary. The panhandle's sun shined warm and bright. She donned her sunglasses and sat back in the creaky, old, wicker chair Sandman had provided for her. If she were home, she'd be wearing winter garb by now and hoping that snow would be delayed another month. The sun would disappear by five o'clock and wouldn't show up again until seven fifteen the next morning. Here, the sun was up much longer. Or did it only seem longer because of the mind-numbing flatness in every direction? If she were three, maybe four inches taller, she could see Texas in one direction and Kansas in the other. Flat plus flat plus flat.

At first, she had found the homogeneous topography calming. Hypnotic and calming, with a dash of mindless monotony. She could sit outside her room, eyes closed for hours, and everything would be the same when she opened them again. After her recent period of cascading changes, blah-blah-blah was a relief.

Until it wasn't. Somewhere along the way, the invisible line between tranquil and tranquilized had been crossed. One day, a fly landed on the post in front of her. She watched it for an hour, and the fly never moved. Finally, it fell to the ground, dead. She understood, completely.

The only thing that made a difference was Maggie. Getting to know her was the bright spot in her day. But Roz was a different story. She thought the dinner with her and Maggie would melt the ice, at least a little bit. Not so much. She was invited a second time, but Roz canceled at the last minute because "the neighbors' chickens got loose."

They did have lunch at Pee Wee's in Righteous, a train car diner. But it was so packed at noon, they couldn't find a booth together. They sat at the counter, two or three stools apart, eating alone together.

She rarely saw Roz, getting glimpses of her from time to time when she drove past the Save-a-Lot. It was different with Maggie. She saw Maggie every day. She would stop by 18 with extra towels and soaps. They'd sit together talking about nothing, sometimes laughing, and seeming to enjoy each other's company. They'd grab a beer at Cooney's or go out for a burger. Laney felt they were getting closer.

But Maggie had fallen from view recently. She arrived and departed from work like a shadow. Never in the office, never where she could easily be seen. She left towels and soap on the wicker chair without knocking on the door.

She started missing work altogether.

"Yeah, she's been out, I know."

"What's wrong?"

"I don't know," Sandman had said, with his back to Laney.

"Is she sick?"

"Yeah, maybe that's it. She's taking some time is all she said."

"Time? For what?"

"Don't know," said Sandman through a hard sigh.

"Where'd she go?"

"Nowhere." He shrugged his shoulder and twisted the mop, water dripping into the wash bucket.

Did I do something? thought Laney. Is she angry at me? Did Roz tell her what had happened, even though it had nothing to do with Maggie?

Maggie's absence was more difficult to handle than Roz's stonewalling. With Roz, the story had been written. It was impossible to un-write it and impossible to add new chapters to it. Maggie was new, though. They didn't have any history together. Their story had yet to be written. Maggie gave Laney something rare—hope.

•   •   •

"What in the hell is going on?" said Roz. "Why aren't you at work?"

"Because I'm not."

"Jesus, Maggie, what's wrong with you?"

Roz stood at Maggie's door. Maggie pulled the covers up so her mother couldn't see her.

"Sandman is gonna be pissed. How long's this gonna go on?"

"That is not your concern."

"What do you mean, it's not my concern? Of course, it is. I'm your goddam mother."

Maggie opened her mouth, then decided the best defense was to say nothing.

"Maggie! Do you hear me?"

Maggie didn't move. She made sleep sounds, heavy breathing, mild snoring.

"Jesus H. Christ. What is gonna become of you?"

Roz watched the lump in the bed, hoping it would move, hoping it would sit up and talk to her, hoping, hoping. What had she done wrong? How had she failed as a mother? Whenever she commiserated with her regulars at the Save-a-Lot, they were unanimous in their opinions. "Don't drive yourself nuts. She's a grown woman. You've done your work. Now it's on her to make a life." She always appreciated them taking her side, but what did they really think? What did they say to their husbands when they got home?

Righteous was small. Town's folk had been watching each other's kids grow up since forever, but they never advised or criticized. They understood life was long. They'd be living side by side for most of it, and no one wanted to make enemies. Best to keep your opinions to yourself.

But you could tell a lot from what they didn't say. If someone came into the store and *didn't* ask how Maggie was, Roz would wonder what was up. If she said hello to someone and they answered without smiling, she'd grow suspicious. If they drove by and nodded instead of giving her a friendly wave, she'd be puzzled.

Roz always hoped she'd be seen as an A+ mother, but she was sure that if the citizens of Righteous had been asked, they would have given her a D+ at best. She didn't have to hear it directly from them. It was in the air. No matter how critical they might have been, no one would have judged Roz more harshly than herself.

Three years before Maggie was born, Roz was still sleeping with her favorite stuffed animal. About the same time, she had her first period. And she bought her first training bra. She knew nothing about life, but life was coming at her fast.

She was fifteen when she met Jackson, who was a few years older. She'd never loved anyone or anything as much as she loved him. She went to war with her parents over Jackson, but they wouldn't budge. Then Jackson was gone. By then, lines had been drawn in the sand, and things had been said that couldn't be unsaid. She moved out and lived with friends. Drinking and drugs followed. Multiple partners, too.

For reasons that didn't make sense to her friends, Roz decided California was the place to be; California was the solution to all her problems. She boarded a bus bound for Columbus, then on to St. Louis. During the long ride from St. Louis to Albuquerque, she first noticed her breasts were swollen and tender. And her belly was the shape of a crescent moon. When they reached the bus stop in

Righteous, she got off, went to the ladies' room at the Texaco station and threw up.

She got a job at that gas station and found a room for rent. She was sixteen. No parents. Boyfriend as gone as gone could be. And someone growing in her belly. She had no idea who put it there.

When the time came, they kept her in the hospital several extra days because she was so young and alone. But soon, she was back in her tiny rented room, a helpless baby in her arms. The baby got pink eye and then a respiratory illness and before Roz knew it the baby was six weeks old and hadn't been named. She settled on Margaret. Later, she regretted giving her daughter an "old lady name," so she called her Maggie.

One day she turned around and that baby was nineteen with the temperament of a two-year-old. On the road to nineteen, there had been birthdays and holidays and picnics and slumber parties and lazy summer days at the public swimming pool. Roz posted school work on the refrigerator and went to band concerts, choral concerts, and school plays. If she thought hard about it, she could remember good times. But it seemed they stood out because they were as infrequent as rain.

Had she told Maggie she loved her?

She went back to Maggie's bedroom. All she could see was a mess of beautiful hair sprawled across her pillow.

"Dammit Maggie, get up!"

Her mother's voice was piercing, like a nail being pounded into her temple. If she lay still, maybe her mother would leave. Then she could close her eyes and disappear.

Recently, Maggie spent most nights sitting on the front porch, her OU sweatshirt keeping her warm. She'd turn off the porch light, pull her knees up to her chest, and let her eyes wander. Trucks rolled by now and then. The air abuzz with moths and mosquitos, fireflies, crickets, and cicadas. The echo of coyotes in the distance, howling mournfully. She'd lean back in her chair, amazed at the star-cluttered sky. She'd close her eyes and enjoy the faint, moist, breeze on her neck and face, sometimes cool enough to curl her toes.

When Maggie was little and her mother didn't hear her calling in the night, Maggie'd get up, all sleepy-eyed and search for her. Her mother would be on the porch sitting on the same chair. Most times, she'd send Maggie back to her room, but sometimes she'd let her stay. Maggie would crawl up on her lap, lay her head on her mother's chest, and listen to her beating heart. Sometimes this memory made Maggie smile; sometimes it made her cry.

Lately, when she sat on the porch, she hoped the Milky Way would point her in the right direction, make clear the path ahead. In the end, though, the plethora of stars, the massiveness of the sky stretching to eternity, made her feel small and insignificant, her concerns human dust.

She returned to bed just before sunrise and fell into a deep sleep. This had been the pattern for several days. First time she did this, she felt guilty not going to work. She called Sandman, using a sickly voice, to say she had a bug. She closed with a cough and an apology, and Sandman said it wasn't necessary. She felt less guilty the next day, so she sent him a brief text with no apology. After that, she didn't notify him at all. And he didn't try to contact her.

The silence between them was like a conversation. The less they said, the more they conveyed. At times, she wanted to call him to ask, "Don't you have anything to say to me?" Two cups of coffee and a hot shower later convinced her that was not the way to go.

"Mom!" she called. When she didn't answer, Maggie knew she'd gone to work. She sat on the side of her bed, head in her hands. Determined to take a shower today, she stood, took a deep breath, then another, and headed for the bathroom.

As scalding water pelted her face, and the room filled with fog, she repeated today's mantra— "C'mon, get going."

She stood on the front porch staring at the chair for a moment, then got in her Saturn. She rolled the window down, letting in the blistering heat. She passed the Save-a-Lot where her mother was leaning against the register gabbing with customers. As she approached the Sunrise Motel, Sandman was on a ladder repairing a gutter. She slowed down but didn't turn in.

Instead, she drove to Garmand, ten miles away. More private. She stopped and parked on the road across from the Garmand Free Clinic. She watched as old people and kids holding their mothers' hands came and went. The side of her face was pink from the sun when she started the car and pulled into the Clinic parking lot.

There was a line at check-in. When it was her turn, the receptionist asked if Maggie had an appointment. Maggie shook her head no. Without a word, the receptionist wrote a number on a post-it and pointed to the waiting area. Maggie found a seat on the end of a row. She looked at her post-it—Number 10.

·   ·   ·

Laney was sitting outside her motel room when Maggie drove by. She edged forward on her wicker chair, ready to stand. She smiled as Maggie slowed down. But then Maggie sped up and kept going. Laney's shoulders slumped in puzzlement. Where was she going? And why? She leaned back in her chair, took another sip of coffee, then sat forward again. She got up, went into the kitchen, dumped her coffee in the sink, then into her bedroom looking for her car keys, which were under the bed.

It was several minutes before Laney could see the blue haze trailing Maggie's car. She kept her distance, twice losing Maggie at stop lights. But Maggie was driving slowly, as if she wasn't sure where she was going. Catching up was easy.

They turned onto a two-lane in the middle of nowhere. No buildings, no houses, no nothing. In the distance, she could see the ominous Black Mesa dominating the horizon. She passed a sign that said, "Garmand, Everyone and Every-gun Welcome." Soon a gas station popped up, then a small plaza with six storefronts, then a stoplight. She pulled to the curb outside the post office until the light changed. She followed Maggie for a couple more miles when Maggie pulled off the road and stopped. Laney pulled off the road, as well, and slid down in her seat, hiding behind the steering wheel.

When no one tapped on her window or accused her of stalking, she raised up and watched Maggie, who was leaning out her window studying a squat, tan, adobe building that had a free clinic sign out front.

Free clinic, she thought. Why would she go to a free clinic when she already has a doctor? She watched a pickup pull into the lot. No one got out for several minutes. Finally, a woman exited on the driver's side. She gestured to someone else who was still in the car. Her hands were outstretched and her fingers were splayed; she thrust her arms forward, then up in the air. She put her hands in her jeans pockets and went around the car to the passenger door. She leaned on the truck and spoke without gesturing.

The car door opened and the woman stepped aside. A girl in her early teens got out. Her head was bowed and her shoulders were shaking. She wiped her eyes with the palms of her hands. The woman put her arms around her and held her tight. She then took the girl's hand in hers and kissed it. The girl heaved a sigh. They entered the clinic together.

Laney's back stiffened. Her eyes were wide and unblinking. Her moist hands were wringing the steering wheel, her white knuckles about to split open.

"No. Please not that," she said.

CHAPTER 16

"I cannot believe you are still doing this." Gretchen leaned against the sink, an iron skillet dangling from her hand. "Franklin, you've gotta get over this."

Franklin had come home from the pharmacy armed with the enlarged photo. On the drive, he had hardened his resolve, convinced there was no other option but to keep going, keep trying, no matter the outcome. It was impossible to imagine himself without her. His life had been one long performance for Laney, he, on stage and in the spotlight and she, the only one in the audience that mattered. It was her smile, her applause, her approval that he sought. She kept him afloat, filled him up when he was empty, made him feel like a man when doubts crept in.

He smoothed the enlarged picture on the kitchen table while Gretchen unloaded the dishwasher. All he said was, "Take a look at this." Then Gretchen exploded.

"She does not want to come back! I'm telling you. She doesn't. That's the goddam truth. Seriously. Why you can't get that through your melon is beyond me."

Franklin leaned over the kitchen table, studying the photo. "What do these look like to you?" he said, pointing at the license plate. "Is that an 'M' or 'N'? And that one, is it a 'C' or zero? I think it's a 'C.' But I'm not sure. And then this one here. An 8? A 9? Maybe—"

"Franklin!" Gretchen slammed the skillet on the kitchen counter. "What is wrong with you? This is embarrassing, the way you pine over that, that…"

"Go ahead and say it—that bitch. That's what you've—"

"That B.I.T.C.H. Yes! For crying in a bucket, why do you insist on making a fool of yourself?"

Franklin hunched over the picture again. He *is* nuts, she thought.

"Are you listening to me?"

"Come 'ere. Look at this one."

Gretchen glared at him, then stood by his side, leaned over the table, and sighed. "It's either an eight or a 'B'."

"Yeah. Yeah, but how do we figure out which one it is?"

"We? There is no 'we' in this snipe hunt."

"C'mon."

"You are on your own, mister."

Gretchen was leaving the room when she heard heaving and groaning. She turned around. Tears flowed from Franklin's eyes, like water from a downspout during a thunder storm.

She put her hand on his back and rubbed it in circles, gently.

"Brother, what is it?"

Was it still Covid? They both agreed that he was getting better inch by inch, although some nights she'd find him standing in the middle of his bedroom humming in the dark.

He was sleeping better, almost five hours a night. The numbness in his hands and feet had subsided. On most days his mind was clearer.

But the clearer his mind got, the more obsessed he became with that woman.

Often, Gretchen found his grief hard to fathom. She knew grief. She remembered what it was like when the musky smell disappeared from the clothes in Gris's closet. She remembered the first time she woke up sprawled across the middle of the bed, no room left for Gris. She remembered thinking she'd seen him at the grocery store. How her heart pounded. And when she realized she was mistaken, she still watched, hoping for glimpses of anything familiar, his nose, his mouth, his hair.

Laney wasn't *lost* lost. It was more like her brother had lost something in a closet or the basement. It was gone but still there. He just couldn't find 'there.'

Franklin caught his breath and dabbed the last of his tears with a tissue. Gretchen stood in the middle of the room, hands on hips. She stared, not at Franklin but through him. She blinked slowly and breathed deeply. She felt old. Old and tired and worn down.

Franklin watched her. His little sister.

"Sister?"

"Please don't ask me to do this."

"Are you okay?"

Gretchen looked sideways at her brother. "What?"

"Just what I said. Are you okay?"

"In what sense do you mean 'okay'?"

"I mean—"

"Like okay with your crazy plans to recapture a love that never was? Or, okay about living with you? Or, okay about the weather? Or, okay about that ridiculous chair of yours? Or, okay—"

"Gretchen. Are you okay?"

His droopy eyes were glued to her.

"No. I am not okay. Okay?"

"I'm sorry."

"Not your fault."

"I miss him, too."

Gretchen couldn't remember her brother saying this before. Recent months excepted, he always played his emotions close to the vest. When Gris died, he stayed at the house with her. He washed the car for the funeral. He grocery shopped. He took charge of her cell, responding to well-wishers, calling whoever needed to be called. He made lists and checked off each item. He was the go-between with the funeral director. He got the obituary to the paper on time. He blocked anyone seeking access to her.

He never asked whether she was okay, or how she felt, or how she was dealing with such a horrific event. He showed little emotion, didn't cry. But he never left her side, and he loved her in the only way he could.

Gretchen bowed her head. "I know."

"The sentencing will be here soon. Are you going to go back for it?"

"Don't know."

"Okay."

He cleared his throat. She coughed. They both harrumphed.

"So, like I said...Do you really think you have a chance with Laney?"

Franklin rubbed the stubble on his cheeks and looked at the photograph crinkled in his lap. His head fell back on the rest, and he studied the ceiling for answers that didn't exist. The resolve he had in the pharmacy had weakened. He looked at the photo again. He held it close to his face and squinted for clarity, but there was none to be found. He closed his eyes, hoping to see Laney, every detail of her smiling face, clear, inviting, and focused on him, but she wasn't there.

"Honest?" he said.

"Honest."

"Probably...not."

Gretchen was glad her jaw was attached to her face. Otherwise, it would have dropped to the floor and shattered into a million pieces.

The only person more surprised than Gretchen was Franklin. The words had trudged to the tip of his tongue, and before he could reel them in, they tumbled out. Was he waving a white flag, a sign of surrender? Was it Covid draining the fight out of him? Was it Laney's absolute, unconditional, unqualified silence, a silence that stung like a hornet?

Forty years. Every marriage has ups and downs, sometimes the downs outnumber the ups, but a good marriage survives. A marriage is relentless, impervious to defeat. Until it's not.

He could see the smirk on his father's face, the smirk, and the dismissive wave when Franklin came home with girls his father deemed "laughable." Franklin never got the game winning hit; he never brought home a stellar report card. He could have jumped over Everest, and it wouldn't have been enough. He could have dived to the bottom of the Pacific and his father would have shrugged in disappointment. But not attracting an "acceptable" girl hurt the most.

Franklin balled his fists as his arms hung at his side.

"Are *you* okay?" asked Gretchen.

There he was, nine years old, his father leaning over him, his hot, foul breath on Franklin's neck as he was about to doze off. The room dark. The house quiet. His mother and sister sound asleep. He could feel his father slipping into bed beside him, pressing himself against Franklin, whimpering like a baby, asking for forgiveness, his arm draped over his son's shoulder, his hand gliding back and forth across Franklin's soft belly. The smell of him, the beer and cigarettes. Franklin would close his eyes tight, waiting for his father to finish.

In the morning, his father would be glum, a cigarette dangling from his mouth, his hands cupping a mug of black coffee. Franklin's mother would have a worried look on her face, like she knew something and was trying to unknow it. Franklin would sit and wait for his scrambled eggs. His juice and toast. Gretchen would still be in bed, her bus coming later.

He tried not to look at his father. Because if he did, he might gouge his father's eyes out with his fork. He might pin his father's hand to the table with a knife. Then he might break into laughter, wild and unstoppable.

His father would sneer. "What are you looking at, my little baby boy? Have you picked out a dress for today?"

Franklin's mother, her face twisted in fear, would treat it as a joke. "Of course not. That is a silly thing to say to your son. Where you get these ideas, I just don't know." Then she'd scratch at her cheek nervously.

At his twenty-fifth birthday party, his father stood to give a toast: "To my little boy, still not quite a man." Then he lifted his beer and said, "Here's hoping you find some sad little bitch to marry you before you're thirty. If not, you might just as well cut that thing off and throw it in the trash." He laughed hard at this, so hard he toppled his beer into his lap. "Goddammit!" he yelled. "Goddammit!" By then, everyone had retreated to their bedrooms. His father stood at the bottom of the staircase. "Goddammit to hell! Do you hear me?" Quiet would follow except for the sound of his sister crying in the bedroom beside his.

His father died two years later. Thank God.

Franklin's only regret was that his father hadn't lived long enough to witness his engagement to the most beautiful girl in the county. The day after Laney said "Sure," Franklin drove to Locust Grove Cemetery, found his father's grave, and took a picture of Laney from his wallet. He leaned over and held the photo close to the headstone. "Look, Daddy. That girl's name is Laney. She's nineteen. Look at her, how beautiful she is. Guess what? She is going to be my wife. She is going to be Mrs. Franklin Stafford." He took a deep breath, then knelt on the damp earth in front of the stone and said, "God damn you to hell."

He had won the battle. He had proven himself.

Franklin's triumph had lasted forty years. Now it was all but gone. He imagined his father laughing at him, a look of vindication on his face.

His only recourse was to get Laney back. That would prove it wasn't the marriage that had failed, but the separation. It was doomed to failure. Laney's return would confirm it.

But he wondered, Can I make this happen? If so, how? Or is Gretchen right? Am I being a fool? Or could all of this be Covid at work, convincing me that her 'no' was really 'yes' in disguise? He shook his head, puzzled.

"Franklin?"

"Huh?"

"Are you okay?"

"It's hard to tell." He put his arms around her. "I'm going back with you for the sentencing."

She leaned away so she could see his face clearly. "Thank you, Franklin."

He unwrapped his arms and kissed her forehead.

"You know, don't you?" he said. "I have to keep…"

"Trying?" What else could he do? What else does he have? thought Gretchen.

"Yes, I'm afraid that's true."

"I don't think it's going to matter."

"I know."

CHAPTER 17

At least she wouldn't have to go back to Ellwood. The thought of seeing her house again was too much to bear. She'd heard the Smedlings had removed all the shrubbery, shrubbery that Gris had carefully planted ten years before. Shrubbery the goddam Smedlings had admired. Even worse, they painted the house gray with white shutters. And a red door. Too show-offy, Gris would have said. They also tore down the front porch that had stretched the width of the house, the porch where Gris had hung a swing. They'd enjoyed coffee there on summer evenings, and the scent of peonies, the shade of an ash tree. (The Smedlings had chopped the tree down; they suspected ash borers; turned out they were wrong.) Neighbors would stream by the house on the Fourth of July, waving and chatting as they headed to the festival. Gris had talked about making it a four-season porch, sliding glass windows and insulation under the floor. Never got to it.

Gretchen had loved that house. It was the first and only house they ever owned. She smiled, thinking of the early years, the move to Ellwood, the success of his new job as an electrical contractor. ("Subcontractor," he'd say. "Don't make it more than it is.") Eventually, Artie Mok's business dried up, so Gris went out on his own. Never looked back. Loved it.

Franklin sat up in the back seat. He'd been asleep for over an hour when Gretchen hit a pot hole. Franklin coughed and cleared his throat, then went to sleep.

"Where are we?"

"We'll be in Erie soon, about twenty minutes."

"Gotta pee."

"Twenty minutes."

"I mean, bad."

"Twenty minutes."

While Gretchen appreciated Franklin's willingness to accompany her on this unpleasant pilgrimage, she had tried to dissuade him. She hadn't wanted to look after anyone but herself.

In recent days, the phone rang constantly. Reporters showed up at the front door, knocking loudly, as if they had some right to be there. It seemed as if every newspaper in western Pennsylvania was carrying the story. Another reason she liked living in western New York where no one knew what had happened, except Franklin.

"I'm glad you get this opportunity to speak your mind. It should help."

"You think?"

"Yes, I do."

Gretchen wasn't sure. She'd been waiting four years. She had planned ten versions of what she wanted to say and how she wanted to say it. Calm, tearful, huffy, furious, dismissive, forgiving, vengeful. Or, would she speak at all? Would she let her silence speak for itself?

Some loved ones had declined the invitation. She'd seen them online. "I don't want to give him any more attention. To me, he's a dead man." "We've suffered enough. Going there would only add to it." "If I went, I'd kill him."

To Gretchen, these were all ways of saying: "I'm afraid. I'm afraid to face it all over again." Who wants to get that close to evil? Who wants to feel it floating in the air, clinging to the walls, the furniture, to everyone in attendance? They'd spent four years trying to wipe away the stain, wash away the dirt, the grime. Trying to negotiate a truce between the guilt of going forward and the terror of never moving again? How do you move and stand still at the same time? How do you remember and forget? How do you grab the clock from the wall and reset it to a time before your life careened off a cliff?

Will this give you closure? some might ask. Nothing will ever take it away, comes the answer. Does this feel like justice? I no longer know what justice is. Does knowing your loved one is in a better place give you peace? There is no better place than in my arms. Does time heal all wounds? Maybe an eternity. What keeps you going? I don't know. I just go, step by step, day by day.

"Sister! I'm gonna spring a leak if we don't get—"

"Here's the exit."

Gretchen pulled into the truck stop. While she pumped gas, Franklin headed to the john. When Franklin didn't return, she parked the car and went inside. Franklin was standing at the magazine rack chewing on some jerky and reading the front page of the newspaper. When he heard his sister, he quickly folded the paper and dropped it on the pile. Gretchen looked, but all she could see was "Sentencing."

"I guess we're back in Pennsylvania," said Franklin.

Gretchen sighed. "Yes, we are, aren't we."

She bought a thirty-two-ounce coffee, then turned to the door. Franklin pulled another jerky from the bag, glanced at the paper again, and then followed her out.

"Want me to drive?"

"Jesus, no."

"Thought you could use a break."

"You probably didn't notice, but since we left home, you've only been able to keep your eyes open for about ten minutes."

Franklin could neither predict when exhaustion would strike nor control it when it did. He'd fallen asleep on the kitchen floor in front of an open refrigerator. He'd fallen asleep lying on the back patio, on the rug in front of the fireplace, on the toilet, on the toilet again, and on the toilet once more. He seemed to give the toilet preferential treatment when it came to sleep. Gretchen would open the door, shake her head, close it, and walk away. His doctor said it was Covid holding on.

Mostly, they both ignored it. Except when he wanted to drive. He hadn't been behind the wheel since his trip to the pharmacy.

Gretchen took a sip of her coffee. It was so hot that a shiver ran down her spine and the tip of her tongue went numb. Franklin tossed his bag of jerky onto the front seat, took a swig of his Mountain Dew, then lay down again. But sleep eluded him.

He was concerned about this trip and how it would affect his sister. When she first arrived at his house, he was overwhelmed by Covid and couldn't think of anyone but himself. Nevertheless, he noticed a difference in her. Her eyebrows were always taut and her lips rarely had the strength to form a smile. When she did smile, she seemed embarrassed, as if she'd broken some rule. She didn't breathe, she sighed. She picked at her food, tossing most of her meals into the disposal.

Gris's death hit like a freight train. She was flattened for months. He visited as often as he could, but with work demands and Gretchen's ban on Laney, it wasn't as often as he wished. He saw her on *CNN* occasionally, commenting on what had happened. *USA Today* ran several stories the first few months after the disaster, sometimes quoting her. She'd declined invitations to appear on the morning newscasts. Others took her place.

Everyone wanted a piece of her grief, everyone wanted to make sure her tragedy remained newsworthy. Her loss trended on Twitter for weeks. Condolences poured in from around the world. So did threats from a smattering of crazies who insisted the whole thing was staged by a cabal of Jewish filmmakers who wanted to "rule the world." It was then that she cut off her links to the outside world.

Would it all start up again? Would everyone scratch and claw at Gretchen again? That was why he insisted on coming with her for this final act. He would protect her.

Franklin heard the click-click of the turn signal and sat up. They were getting off 79 and onto 422, just a few miles from their destination. Franklin Googled New Castle. In "What to do" he found directions to several places, none of which were in New Castle. There was Amish country in New Wilmington and Volant; Youngstown, Ohio was a half hour away; and Pittsburgh, the best option, was one-hour south. He also read that, once upon a time, the town had been called "little New York City." Clearly an aspirational rather than descriptive title. Like many western Pa. towns in the post-steel era, New Castle looked like a struggling old man who'd lost his cane.

MapQuest guided them through a maze of streets and past empty storefronts and shuttered mills to the County Court House, appropriately located on Court St.

"Handsome building," said Franklin. And it was. Set on a rise, the courthouse overlooked the town. It's pillared front suggested strength while its cupola, with clocks on every side, suggested vision. The lawn was covered with American flags and at the corner was a war memorial. This was where justice and patriotism resided in Lawrence County, Pa.

Gretchen drove slowly past the building, her jaws clenched, her shoulders stiff. Franklin leaned forward in the back seat and placed his hands on her shoulders. She pulled to the curb and put the car in park. She was breathing rapidly, and her body was shaking. Franklin opened the back door and got into the front seat beside her. She rested her head on his chest and wept quietly.

"Maybe we should head to the motel," said Franklin.

Gretchen wiped her face dry. She pulled into traffic and turned at the next corner. Beyond the modest frame homes, and within view of the courthouse cupola, stood the county jail, a long, two-story building with slit cut windows. They watched prison guards coming and going during the shift change, family members huddled together, some in tears, lawyers with thick folders under their arms stopping to talk and joke.

Gretchen leaned back in her seat, letting her hands rest in her lap. She felt an unsettling calm sweep over her, as if she had entered the eye of the hurricane, the safe zone where there was no wind and the sky was blue. In the distance, an angry patchwork of smokey gray clouds crawled toward the city.

Gretchen pressed her temples with both hands.

"Do you want me to drive us to the Hampton Inn?" said Franklin.

As if on cue, they got out of the car and exchanged sides. Franklin studied MapQuest while Gretchen dug deep into her purse, pulling out a folded piece of paper. As she opened it, Franklin saw the heading: Edgar "Edge" Stinson-Golding.

CHAPTER 18

Maggie pulled into the motel lot, turned off the engine, and sat. Laney arrived several minutes later and remained in her car, as well, wondering if somehow her granddaughter knew something. Sandman looked out the office window, puzzling over what was going on.

The nurse at the clinic asked Maggie if she was using birth control. Maggie said, no, because it made her gain weight.

"Okay. Have you taken a home pregnancy test?"

Maggie hesitated, embarrassed that she hadn't. "I was going to, but I thought it would be better to see someone."

"Okay." The nurse sat with her back to Maggie, entering data into the electronic record. "Have you been sexually active."

"Yes."

"Did you or he use protection."

Maggie remembered laughter as she and Sandman crashed into his room. In the pale moonlight, with little of his face showing, he looked vaguely like Brad Pitt. On a bad day, but Brad Pitt, nonetheless. They undressed and got into bed. Sandman left his socks on and, for some reason, asked if she wanted a drink of water. Everything after that was fast and awkward, like two puzzle pieces being forced together even though they didn't fit. When they were done, she was on top. The next thing she remembered was waking up midmorning the next day, Sandman having already left.

Among the splinters of memory that remained, she couldn't find any that suggested Sandman had used a condom.

"I'm not sure."

"You're not sure?"

"No."

"Was this consensual or forced?"

"Forced?"

"Yes, against your will."

"Was I raped?"

"Uh-huh."

"No, no it wasn't forced. At the time, I wanted to…go ahead with it. I mean, I had a lot to drink that night, but…yeah, I knew the guy and both of us wanted to…you know."

"You remember having sexual intercourse and being a willing participant."

"Yes, you could say that. I mean, I didn't sign a legal document, but…"

The nurse sighed. "Okay. How long have you been together?"

"We're not together."

"Oh." She stopped typing and crossed her arms. "Does he know you're here?"

"Huh-uh."

"Okay. You knew this guy, but there wasn't anything between you two. As the night went on, though, he started looking better and better and the rest is…history."

"I suppose."

"Okay. It happens. It does. Tell you what, I think we both know what the test results will be, but let's take it and see for sure." She smiled at Maggie. "So, you had sex with this man just the once, right?" Maggie nodded. "Since then, what have you noticed?" She turned back to the computer.

"I missed my period."

"Okay. Anything else?"

"I can't hardly get out of bed, and I've thrown up a bunch of times. My breasts are sore."

The nurse took a deep breath as she finished her notes. Then she drew blood.

"How quickly will I find out?"

"Come back tomorrow."

Tomorrow? thought Maggie. How will I make it until tomorrow?

•   •   •

Maggie glanced at the office and saw Sandman peering out the window. They had not spoken since that night. He waved. She held up a stiff hand.

Sandman didn't know what to make of Maggie's behavior. She'd missed work, saying she had the flu. The flu doesn't hit one day this week, then another day the following week and finally two more days the week after that. He knew she was processing what had happened. So was he.

Sandman had been enamored, perhaps obsessed, with Maggie from the first time he saw her at the Save-a-Lot. She was a long-stemmed rose, her beauty so simple, so spare that the word 'perfect' came to mind. She was barking back and forth with her mother, who stood behind the counter, arms folded, face determined. He stood in the back of the store, near the Twinkies, and listened. The word 'job' came up repeatedly. The tone of their voices suggested long-standing differences.

He approached, Twinkies in hand. Neither woman noticed him. He was about to put some money on the counter and leave, but then he spoke. Both women stopped. He cleared his throat into his fist. "It doesn't pay all that much, but I got an opening at the motel..." Her mother unfolded her arms and smiled. "Ain't any jobs, huh?" Maggie glared at Sandman and shoved her hands into her jean's back pockets. "Sounds to me like this guy, Sandman," she said, raising her eyebrows for him to confirm his name, "has a job for you." She grinned. "How 'bout that?"

In the beginning, Maggie was little more than polite with him. She came, she cleaned, she went. She asked questions but little more. Eventually, she became (almost) friendly. They talked, mostly about work, sometimes about life outside of work. He knew living with her mother was problematic, that Maggie was unhappy living in Righteous, that she'd held out hopes of leaving, but had never taken the leap.

He was painfully aware of their age difference, something that losing weight and shaving off his beard wouldn't hide. He looked at his mid-section and hoped it was more like an appealing "paunch" than a "beer gut." If he wore his baggy flannel shirt, no one would know the difference. There were streaks of gray in his beard and hair. When he added it all up, Sandman knew he fell into the "much older cousin" or "youngish uncle" category, neither of which were satisfying to him.

In time, he understood they would never be a couple, so he settled for what she was willing to give. A modest friendship.

Needless to say, he was taken by surprise that night, the night she came into the bar alone and sidled up to him, a sad smile on her face. He didn't ask what was wrong. But he offered to buy her a drink. By the fourth beer, she was laughing and dancing, even when no music was playing. She threw one arm around his neck and leaned so close that Sandman's whole body skipped a beat.

Sandman kept pace with her, drink for drink.

They played pool until the barkeep blinked the lights for closing time. They left together, arm in arm, holding each other up, wending their way down the road to the motel parking lot. She tossed the keys to him, thinking he was in better shape to drive her home. After four failed attempts at starting the car, they both snickered and realized they weren't going anywhere.

When they got to his room, she kissed him and then he kissed her. He remembered they both held their breath as if they were about to take a leap into the void. The rest was hazy, treacherous, and as powerful as an Oklahoma tornado.

When he woke up in the morning, he remembered enough to know something had happened. He lay beside her, wondering whether to awaken her. He gently slipped her hair behind one ear, listened to her breathing, and watched her sleep. When it became clear that she would be gone for a long while, he washed and dressed quietly and headed down the walkway to the office, an extra hop in his step.

When she didn't drop by the office that morning, when she went about her work routine without checking in, when she didn't once make eye contact or acknowledge his presence, he knew there wouldn't be a happy ending to their once-upon-a-time tryst.

As the next few days passed and the fence between them remained, he got worried. She looked different. Haggard was too harsh a word, but it was the first one that came to mind. She was beyond exhausted some days. Once he spied her napping in one of the rooms. Another time, he heard retching sounds coming from a bathroom she was trying to clean. He sat up nights, unable to clear his mind. She's got to be, he thought.

Sandman had been through this twice before. Once on a three-month hiatus to Tijuana. And again, with his best friend's mother. Both were long ago. He left Tijuana as soon as she got the news, and never went back. He didn't find out about his friend's mother until after she'd miscarried. Feelings of guilt and sighs of relief.

Guilt and relief had a lasting impact. He made sure he was better prepared for the occasional one-nighter. Protection always in his wallet, just like high school days. Lessons learned, he thought his youthful stupidity had run its course. But it had given way to middle-aged stupidity. He'd looked everywhere, the toilet, the tub, both wastebaskets, the bed, under the bed, but found no evidence to suggest he had worn a thing.

Laney couldn't resist her budding grandmotherly instincts. She got out of her car and called to Maggie, innocence in her voice. Maggie turned, shielded her eyes and, when she recognized her grandmother, nodded. Laney pulled the mask from her purse, put it on, then took it off and put it back. She wanted to wrap her arms around Maggie, and squeeze with all her might; she wanted to reassure her that, no matter what happened, all would be well. But Maggie didn't make a move toward her grandmother, and Laney knew she couldn't reassure her granddaughter about anything.

Maggie, shoulders stooped, head tilted to one side, face hidden behind a veil of hair, didn't speak. Her arms dangled in front of her, her left hand clutching her right pointer. Tears came to Laney's eyes. The hand clutching the finger. She remembered another girl who, when she felt helpless and needed someone to hold her, would grab that same finger and hope to be saved.

Why hadn't Laney taken Roz into her arms more often? Why hadn't she crossed the invisible line that separated them and held her daughter and whispered in her ears that she loved her and that everything would be alright? That's what good parents do, isn't it? They comfort and reassure their children even when they have no idea what the future holds. They bet that tomorrow will be better, that their promises will be magical, that, as a parent, they have the power to create the best of all possible futures for their child, just by holding them close and telling them it will all come true in time.

Laney took her granddaughter in her arms and held her tight, and when Maggie tried to pull away, she held her tighter still. She knew she couldn't let go, because if she did, they'd both fall apart. "There, there," she said. Maggie sighed and rested her head on her grandmother's shoulder.

CHAPTER 19

Laney adjusted her mask, crossed her legs, and picked up the six-month-old *People* magazine from the table beside her. There were two teenage girls in the waiting room. Both with knees held tight together and arms crossed in front of them. Each pale and unsure. A single table fan arced back and forth, battling the stifling heat. The girls were with their mothers, who wore masks to defend against both Covid and shame. They stared straight ahead, their eyes downcast, their demeanor bleak.

Maggie sat beside her grandmother, head leaning back against the wall, arms folded, her left leg jackhammering the floor.

"What's up with you?" her mother had asked the day before. She pointed out the kitchen window. "See that sheet on the line? That's how pale you look." When Maggie didn't answer, Roz frowned. "Okay. You don't have to tell me. But I know something's up." Maggie walked slowly to her room and closed the door behind her.

"What did your mother say?" Laney had asked earlier on the drive to the clinic.

"Nothing."

"Nothing? That's not like your mother."

Maggie looked out the window. "I didn't tell her. She was in a mood."

Laney didn't have to ask her granddaughter what she meant by 'mood.' Roz was born in a mood. Laney had tried to love that mood away, ignore it until it was gone, or threaten it if it didn't cease and desist. All to no avail.

•   •   •

Roz stood on the front porch, coffee mug in hand. One, two, three semis passed, then a Greyhound. She took a slow, deep breath and arched her back. Another day.

When she'd looked in Maggie's room earlier and found only her unmade bed, she'd felt relieved. No cajoling this morning. No begging her to get up. No screaming. No fighting. Her insides uncoiled. She sat on the porch step and turned her head side-to-side until her neck stopped cracking. She closed her eyes and listened to nothing at all.

Maggie had heeded her words. She'd gotten herself up early so she'd get to work on time. If she did the same thing tomorrow and the next day and the next, maybe it would become a habit. And if it became a habit, Roz wouldn't wake up with a headache every morning. And if she didn't wake up with a headache every morning, maybe she could smile. And if she could smile, maybe she could see her daughter differently.

•   •   •

The exam room door opened and the nurse waved for Laney to come in. Maggie was staring at the floor. Laney tried to smile.

"You're the grandmother, right?" The nurse shook Laney's hand. "Nice of you to come in with your granddaughter." She turned her attention to Maggie. "So, the results are in. You are pregnant."

Maggie didn't respond. Laney slid her chair closer to her granddaughter. The nurse talked to Maggie about making an appointment with her own doctor. Then she noted Maggie's mood.

"You don't seem at all happy about this." The nurse folded her arms.

Maggie sat up, rubbed her palms on her jeans, and wiped her eyes. She blew air through her pursed lips and tossed the tissue into the wastebasket.

"You okay?" said Laney in a whisper.

"I don't know."

The nurse leaned in. "Feeling unhappy about being pregnant can be caused by any number of things. Is there a particular reason you're not happy?"

"I think she's just a little overwhelmed," said Laney.

"Let's let her answer." She raised her eyebrows at Maggie.

"Is this your first?" she asked.

Maggie shook her head.

"Is the daddy involved?"

"Not really."

"Maybe that's what's got you down."

Maggie didn't respond.

"Is your mama around?"

"Uh-huh."

"And you got your grandma, too, right? They'll help you out."

Maggie blew her nose again. She sighed and looked at her grandmother.

"I don't know what to do."

Before Laney had a chance to respond, the nurse spoke again.

"About what?"

"Huh?"

"You said you didn't know what to do and I said 'About what?'" She gestured with one hand, urging Maggie to answer.

"About everything."

"What is 'everything'?"

"Look, this is life changing news. It's not the time to play twenty questions." Laney put her hand on Maggie's shoulder. She glared at the nurse and widened both eyes as if to say, 'Please, back off.'

"What is 'everything'?"

"Please!" said Laney.

"I don't know if I want to be pregnant."

"Is that so?"

"Yes."

Laney shifted in her chair. "It's none of your—"

"Well, in the state of Oklahoma when you are pregnant, you are pregnant, and that's that." Maggie folded her arms across her stomach. Laney pulled her close and helped her to her feet. "There is no decision to be made," said the nurse.

"Okay, enough," said Laney. "This is no longer any of your business."

The nurse reached for her folder as the two women turned to leave. "Wait one minute," she said.

CHAPTER 20

Edgar Stinson-Golding, known as Edge, had been a "colicky baby." Those were his mother's first words when she was interviewed by the TV network talking heads. "He was always colicky." She didn't take time to think about what she was saying. The lights were bright. The cameras were rolling. The microphones covered her face like a swarm of bees. Later, she wished she'd thought of something else to say, something that might have explained why he did what he did.

He became known as the "Colicky Killer." The name was demeaning, she thought. Not only to him but to her. It didn't explain a thing. What she wished she'd said was that his father, long ago imprisoned, had beaten him regularly since the age of two; that his "lazy eye" had made him the target of bullies; that when his grandfather, his one and only friend, died, he lay beside him on the floor for hours until someone discovered them; that his father gave him his first drink when he was eight; that, she couldn't lie, when Edgar got out of control, she would lock him in his closet, sometimes for hours, while she cried and slept.

What she had to say didn't matter. She took one look at the jury and knew what the outcome would be. They could have voted before the first witness was called. Everyone's mind was made up. He didn't stand a chance. He wasn't a human being to the jury. He was a monster. They licked their lips at the thought of putting him away forever, or even better, executing him.

He *was* a colicky baby. His whole body spasmed randomly, and he cried without pause for hours. Sometimes it seemed like days. How to describe it? Nails screeching across a chalk board the size of the Empire State Building? Chainsaw grinding inside her head? Other mothers would smile and say, "I know what you're going through," as if that made any difference.

He was little more than a toddler when neighbors started calling her—he's out in the street, he hit the little Kiner girl again, he kicked our dog so hard we had to take him to the vet, he tried to strangle our cat. And, at the age of nine, he successfully strangled a cat to death and set it on fire.

They evaluated him and sent him to "kiddie jail," his father's term, for rehabilitation. His mother was inconsolable. She wept until no more tears would come. She didn't go out for days. She couldn't eat. The headaches were so bad, she could only open her eyes in the dark.

The court decided she was an unfit mother. They didn't care about all the sleepless nights, worrying about her boy, worrying and wondering what she should do, who she could turn to. They didn't care that some mornings, when she saw a storm building, she'd keep him home. She'd hold him and rock him for as long as he'd let her. They didn't care that she loved him, that she was the only one who could see the good in him. They didn't care about the pictures he painted, the ones she left on the refrigerator until they turned yellow, or the "I love you" cards he'd make for her birthdays, or the way he would cuddle beside her when he was afraid. Or the way he'd cry inconsolably but couldn't say why.

He entered the foster care system at nine, lived with a carousel of families over the next nine years. She saw him on a semi-regular basis, depending on the whim of the court. In the beginning, he would run and jump into her arms and kiss her. Eventually, though, when he knew he'd never go home again, he would refuse her visits or not speak to her at all.

The foster homes never lasted. The consensus opinion was: "He doesn't feel anything; he doesn't care; our children aren't safe around him; if something doesn't change, he's going to kill someone someday."

He spent a disastrous two years in halfway houses before he was regurgitated out of the system and back into the world. Ask him how he was doing, he'd say, "Fine." Ask him if being in the system had been as awful as one could imagine, he'd say, "Nope." Ask him if he had any regrets, he'd say, "Naw." Ask him if he missed his mother, he'd say, "I don't know." His father? "I don't have no father." Always with a smile as if his every answer was a punchline to a joke no one understood.

His mother, Edith, was ringside for her son's every battle. She held her breath until she thought her lungs might explode, waiting for shoe after shoe to drop. And when they did, she was always surprised that she was surprised. Despite the evidence, she clung to a shred of hope that things would work out for her boy.

Edge barreled through job after job—church janitor, garbage collector, lawn mower, carnival barker. Keeping them was never part of the plan. Some bosses would pay him a handsome severance because they were afraid they'd find a horse's head in their bed if they didn't.

When he came knocking at his mother's door, she'd open it wide. He didn't have to explain why he was there. She knew no one else would take him; no one else wanted him; no one else cared a whit about him. She moved out of her bedroom and onto the couch. She wanted the best for her boy, now twenty-eight years old. What could be better than a room of his own in a house where he was loved.

He said little. He never thanked her. He ate her food and spent what little money she had. If she asked, he would give her a peck on the cheek before leaving the house, heading God knows where. Each night, she awaited that call: "We've arrested..." "We have sad news about your son, Edgar..."

He got a job stocking shelves at the Busy Beaver. He even moved to his own place. Edith cried. "What's with the tears?" he said. "I'm just so happy," she said. He laughed and shook his head. "I ain't runnin' the place, or nothin'."

Had it for four months. In the first week, he was late for work twice and got a warning from his boss, Delbert. Two weeks later, he got into a pissing match with a co-worker, so Delbert docked Edge's pay. "I didn't do a damn thing!" Shortly thereafter, he took ten days off, claiming he had Covid. He told his boss he'd get a note from his doctor. There was no doctor. Delbert put him on probation. "I should have fired you, but I'm gonna give you another chance." Edgar grinned at him.

Things quieted down over the next two weeks. Delbert told him he was glad that Edgar was "finally getting his act together." Edge thought about what he had said, the words he'd used, the look on his face. Was Delbert making fun of him, like he was his pet dog, ready to obey his every command. What gave him the right to tell Edge he should get his act together? What's he mean by "act," anyway? It seemed to Edge that after that, Delbert smiled at him all the time, not a friendly smile, but a smile that said, "You're an asshole."

He came into work the next morning, grabbed his boss by the lapels and slammed him against a wall. "Hey, what's all the smiling about? Huh? What's so funny about me? Huh? You think I'm some kinda joke, don't you, you fat shit."

Several co-workers pulled him off Delbert and pinned him to the floor. Delbert gasped for air and then stood over Edge, finger in his face.

"You get the hell out of here and never come back, you hear me? I knew it was a mistake, hiring you. I thought, Give the guy a chance, but, no, you couldn't handle it, you couldn't even stock my goddam shelves without causing trouble. I've known about you since you were a kid, always in trouble, never doing anything right, just a loser, a worthless, goddam loser."

Delbert and the others forcibly ushered him to the exit and tossed him onto the pavement. Customers gasped and watched and then went about their business.

Edge went back to his rented room over the liquor store. He couldn't eat. He couldn't sleep. He paced the floor for hours, fuming. He wrote down his plans and packed everything he owned into the backseat of his car. He fell asleep at 4:00am and was up at 7. He whisked three eggs, poured them into a pan and lit his hot plate. He measured some coffee into a filter. He added water to the coffee maker and pushed the button. He checked to see if the light had come on, then waited for the first gurgling sound. He shredded cheddar and Swiss cheese, then sprinkled them on his eggs, covered the pan with a lid, and waited one minute. During that minute, he grabbed a paper plate from the cupboard, plastic utensils, and a napkin from the leftover MacDonald's bag, then put them on the kitchen table, which his mother had covered with a bright, yellow, vinyl cloth. He pulled up a straight back chair.

Before eating, Edge bowed his head in prayer, then crossed himself with his middle finger. He scooped eggs into his mouth with a spoon, then washed them down with a slurp of black coffee. He took another bite. Then another. Bite, slurp, bite, slurp, bite, slurp.

He sat in his car for several minutes watching people come and go at the Busy Beaver. A middle-aged guy wearing a ballcap and overalls. A young mother, probably Hispanic, with a baby in tow. Two teenage boys, jabbing and poking at each other. A stocky guy wearing biker-gang leathers. Two black women with two young girls in flowery dresses.

He wore a long, black, double-breasted Macintosh as he walked across the sun-drenched parking lot, his arms tight against his sides. He smiled and said "Hello" to several exiting shoppers. One of those shoppers later told police that the man "was friendly, like he didn't have a care in the world."

He stood near the cart rack inside the auomatic doors and smiled at what he saw. A rifle was at his side now. Several customers strode past him, unaware. Then a woman screamed, but it was too late. He had shouldered his rifle and was looking down the barrel at his boss. Delbert nodded at a customer, then turned around to see what the commotion was all about. One shot and he went down. Then another and another; more bodies on the floor. He aimed and shot, aimed and shot, until the rifle jammed. Click, click, click. He dropped it on the floor and walked out. He was sitting in his car when the police arrived.

When Edith turned on the morning news, she was surprised that the network was broadcasting from the Busy Beaver in Ellwood. At first, she felt a sense of pride that her town was getting attention about something. But the look on the reporter's face and the array of local and state police cars behind her, sent a chill down Edith's back.

At the same time, a mile away, Gretchen was pouring herself a second cup of coffee. She stirred it slowly as she added half and half. She looked at the clock, and realizing she had time before she needed to leave for work, turned on the TV. She was surprised that the network was broadcasting from the Busy Beaver in Ellwood.

CHAPTER 21

Laney offered to drive. Maggie, the window down, her head at rest on the black leather upholstery, was comforted by the warm sun and the rhythm of the wheels. It reminded her of when she was little and couldn't sleep. Her mother would bundle her up and take her for a ride. She always put the window down, even when the air was brisk and chilly. Maggie loved the feel of a warm blanket around her body and a cool breeze on her face. She'd wake up the next morning in her bed, wondering if it had all been a dream.

Every few seconds, Laney side-eyed Maggie. The appointment at the clinic had been disastrous. As they stood to leave, the nurse had gotten up, folder of pictures in her hands. Laney ripped the folder from the nurse and threw the pictures across the room.

"I know you," said the nurse, infuriated. "Everybody in these parts knows you. And your fancy car and your New York ways. You think we're all idiots, don't you? Well, we're not. Life is a gift from God. You don't just throw a gift like that out with the trash. Out here in America, certain things are sacred."

Laney was sucking air so hard her mask disappeared into her mouth. She took it off and crumbled it in her fist. The nurse glared at her. Laney took several breaths, trying to regain her composure.

"It's God's law and now it's the state of Oklahoma's law!"

"Don't you have any human decency, any compassion or understanding?"

Just as the bell was sounding for round two, Laney put her mask back on, reached for Maggie's hand, and headed for the door.

Laney took the long way back to Righteous. They stopped in Hollow Hill for a burger at Tommy's Eats. They headed down highway 270, both still nursing their milkshakes. Twenty miles later, Laney spied a park entrance and turned into the lot. They hiked up a sandy path to the top of a great dune. They sat on a bench, shielded their eyes against the sun, and gazed at several hundred acres of rippling sand. There was a lake in the distance, a shimmering, narrow, blue ribbon on the horizon. The wind blew up and the sand dunes started to sing. Clumpy, unkempt, scrub grass fluttered in the breeze.

"So," said Laney.

"I don't know," said Maggie. She combed her hair with her fingertips.

"Uh-huh."

"Looks like I'm pregnant."

"Yes, it does."

"When my mother finds out, she's going to..." Maggie folded her arms and shook her head.

Laney thought of her own pregnancies. How excited she had been the first time, less so the second time, and not at all the third. Franklin never shared his disappointment about their losses, but she could see it in his face, she could see it in the way his eyes avoided hers.

She hated her friends' sympathy, how they doted on her, and tried to minimize her grief. "You are young. You can always try again." What was wrong with me? thought Laney. Why am I such a failure?

She turned to her doctor. "When I see a pregnant woman at the grocery store, I think, Why can't that be me? Why can't I be normal, like everyone else? Why am I the exception to the rule?"

Her doctor took off his glasses, folded them, and tossed them onto his desk. His smile was sad.

"You are not the exception. All those women you see, all those women who give birth, they're the exceptions. Every time you try to make a baby, about three hundred million sperm have a chance of fertilizing that egg. But only about two hundred will reach it. There is less than a one in three chance any of them will succeed. That's how unlikely it is. And if they do succeed, the odds of making it to term are, well, you get the picture."

This explanation didn't make her feel better. All she knew was one sperm had successfully impregnated one egg inside her body. Why couldn't she be one of the women, chosen by fate, or the universe, or God, or dumb luck, to bring a child into the world? Why was she in the 'step aside' group?

When she told Franklin, he said, "You're fine; he's an idiot," which helped even less.

All of this changed when she became pregnant with Rosalyn. She felt like Cinderella. Out of all the girls in the Kingdom, the slipper fit her foot and her foot alone. And in the blink of an eye, all her fortunes were reversed. And she would live happily ever after. She was never more content than during that pregnancy. Even Laney could see the glow when she looked at herself in the mirror.

But much as she tried, she never experienced the happily-ever-after she'd hoped for. Her plump, impish, baby girl with the rosebud mouth and the most beautiful gray/blue eyes, would come to hate her mother by the time she was fifteen and by sixteen, she'd be gone.

Twenty years later, here she sat with her nineteen-year-old granddaughter who was pregnant (after one try, no less), staring at sand dunes in the middle of America, her marriage in shambles and her daughter's disdain still full-fisted.

She looked at her granddaughter, who seemed mesmerized by the view. Her hair, caught by a breeze, glistened in the midday sun.

"Do you have gold strands in your hair?"

"What?"

"Your hair, it looks like you have gold streaks." She reached for her granddaughter's hair and held it gently. "It's beautiful."

"Thanks."

Who was this woman who took so much interest in her, who showed so much care? It was hard to believe that her mother had come from this person, her mother whose insides were made of leather, who was always ready for a fight, never willing to back down.

By contrast, everything about Maggie seemed soft, doughy, mushy. Her mother had said as much. "Is there a backbone in there somewhere?" Her instinctive reaction to being challenged was to back away. "I can't always be there, you know, you've gotta step up," her mother would say. Maggie heard this for the first time in second grade when she was afraid to give her science report in front of the class. Her mother said this so often that the words became a jumble in Maggie's mind. Eventually, all she heard was 'you can't step up, you can't do it, you'll always need your mother.'

And here she was a grown woman, a pregnant one at that, still feeling like a second grader who wanted to back away rather than step up, who wanted a place to hide for fear of doing something wrong.

"Do you do anything special with your hair? Wonder water, maybe? A hair mask?"

"I wash it."

"Oh. What do you use?"

Maggie smiled. "Shampoo from the Dollar Store."

"Oh." They laughed.

Laney looked at her granddaughter's profile, her perfect nose, smooth cheeks, and dark brows. This beautiful, complicated girl would not be alive, and would not be carrying another life inside her, if Laney's final pregnancy hadn't gone to term.

"Have you thought about what you're going to do?"

"About this?" She pointed at her soft belly.

"Uh-huh."

"Yes."

"And?"

She looked at her grandmother and nodded slightly. "I don't know."

Maggie was only three years older than her mother, when Roz became pregnant. It had been an awful year. One conflict had led to another and another. Laney and Franklin were at their wits end on the final day. Roz had screamed at them for an hour before retreating to her room. A few hours later, she came out with a backpack over one shoulder and a duffel bag over the other. She didn't say a word as her parents called after her. She didn't say a word when she walked out the front door and got into her friend Alison's VW.

She'll be back when she cools down, they both had thought. This is just a tantrum. It will pass. She's just a kid. She stayed at Alison's until the end of the school year. She made her point.

Laney asked Roz if she'd come home for the summer. Roz did not say she wouldn't. In anticipation of her return, Laney and Franklin painted her bedroom, including a black accent wall. Franklin created a summer job for her at one of his stores. Laney planned a shopping spree. They would press the restart button. Maybe even go to the lake for a family vacation.

When the last day of school came and went and Roz hadn't returned, Laney called Alison. Alison had no idea where Roz was. "I thought she was going home, but she didn't say."

Roz sent them postcards from Columbus, Ohio and then a small town in Missouri. No note, no update, just her signature. For a while after that they didn't hear a thing.

Franklin and Laney didn't sleep. He gained ten pounds, she lost ten. Laney wondered how things could have gone so wrong, Franklin wondered how Roz could have been so obstinate.

The next postcard came from Oklahoma. "Staying here for now. Am pregnant."

•   •   •

"Do you need to tell anybody about this?" said Laney.

"You mean my mother?"

Laney shook her head. "Anyone else?"

Maggie folded her hands in her lap and looked at the distant dunes.

"Do you mean the father?"

Laney nodded.

"I don't know."

"You don't know who—"

"I know who the father is. I'm not a whore. I'm not like my mother."

Laney bristled.

"I know you're angry, but please don't use that word. Please don't say that about your mother...my daughter." She looked at Maggie, her eyebrows raised.

Maggie was startled by her grandmother's tone.

"Okay...Okay, I won't. I won't say that." Both women leaned back on the bench, and for a moment it was quiet.

Then Maggie turned to face her grandmother. "Don't take this wrong, but you don't know her," said Maggie.

"How's that?"

"You don't know her. What she's like, I mean. She can be so mean, so awful."

"I know she can. I know. But I love her. And she loves you."

"Easy to say. Been a while since I've felt much love from her."

"It's hard not to feel love for so long. I know."

Laney's face looked drawn and tired.

"I don't understand why she ran away from home, why she left and never looked back," said Maggie.

Laney's eyes welled with tears.

"That's a story for your mother to tell. But I'll say this much. We, all of us, made mistakes. Regrettable mistakes."

Maggie leaned over and scooped some sand in her cupped hands, then opened them and watched the grains scatter into the wind.

"Sandman."

Another car pulled into the lot.

"Sandman?"

"Yeah."

The car door slammed shut.

"What's going on here?" Roz, her arms hanging limp, her shoulders rounded, her face coarse, approached them. "Huh?"

CHAPTER 22

Two corrections officers, one with a tray in his hands, approached the cell.

"Step back," said one of them. Edge didn't move. The first officer pushed him out of the way. Edge had been the smallest in his class throughout school. He'd been skinny and awkward and wore bulky glasses for his lazy eye. He was always being pushed. Other people always tried to walk *through* rather than *around* him.

"Room service today," said the officer, as he put a breakfast tray on the metal platform that served as a bunk. This was Edge's third day in confinement, a decision made by the warden to protect him from threats that had been circulating among inmates and locals. Everyone wanted a crack at that "pussy," "loser," "scumbag," "piece of shit."

In the penitentiary, Edge was just one among many. He kept to himself. Stayed out of trouble, unless trouble came looking for him. But here, back in the county jail, he was a notorious celebrity. Everyone knew Edgar Stinson-Golding. Everyone knew about Busy Beaver. Everyone remembered the trial. And everyone had celebrated the verdict. Front page news in the *Ellwood City Ledger* for months.

His mother, Edith, moved to Ohio and stayed with her cousin for a time. She couldn't remember how many rocks had been thrown through her windows. How many fires had been set in her yard.

How many vile phone calls she'd received. Her son was the criminal, no one suggested otherwise, but many thought she was guilty, too. She was the bad mother behind the bad seed.

Once the officers left his cell, Edge sat down beside the tray. He had a bowl of Wheaties, a stale cheese Danish, a half-pint of milk, a cup, and a spoon.

Edge stood on his toilet and peered out the narrow, reinforced window. It was raining hard. Some of the flags that usually adorned the yard had fallen. Water streamed down the sidewalk. He could hear rumbling in the distance. There were several cars in the lot already. His mother was sitting in one of them.

•   •   •

Franklin and Gretchen parked across the street from her former home in Ellwood. She hadn't wanted to visit, but since New Castle was only twelve miles away, she couldn't resist. With all the changes the current owners had made, only the house's shape and address were familiar. Porch gone, shrubs gone, new color, new double garage, a fence around the backyard. It looked so different she didn't feel the sadness she'd anticipated. All she felt was empty.

"Was coming here a good idea?" asked Franklin.

"I don't know what a 'good idea' is anymore."

She insisted on driving down the street past the Stinson-Golding house. Despite all the years and the changes in ownership, the place looked the same. There were toys and bicycles and boxes strewn across the front yard. The grass was a foot high. Paint was peeling. The roof sagged. Some bricks were missing from the chimney. Two old sofas were on the porch and Christmas lights dangled from the roof.

The first time she met Edith, Gretchen and Gris were canvasing the neighborhood for a City Council candidate. She remembered the inside of the house, with all its blinds and curtains pulled, looked like a cave, and smelled like soiled clothing. Edith's little boy, Edgar, stood in the middle of the room, bare feet, and no shirt. He must have been five, maybe six. He didn't smile when Gretchen said hello.

"Don't mind him," said Edith. "He's shy."

"And we're strangers, so that doesn't help."

Gris was the first to extend a hand to Edith. Then the boy came forward and stood, partially hidden, behind his mother, his arms around her waist. He kneeled. "And who are you?" said Gris. He took off his glasses and rubbed his eyes. "I don't know," he said. They all tried to chuckle.

Edith looked too old to have such a young child. Her hair was disheveled and her skin was gray. Her eyes sagged. The house dress she wore was at least two sizes too large.

Gretchen knelt and tried to get the boy to say his name. He walked away.

"Edgar," his mother said. "He's my Edgar."

•　•　•

Edith got out of her car. She opened her umbrella and walked half way up the sidewalk. And just as she had done the last two days, she waved at the windows, not knowing which one was her son's. She hoped he would see her. She hoped that, if he did, he would feel less alone.

They had warned her not to touch him, but she couldn't help herself. As soon as he entered the visitation room, she threw her arms around him. He seemed shaken, his shoulders tightening under her touch. He patted her back before he stepped away. He looked smaller than she remembered. And thinner. Older, too. Edgar looked like a ragdoll in his tattered gold jumpsuit. His brown hair had receded and thinned. It hadn't been washed or combed. One of the hinges on his glasses was taped. He glanced at her, and managed a half smile. He looked like his father, the rounded shoulders, the 'S' shaped posture, the yellow smoking stains on his fingers. She fought back tears. Once she had driven eight hours to see him in the state penitentiary, but when she started crying, he ended the visit immediately. "Don't," was all he said.

She took his face in her hands and looked hard at him, trying to find the little boy that was there so long ago. He was never a happy boy, but there were times they laughed together and played games, like *Checkers* or *Chutes and Ladders*. They'd go to the toddler pool in Ewing Park when he was barely old enough to walk. He always shied away from other children, but he had fun, she was sure of it.

When Edgar looked at his mother, all he saw was sadness and disappointment. If he could undo everything, he would. Not because he felt guilty, but because he couldn't stand how she looked. He could handle all the threats and fights and abuse he faced in prison. But he could not handle his mother's furrowed brow, weepy eyes, and downcast mouth.

They got coffee from the machine and sat opposite each other at a small table. It was quiet as they drank.

"Are you okay, Edgar?"

"Yeah, Ma, I'm fine."

"I mean, are you ready for this thing, these victim impact statements or whatever they're called?"

"It's okay."

"I mean, you know they're gonna say a lot of things, a lot of very bad things about you, stuff that could hurt you or make you so angry that..."

Edgar didn't understand why his mother was concerned. He tried to imagine what it was like to feel hurt because of what someone said about him, but he couldn't. Edgar was Teflon coated. Things seldom stuck to him. Neither good nor bad.

If something did stick, though, he dealt with it quickly and decisively. Once he'd taped a jagged piece of broken glass to a toothbrush handle and stabbed an inmate who had pushed him on the yard. Only once, but it was enough to make his point.

It was the same with Busy Beaver. Most of the time, he let his boss's jibes and jokes slide, but when he fired Edge for no reason, he had to do something. He had to make him pay. When he went to the store that morning, he only meant to teach his boss a lesson, but when he started shooting, he couldn't stop, he didn't want to stop. The crackling sound of it. The feel of the rifle's kickback. The sulfuric smell filling the air. And all those people running, scrambling, hiding. They understood. He wasn't a nobody. He was a somebody. When his rifle jammed, he dropped it and walked across the lot to his car.

Everyone was still screaming and tripping over each other. They must have thought the shooter was still in the building. It was like watching rats scurrying through a maze that had no exit.

No one noticed him sitting calmly in his car. Were they too afraid to look? Too stupid? He turned the radio on, waiting for the news. He opened an energy bar and ate it.

•   •   •

There was a knock on the motel door.

"It's open!" said Gretchen.

"Got you something." Franklin walked in with a fist full of candy bars. "These are yours." He tossed a Snickers, a Twix, and a Butterfingers onto the bed. He tore open the first of three packs of Reese's Peanut Butter Cups and put one in his mouth.

Gretchen opened her Snickers, then laid it on the bedside table. She got up and walked to the window. Franklin popped another Peanut Butter Cup into his mouth and tossed the wrapper into the wastebasket. He stared a hole through his sister's back, trying to think of what to say.

"Are you okay?"

"Are *you* okay?"

"Not really," said Franklin as he tore open another pack.

"Me neither."

"We should start a club." He waited, but she didn't laugh. "I'm here, you know."

"I know."

"Okay. I think I'll take a shower."

Gretchen looked at the gray clouds, like elephants, swallowing the sky. Steady light rain became a downpour again, this time with stiff winds. People scurried to their cars, pulling their jackets over their heads. Umbrellas, blown inside out, sailed across the parking lot like makeshift drones. Scribbly lightning lit the sky. She counted—one, two, three, four, five—and thunder followed. The lightning was a mile away.

Five seconds, Gris had said. It had been a humid July day. They had gone to Conneaut Lake Park. When the rain started, they took shelter under the merry-go-round. There was a streak of lightning followed shortly by a clap of thunder. That means it's one mile, he'd said. One mile what, she said. The lighting, it's a mile away. She laughed. He explained the simple math involved in his calculation. And it worked. Almost always. You didn't know you married a genius, did you? Trust me, when we met, there was nothing about you that suggested genius, she said with a laugh.

Sitting on the window ledge of the Hampton Inn watching the rain, a smile crossed her face. And then it went away. She looked at the clock—6:00pm. Sixteen more hours. She knew there was another mother counting the hours, as well. She had not spoken to Edith since that day in the Busy Beaver parking lot.

Gretchen had pulled in first. She watched from behind the police tape, trembling. She could see bodies covered in plastic near the checkout. A woman beside her was crying. Gretchen tried to convince herself that it was too early to cry. Police raced back and forth inside the Busy Beaver, guns drawn, rifles at their shoulders. They ran hunched over up and down the aisles, signaling the all clear to the Chief. Frowns of worry covered their faces. Hands went up in frustration. Heated words were exchanged. The search continued, while bodies lay still.

Gretchen studied the size of each blanketed corpse, convincing herself that none of them were the same as Gris.

She startled when she felt a tap on her shoulder. It was Edith, her face contorted, her arms wide, seeking a hug. She looked so sad, so forlorn, that Gretchen took Edith in her arms.

"I had to come," said Edith. "I don't know..."

"No one knows."

They stood side by side, a strange duo, arms around each other's waist. Gretchen looked at Edith's pained face. Firetrucks screamed into the parking lot, lights flashing, wheels screeching. Police from New Castle and Beaver Falls arrived in full force. Gretchen looked at Edith's face again. Is she breathing? Edith's fingers dug into Gretchen's side. A dozen police rushed across the parking lot, weapons raised, heading toward a parked car in the far corner.

"Look," said Gretchen, pointing. "They've found something."

"What?" said Edith as she turned.

"They've found..."

"Oh my God no!"

She let go of Gretchen and ran, her arms waving frantically.

Gretchen's back straightened as she watched Edith. It's him, she thought. She looked back at the bodies now being lifted into ambulances. She looked back at Edith, who was on her knees pounding the car, pleading with the police— "Please don't shoot! It's my boy."

Several ambulances sped by, sirens raging. Gretchen got back into her car. She sat still, holding the wheel, as if to steady herself. A dead calm came over her. If she didn't follow the ambulances, she would never have to know. She could go back home, clean the house, and wait. Gris came home every day at 5:30pm sharp. She looked at the time on the dashboard. Five-thirty was forever away. She took her cell phone from her purse and tried his number. She was pleased that it rang, a good sign, she thought. Then Gris's familiar voice came on, "Hi, this is Gris. I'm afraid I can't talk with you now. Leave a message and I'll call back as soon as I can."

"Gris?" she said. "Are you there?"

CHAPTER 23

What the hell? thought Roz, as she watched her daughter and mother cruise by the store and down the road past the Sunrise. Her insides began to twist. What are they up to?

Roz paced back and forth behind the counter, unable to settle herself. Seeing her mother again after so many years had awakened feelings she thought had died. It took years of being on her own to put those feelings to rest. Giving birth to Maggie had helped. She had brought a life into the world, she had raised that child without help from anyone, proving what her parents never thought possible, that she had a good head on her shoulders, that she was responsible, that she could make her way in the world.

To do this, Roz had cut her family tree off at the roots and transplanted herself to another world, her own world. She wasn't a wandering nobody, as her parents might have assumed. She'd made her own decisions for years. She had standing in her community and was a respected business woman, fellow citizen, and Oklahoman. She was somebody.

She bristled at the thought of Maggie getting close to Laney. Her parents had chased away her first love. Now her mother was trying to take away the only love she had left.

She put the "Closed" sign on the door, got in her car, and lit out after them. The road was straight as a ruler for miles. This was the road that would have taken her to California. She had thought of heading for the coast many times since then. But Maggie was barely a peanut in those early days, and even when she was a youngster the thought of a twelve-hundred-mile bus ride seemed foolhardy. Later, she realized that everything before she arrived in Righteous had been foolhardy, as well. Even her friends told her that leaving for God-knows-where was "stupid." She was going to "ruin" her life. And for what? Just to spite her parents. This convinced her she no longer had any friends. It hardened her resolve to prove them all wrong.

She imagined herself as a successful-something, one day returning to western New York in a flashy car and wearing the finest clothes money could buy. And Maggie would be by her side, a perfect child, smart, beautiful, attentive to her mother. And everyone, her parents and her friends, would see how wrong they had been. They would beg her to stay, but she would turn away from them once again, victory in her hands, and head west to that golden paradise on the pacific coast.

She *exhaled a low, breathy laugh and shook her head with disdain. These were the times when self-loathing, like bugs crawling under her skin, consumed her every thought. These were the times when she held the steering wheel tight so she wouldn't veer into oncoming traffic. These were the times when reviewing every decision she had ever made showed what a fool she had been. Tears followed and after the tears, anger, anger that often found its target in Maggie.*

Roz pulled off the road, the car jerking to a stop. She couldn't catch her breath, perspiration dripped from her chin. She lay across the seat and tried to breathe slowly, tried to collect herself. The breeze through the window dried her dampened skin. She closed her eyes. She felt limp and lost.

She continued west for miles, eventually reaching Hollow Hill. Discouraged by then, she paid little attention to the people and the cars and the possibility of finding her daughter and her mother.

When she saw the sign for Dunes Lake Park, she gave up. She pulled into a parking lot so she could turn around and head for home.

In the far corner of the lot, there was a familiar car covered in dust and sand. She pulled in beside it and got out. She walked up the path slowly, cautiously. She stopped when she saw them sitting on a bench at the top of a dune. She could hear the murmur of their voices. She stopped, unsure whether to stay or go. She continued up the path, then stopped again.

"What's going on? What are you up to?" Roz, her arms folded, her feet wide apart, her shoulders rounded, came forward. She spoke softly even though she was screaming inside.

"Just enjoying the view." Maggie said this as matter-of-factly as she could. "Remember we used to come here?" She smiled.

"Long time ago." Roz took several more steps forward.

"Hello, Roz," said Laney. The words came out flat.

"Surprise." Roz's anger, like mercury in a thermometer, was rising.

"Maggie wanted to show me this place. It's so different, like an oasis…"

"Mom?" said Maggie.

"You two have gotten real buddy-buddy, haven't you?"

"Mom, I…"

"A regular dynamic duo. Maybe you should get matching BFF bracelets."

"Look, Roz, I can explain."

"Of the many things you need to explain, which one would you like to start with?"

Maggie, head tilted, watched without moving. Growing up, she had assumed the geographic distance between her mother and grandmother explained why they had little contact over the years. But since her grandmother had arrived, she realized she had been wrong. It wasn't the geographic distance that mattered. The emotional distance was more daunting than the miles. Maggie was confused. It seemed the further apart they were emotionally, the tighter their hold on each other was.

"Roz, I'm just getting to know my granddaughter, that's all." Laney didn't bother to smile.

"Why?"

"Because that's what grandmothers do, they get to know their grandchildren."

Maggie could see the line being drawn.

"I guess I should have been your granddaughter instead of your daughter. Maybe then you would have taken the time to get to know me a little."

"My God, Roz, it's been years and years..."

When Laney pulled out of her driveway and blindly headed toward Oklahoma, she hoped the surprise of showing up would be enough to shatter the wall that Roz had built around her. She hoped enough years had passed, that seeing each other face-to-face would make the difference. She hoped that what had long been lost would be found. But her hope was misguided. Roz was still that stiff-necked girl who'd walked out the door without so much as a goodbye.

"What does that mean? Years and years? Time heals all wounds, is that what you're saying? Mom, that's bullshit and you know it."

All Laney heard was 'Mom.' It had been years since she'd heard that word.

"Time heals nothing. Anyway, some things shouldn't be healed. Some wounds should stay open."

"My God, Roz, your father and I always wanted the best for you. That meant we had to make decisions you weren't capable of making when you were fifteen. Simple as that. You make decisions for your child and hope they're the right ones."

"You do, huh?"

"Don't act like you don't understand. You're a mother. You've got a daughter. Think about it."

"I get it. You make decisions to protect your kid. But you don't make decisions that are gonna destroy your kid."

Maggie flinched, as if someone had smacked her face. Her eyes locked on her mother. She took one step toward her.

Laney's mouth fell open.

"What do you mean? Roz, what do you mean we 'destroyed you'?"

"He's dead, isn't he?"

"Roz, for God's sake."

"Right? He's dead?"

"We didn't kill him."

"Mom?" said Maggie.

CHAPTER 24

Franklin stood in the Hampton Inn parking lot, hands in his pockets, jacket flapping in the wind, Styrofoam cup of cold coffee in his hands. Drizzle dampening his hair and glasses. He sat the cup on a nearby car, took out a tissue, wiped the lenses, and put his glasses back on. It was 3:00am. He sipped the coffee.

He had tiptoed out of the room, not wanting to awaken Gretchen who'd been chasing sleep for several hours before turning off the TV and falling silent around 1:00am. By then, Franklin had given up trying.

The tingling in his hands and fingers had returned. The headaches, too. He had a bout of coughing earlier in the day after breakfast. Eyes wide, Gretchen had watched, saying nothing. He assured her that he'd swallowed wrong, that he was fine.

· · ·

Gretchen was standing outside the Busy Beaver again. Gris saw her, "I love you!" he called. She tried to answer, but her tongue was too swollen to speak. He cupped his hands over his mouth and shouted again and again. When she didn't answer, a look of confusion and dejection replaced his smile. Gretchen was watching another man, a man who was raising a rifle to his shoulder. She panicked and tried to wave to Gris, but her arms hung dead at her side. Shoppers were coming and going, but no one noticed. She tried to scream, but couldn't make a sound. She couldn't move. All she could do was watch. The shooter sharpened his aim and was about to pull the trigger when Gretchen gasped and woke up, tears blurring her eyes.

The room was pitch black except for the tiny fire alarm light flashing on the ceiling. She listened for her brother, but heard nothing. She sat on the side of the bed, catching her breath. She reached for her cell. It was 3:45am. She turned the flashlight app on and went into the bathroom, closed the door, turned on the light, and splashed cold water on her face. She pressed a cold washcloth on the back of her neck. Only then did she realize it had been a dream.

•   •   •

Franklin dumped the remaining coffee on the asphalt and started walking the perimeter of the parking lot, hoping the brisk air, cool mist, and exercise would wake him from his funk, and clear his puzzled mind. He looked down the hillside toward Washington St., the traffic lights on blink. There weren't any cars, only a city garbage truck starting its morning rounds. In the distance he could see a hilltop silhouetted against the faint predawn light.

He turned when he heard someone clearing his throat. A man was standing near the motel entrance. The man waved and spoke indistinctly. "What?" called Franklin. The man started walking toward him. "What do you want?" said Franklin. The man's head was down. He wore tattered jeans and a sleeveless T-shirt. "Don't come any closer," said Franklin. The man didn't stop. "I'm telling you, please go away."

The man raised his head, a sneer crossing his face. Franklin heard a familiar guttural laugh, and recognized the man's shadowy bulk. The man's shoulders were rounded and his arms were bent, his fingers splayed.

Franklin backed away. It's me, said the man. Just you and me, little boy.

"Is that?" Franklin covered his mouth and shook his head, no, no, no.

The man kept coming. Franklin wanted to escape, but there was nowhere to go. The man picked up his pace. His grizzled face and narrow-set eyes became clear. "Stop, for chrissakes!" Is he laughing? wondered Franklin. He bent over and charged, hitting the man full force in the belly with his shoulder. From deep inside Franklin, a gravelly yowl rose as the man hit the pavement, his head bouncing, his arms flailing. Franklin stood over him and bellowed, his face contorted, his sides aching from the strain.

·   ·   ·

Gretchen saw lights flashing against the closed curtains. She drew them back slowly. Police officers were scrambling from their cars and rushing toward the men lying on the pavement. Gretchen's stomach turned over. She stood back and shut the curtains.

She looked at her brother's bed. "Franklin," she said, her voice a breathy whisper. When he didn't reply, she called again, "Franklin!" Nothing. She turned on a light and bent over the pile of bedsheets and crumpled pillows. He was gone. She went back to the window and drew the curtains again. The police were holding one of the men by his arms. The other was gesticulating dramatically.

"Look, mister, please, just stop!" said one of the officers.

"But I can explain," said Franklin.

"Just be quiet!"

Franklin sat up, pushed the cop, and tried to pull away. "Look, I'm telling you, I thought he was gonna kill me; he kept coming and I didn't know what else to—"

"Sir! Goddamit!" The officer pulled a Taser from his belt. "Don't make me use this."

Gretchen ran across the parking lot, her terrycloth robe flapping behind her. She knelt beside her brother. "Franklin, are you...what happened?"

"I...I...it was him, I know it was."

"Who?"

An EMT was working on the other man. He had a large gauze wrap, white as a full moon, across the back of his head. He was tall and thin and clean-shaven. He wore a uniform of some kind and was reaching for his cap, the word SECURITY stenciled across the brim.

"Jesus," said Gretchen. "Franklin, what were you..."

Franklin's lips quivered, and his hands were balled against his chest. His eyes darted back and forth, and his face was white with terror.

She put her hand behind his neck and lifted his head. "Franklin?"

•   •   •

Turned out, Gretchen knew Stanley Grinding, the security guard. He was one of Gris's old bowling buddies.

"How can I put this, Stanley? His wife left him without warning and then he got that kind of Covid that never goes away and ever since, he's been crazy as crazy can be."

Stanley shook his head and took the gauze off to see if he'd stopped bleeding.

Gretchen continued. "And you're right, he should be in jail. He thought you were someone else, for sure, but that doesn't change the facts, does it? I mean, it's up to you. I get it. Charge him if it makes sense."

Another ambulance arrived on the scene. They put Franklin on a gurney and hoisted him into the back of the ambulance. He was docile as a kitten by then.

"Look at him. He is way off his nut," said Gretchen.

"Look, Gretchen, Gris was one of the best guys I ever knew. I mean, he was, well, you know, he was something else." He shook his head and rubbed his eyes. "What can I say, you been through plenty. I mean, they shoulda taken that kid out and blown his head off. That's what I woulda done, you know what I mean? And I wouldn't've given it a second thought."

Gretchen nodded solemnly.

"I'm not gonna press no charges, I'm not."

●   ●   ●

By the time Gretchen reached the hospital, the ambulance had come and gone. Franklin sat on a curb near the entrance, two women and a man clothed in crisp blue scrubs surrounding him, their hands on their hips. When Gretchen pulled up, Franklin stood and the emergency room staff closed in. They wanted to keep him for observation.

"Who are you?" said the doctor.

"I'm his sister."

"Okay, then. From what he's told us and what the EMTs reported, I think your brother has had a mental health event."

"A what?"

"I think he may have had a psychotic episode."

"That's ridiculous. I know my brother. His brain is foggy from Covid, but he's not crazy."

"We're not saying he's crazy."

"I think you are."

"We're not."

"Yes, you are."

The doctor heaved a sigh, looked at the ground, and collected himself. "Look, all I'm saying is that he could be a danger to himself and others in his current condition."

"Let's get out of here!" Franklin was pacing back and forth, the nurses following.

Gretchen held up one finger— "Just a minute."—then turned back to the doctor. "What do you mean, he could be a danger to, whatever?"

"He attacked that man and knocked him to the ground."

"That may be stupid, but it's not crazy."

"He thought the man was your father."

Gretchen grimaced. "He what?"

"Yeah. He thought the guy was your father. He got agitated and attacked him."

Gretchen looked at her brother, who had stopped pacing, and was talking with the nurses, his tone now friendly. The muscles in her jaw were granite hard. She wiped sweat from her brow. Our goddam father, she thought. She kicked a stone across the pavement.

"Does this happen often?"

"No." Gretchen's shoulders sank. "No, it doesn't. They had their problems, yes, but...no."

Franklin and the nurses were laughing. He was telling stories about his shoe store escapades. Gretchen watched. He was just a guy regaling his audience about past glories. She explained to the doctor what had been going on in the last several months, including why they were in town. She told him she'd look after her brother and if anything happened, she would get him to a psychiatrist when they got back home.

The doctor rubbed his cheeks. "Okay, well, I'll let him go. Good luck."

"Good luck? There is such a thing?"

CHAPTER 25

Roz sat in her car after Laney and Maggie had left. She took the keys from the ignition and went back to the bench where they'd been sitting. She sat, half folded over, her hair fluttering in the breeze. "We didn't kill him," her mother had said. She shook her head, thinking of the look on Maggie's face, the shock and confusion. She walked down the path and into a field of dunes. Hawks circled, searching for prey. She could taste sand; she could feel the grit on her teeth.

Once she reached the lake, Roz sat on the hot sand and watched the cloud shadows racing across its surface. She lay back, her hands behind her head, and pulled up her knees. She closed her eyes. She could hear her father's laughter. They were running to the dock, a race she won every year, then dangling their feet in the water while her mother opened the cabin. "You get faster and faster," her father said, admiringly. "Maybe you're just getting slower." She nudged his ribs and they laughed some more.

Soon, her mother joined them, picnic basket on her arm. She spread a blanket on the grass while Roz and her father looked for dry twigs and small branches. Her father lighted the fire, and Roz added kindling to keep it going. Her mother opened the basket, took out the paper plates and cups, the plastic silverware, the iced tea, the fried chicken and potato salad, the spice cake wrapped in saran.

Later, they sat on the porch, each in their Adirondack chair, listening to the rain patter on leaves and the mournful call of loons swooping over the lake.

Roz sat up in the sand. She crossed her arms and leaned on her knees. That was their last vacation as a family. She was thirteen and had finished junior high school with a 3.95 grade point average. The future seemed bright as she anticipated going across town to high school in the fall. She didn't know it then, but this was her last summer as a little girl, the last summer as a daughter who worshipped her parents and thrived on their approval.

They never made it back to the lake again. Her parents blamed this on their busy schedules. They apologized over and over to Roz. They promised the following year would be different, and the year after that. And then they stopped making promises.

Roz knew that her parents' work wasn't the reason they never sat on the cabin porch together again. The fabric of her parents' marriage was torn. She could feel the emptiness engulfing them. Their tongues were barbed and their hearts stopped beating for each other.

Roz needed them less and less. Or were they less and less available? Friends filled the void. She was a feral teen, drinking, drugging, staying away from home as often as possible, experimenting with life.

It wasn't until she met Jackson, that life made sense again. She was fifteen, and he was a nineteen-year-old boy who worked for the town. "I'm a refuse engineer," he joked. His parents divorced when he was fourteen, so he dropped out of school. To escape the turmoil, he moved in with his aunt who was barely out of high school.

He was tall, long-necked, hipless, and tatted. He wore horn-rimmed glasses and a bandana on his shaved head. He wrote poetry and dreamed of going to Greenwich Village to become the "next somebody."

When they met, she was standing outside the drug store in the rain. She huddled in the cold, waiting for the storm to break. She didn't notice him when he came out of the store. "Hey," he said, "you look like you're freezing." She didn't respond. He waited, but then walked away. A few minutes later, he pulled up in his truck, rolled the window down and said, "I'll give you a lift." She hesitated at first. "I'm not an ax murderer or rapist. I quit all that." She laughed and got in his truck.

Roz closed her eyes. It was all so mournfully beautiful. She kept Jackson a secret. He'd pick her up after school, and they'd ride for hours in the country, just talking. She told her parents she was working on a school project, had to stay after so she could do research. After the third time she used this excuse, her father asked, "Where do you actually go every day after school?" "I told you. School work," she answered. "Roz, c'mon," her mother said.

Soon their rides ended at his grandfather's hunting "shack." Jackson would make a fire. They'd drink black coffee and he'd read her his poems, mostly about lone wolves and painful deaths. They'd share a joint and lie together on his bed. The first time they made love, Roz trembled with anxiety. He told her they didn't need to do anything, but she said she wanted to. He went slowly, gently, touching her with his finger tips, kissing her, easing her on top of him. Each time, she felt a whirling sensation in the pit of her stomach that she called love. But she didn't tell him, fearing he might laugh.

Roz opened her eyes and shook her head, thinking how young she had been no matter how grownup she'd felt. Maggie was invited to her first school dance when she was thirteen, the boy was fifteen. She'd seen him in the store from time to time. Pimply, gangly, a mouth full of braces. He was polite and seemed immature, which she liked. She gave Maggie the okay.

The next morning, Roz noticed a dark red mark on one side of Maggie's neck and a purple one on her chest. "Why do you have to make a big thing out of nothing! They're just scratches, or bug bites, I don't know. They're just there, who cares? Really." Roz grounded her for a week.

Maggie found out that her mother had confronted the boy at the Save-a-Lot: "Were you sucking on my daughter?" She didn't go back to school for a week. And she didn't talk to her mother for a month.

Even then, Roz knew she couldn't win the battle over boys. No matter how hard she tried, it was like digging a well with your elbows. Her parents' attempts had failed and so would hers. And yet, she persisted.

It wasn't until junior prom that Roz gave Maggie permission to go out with a boy again.

Maggie didn't come home for three days. Roz sat on the porch until Maggie returned. Day and night. Heat and cold. She was too angry to speak when Maggie rolled out of a car (driven by some boy Roz had never seen before) and tiptoed across the gravel driveway, dance shoes in her hands, tulle trailing behind her like a kite's tail.

"I sure hope he didn't knock you up."

One of those times she wished she'd given more thought to what she'd said.

Maggie stopped, dropped her shoes on the ground, took her clutch from under her arm, opened it, and dumped a dozen condoms on the ground. "I started out with a lot more than that. I'm not stupid. Like some people."

Roz was relieved (and appalled) by Maggie's answer. Her daughter's sexual exploits as a teen seemed like sport, just notches on a belt, while Roz's love-making with Jackson had been like picking forbidden fruit from the Tree of Knowledge. Innocence, discovery, awakening; it was the break of day.

The wind was picking up. Roz got up, dusted herself off, and walked back to the bench. She looked down the path to her car, thinking about what awaited her at home. She sat down again.

Jackson was the first man she'd ever loved. And the last. And Jackson was the first man who ever loved her. And, as far as she knew, the last. The flame burned bright, but the wind was unrelenting. Darkness returned quickly.

"What in the world?" Her mother's voice seemed angry or blaming, rather than incredulous or despairing. Roz could feel the floor disappear below her.

•   •   •

"What the hell was she thinking?" her father had said. "I mean, really?"

Roz shook her head. She sat down at the kitchen table. Her mother wrung a dishcloth, while her father poured his martini down the sink drain. The refrigerator buzzed and Roz tried to swallow and her mother inhaled like she was about to burst a balloon and her father cleared something from his throat.

"Did he say anything to anyone? To you?" Her mother reached for Roz's hand just as she buried it in her lap.

"If he had said something to me, do you think he'd be dead now? Do you? How stupid are you? If he had said something to me, I would have stopped him. I would have stopped him. I would have."

"Does anyone know where he got all the pills? I'll bet it was his mother." Laney tilted her head toward Roz in sympathy.

"Please don't do this?"

"Do what?" said her father.

"Pretend you give a shit."

"Now wait a—"

"Because you don't. You never did. You hated him from the beginning."

"That's not fair," said her mother.

"Roz, this is not the time—" said her father.

"Time for what? Time to tell the truth?"

"C'mon."

"I asked you a simple question. You could have said 'Yes' or you could have said 'No.' You chose 'No' and now Jackson's dead."

Roz sat up, the shadow of a hawk rippled across the dune. "You said no," she whispered. "No."

. . .

Maggie sat on the porch rocker waiting for her mother to come home. Her grandmother said she'd sit with her, if it would help, but Maggie declined. She checked her phone for messages. Nothing. She'd been waiting an hour. Where was she? She went in the house for a beer. When she came out again, Sandman was passing. He blew his horn, waved, and then U-turned and pulled into the driveway.

Not now, thought Maggie.

Sandman stopped to tell her about the couple from Missouri, the one's who'd passed through the previous week. They'd stopped the night before and asked for Maggie, by name, no less. They went on and on about what a "lovely girl" she was and how she had come in the middle of the night to fix the toilet, something that Sandman didn't know. "I told them you were the best," he said. "I told them the place couldn't run without you."

Maggie breathed in sharply.

"And that's true, Maggie." He waited a beat and when she didn't speak, he said, "I told 'em you were on a well-deserved vacation. When they asked where, I said, 'the Caribbean.' I figured if I was going to lie, I might as well lie big." He chuckled into his chest.

"You want a beer?"

"If you don't mind." Sandman sat sideways on the top step of the porch and leaned against the post.

Maggie laid her beer can on the arm rest. "Lone Star, okay?"

"Yeah."

She put his bottle on the porch beside him, sat down in her rocker, a second bottle in her hand. She finished the first in one gulp, looked at the second, and let it rest in her lap.

"Yeah, folks been missing you..."

"Sorry, I haven't been around. Busy is all."

"I figured." He tipped the bottle, then wiped his mouth on his sleeve. "What do you think? Coming back?"

"Every day, when I wake up, I'm coming back, but I never make it."

"Yeah, I get it."

"You do?"

Sandman's beer dripped off his chin.

"Well, a lot happened, I guess. Sometimes it feels like nothing happened, but it did." He tried to catch her eye. "I mean, of course, it did, but we never..."

"No, we never."

They both drank more beer. The highway was quiet. Birds gathered on the telephone wire.

"I don't know...maybe we should." He looked away as he said this.

"You know it was a one-off, right? I don't mean that the way it sounds, but it *was* a one-time thing."

"Sure, yeah, no, I know that. I mean, yeah." His bottle dangled from his hand. He stood and raised his eyebrows at her, a soft grin on his face. "Of course." There was finality in his tone.

"Look, Sandman—"

"You don't have to say anything."

"I'm pregnant."

He sat down again. He took a deep breath and held it. "You're sure?"

"As can be."

"Hm. I wondered. I mean, when I didn't see you and all."

"You wondered right."

He scuffed his bootheel on the step. "You know, that wasn't, I wasn't trying to—"

"Neither was I. But it happened."

"I'm sorry, Maggie, I should have been—"

"Me, too." She got up from the rocker and leaned against the porch column. "Sometimes you just do things. You don't think about them. You just do them. And if someone asks you 'Why?' you say, 'I don't know'."

"Yeah. I guess that's true."

Sandman wanted to do something, put his arm around her, tell her everything would work out, help her in some way.

"You know, Maggie, I'd like to—"

"I don't need any help, Sandman. I don't."

"But—"

"What?"

"I'm, you know, I'm part of this thing."

"I know you are. And I know you want to do something. But it's not going to be like that. We're not going to be, you know, we're not going to be, I don't know."

"Parents? You mean parents?"

"I don't know what I mean yet."

"Are you gonna keep—"

"Don't ask me that. Please."

"But—"

"I don't know what I'm going to do. About anything."

Sandman stood and leaned against the opposite column. "Well. I'm here. You know that. I'm here."

Maggie looked at Sandman. His head was bowed, his mouth open slightly. She took a step towards him and put a hand on his shoulder. "I know you are."

They both turned when they heard car wheels humming and then a horn blowing.

"You should go."

"You sure?"

"Yeah, go. I'll try to get back to work," she said, knowing it was a lie.

Sandman headed to his car as Roz skidded into the yard, raising a storm of dust and dirt that enveloped him. Sandman coughed, but kept going. Roz pointed at his car as Sandman sped away. "What'd he want? Huh?"

"Nothing."

"Don't 'nothing' me. What did he want?"

Maggie crossed her arms and tightened her jaw.

"He's the one, isn't he? Jesus Christ."

Maggie retreated into the house.

CHAPTER 26

The officer rattled the jail cell with his night stick. "Time's comin'."

Edge, lying down, hands behind his head, didn't respond.

"Hear me? It's sentencing time."

Edge didn't answer.

"I'm tellin' you, you'll never see the light of day again. That's for sure."

The officer adjusted his belt, shuffled his feet back and forth, then walked away.

The trial had gone on for weeks. Witnesses came and went, angry, tearful. Experts, laser pointers in hand, went through slide after slide of their power point presentations. Then there were the crime scene photographs, blown up to poster size. People squirmed in their seats. Edge remembered the courtroom lights buzzed constantly, and when he asked the bailiff if something could be done about it, he sneered, "You fucking kidding me?"

It had been an old, church-going, eye-for-an-eye jury. "All we need to do is convince one," his public defender had said. One juror, belt cinched tight, collar buttoned up, pencil straight part in his pasty combover, stared at Edge continuously. It stopped when Edge glared back at him once. He won't be the *one*, Edge thought.

The jury came back so quickly that Edge hadn't had time to finish lunch. The foreperson, chest puffed up, crowed "Guilty!" eight times, one for every person he'd killed. The courtroom erupted, like someone had hit a grand slam in the bottom of the ninth to win the World Series. He did hear one lone voice say, "Oh...no." He turned and caught his mother's eye. And then they took him away.

Appeal denied, appeal denied, appeal denied. Birthdays came and birthdays went. His father wrote three letters. He didn't open any of them. His mother wrote often. She visited four times. It was a long drive for a short stay. She cried. He clenched. She told him his friends were thinking of him but when he asked, she couldn't remember their names.

He spent his afternoons in the yard working out. After the broken arm, he went to voluntary segregation for safety. Two hours a day outside the cell. He paced the perimeter of an eight by ten space, concrete block walls all around, a sliver of sky above.

He returned to population at the end of the year, but seldom left his cell. He did Sudoku, read Stephen King, tried his hand at Wordle, took online drawing classes, watched soaps, lay on his bunk curled in a ball, did Sudoku, read Stephen King...

"Get up, goddamit!" There were two officers this time. "We're late."

Edge sat up. He pulled on his jump suit and slipped his plastic slides on. He took a piss. "I'm all yours," he said, as he crossed his arms behind his back. The officers came in the cell, while two others waited. They cuffed him and shackled his ankles. He shuffled along, his escorts trotting him in front of a holding cell, a dozen small-timers watching. "You're done, son!" "Feeling a little colicky, are we?" "Good luck, motherfucker!" "You killed my cousin, you fucking piece of shit!" He walked on, his face expressionless.

• • •

Gretchen turned over and looked at the clock. She sat up and listened to her brother's thick, steady breathing. She rubbed her face with both hands then stood. She tapped him on the back. "Franklin," she whispered. He didn't move a muscle. She tried again. "Hey, Franklin." Didn't flinch. Thank God, she thought.

She picked up the bottle of pills and put the cap back on. She had told him they would help him sleep, but she didn't say for how long. She figured a double dose would be enough to keep him away from the courthouse and off her mind.

•   •   •

By the time they returned from the hospital the night before, he was in tears. "Why did he do that?" he kept saying. "It was long ago," she said. "Was it?" Franklin was lost again in a spectral haze. He hadn't talked about their father in years. Not since his death.

Long ago, she'd intended to tell him she knew what had happened. She wanted to tell him how sorry she was. But the timing for that conversation was never right and, eventually, life took over. She and Gris moved out of state and Franklin and Laney had their troubles with Roz. New worries replaced old ones.

She sat on the bed beside her brother, leaned over, and softly rested her head on his shoulder. She closed her eyes. She had been a little girl and he a little boy, a little boy with spirit and drive, who didn't know a thing.

At first, she didn't understand what they meant, the sounds that came from her brother's bedroom. She went to her mother who said she must have been dreaming. When she insisted otherwise, her mother abruptly told her to go back to bed and stay there. Her mother's voice was angry, but the look on her face, it took a long time for Gretchen to name it, was fear, even terror. For days, her mother didn't look at her. Gretchen soon understood there were things you shouldn't talk about, things that no one should talk about, things that were, what was the word, too unspeakable? Only later did she understand the cost of not talking. Only later did she understand that silence couldn't defeat cruelty.

Her father preferred her. He was kind and humorous, and he'd give her gifts and do things with her. He never disciplined her and chided her mother when she tried to. And yet, there was something empty in the attention he gave. It was like he was showing off, or trying to prove something, or using her to make himself look good. She never noticed this as a girl, but in her teens, it became clear. He was on stage when he treated her well, and she was merely a prop. He was playing to an audience of one, their mother, trying to convince her he was a good father or, at least, confuse her.

They grew up. Their father finally moved out. It seemed to clear the air. Until that birthday party, Franklin's twenty-fifth. Their father had been slobbering drunk. He humiliated his son with vulgar, slashing snipes about his manhood, his worthlessness, his failure to be anything. Franklin stared at their father, expressionless, his face turning red, then ashen white. Their mother cleaned the table while their father went on. Unable to take it any longer, Gretchen left the room in tears. She didn't speak to him again for two years, not until the day he died.

She stood over her brother a moment longer, remembering. She pulled the cover over his shoulders, grabbed her jacket, purse, and keys, opened the door slowly, and closed it gently.

· · ·

The court house parking lot was a gaggle of news trucks, a tangle of antennae, and a cluster of well-coiffed news anchors and reporters. A few hundred observers filled the lawn, most of whom were more interested in the news celebrities than the news itself.

Gretchen finished her first cup of black coffee and opened her second. She unwrapped a breakfast sandwich, smelled it, and took a bite. She had parked down the block, farther away from the hubbub. The caffeine offset her sleepiness making her uncharacteristically calm. Her wait was over. The time had come. She unfolded two sheets of paper and read them slowly, her lips moving. She took a pen from the glove box and scratched out some sentences and added others. She folded it up again, put it back in her purse, then abruptly took it out again. She turned the second page over and began writing. And then she was done. She took a deep breath as the court house door opened, sucking everyone in.

She was told she would be third in line. There were five victim impact statements. The others had spoken to the press, but declined going through the horror of seeing their loved one's killer again. Given the option of sitting in the courtroom or waiting in the hall, Gretchen found a bench in the hall where she sat, legs crossed, sipping her lukewarm coffee.

A pair of women's square-heeled black shoes with scuffed toes appeared in front of her. She looked up. Edith Stinson-Golding leaned forward, her hand outstretched. Her face told a story of excruciating love and inescapable pain. Her hand shook, and as she tried to smile, the corners of her mouth trembled.

"Hello," she said in a whisper. "May I sit with you for a moment."

"Yes, yes, of course." Gretchen moved her jacket aside. "Please."

Edith sat close and took Gretchen's arm in both hands. She started crying, then abruptly stopped. "I never told you how sorry I am." She began to weep again. Gretchen put her arm around her and rocked her slowly. Someone leaned out the courtroom door and called for Edith to come. She squeezed Gretchen's hand and walked away.

She sat all morning, then court broke for lunch. The bailiff told her she would be next. He gave her directions to the snack bar in the basement. She thanked him, but knew she wouldn't eat. She went to the ladies' room, washed her face, and sat in a stall for a long while collecting her thoughts. When she came out, people were scurrying back into court.

The room seemed small when she entered. Perhaps because it was so crowded. There were two ceiling fans, one turning slowly. The American flag and the state flag hung listlessly. She had expected church-like benches, but, instead, there were individual plastic chairs pressed tightly together. Heads turned. The judge, a woman, leaned on one elbow, her glasses hanging at her chest, her black robe enveloping her. There were two opposing tables. At one was a pony-tailed lawyer, a man in an orange-striped jump suit sitting beside him. His hair was longer than she remembered and his face was full, even jowly. The skinny boy was gone, replaced by a man-sized version. He sat with his arms on the table, fiddling with a pencil. His ever-present smirk had been replaced by the indifferent stare of a man whose life was over.

The bailiff opened the gate and gestured to the podium. She stepped onto the podium, laid her jacket on a nearby chair, removed her mask, took her papers from her purse, and flattened them on the lectern. Across the front edge of the lectern were a cluster of microphones linked with duct tape. She took a breath and looked around the room. She glanced at Edith, but tried not to make eye contact. She imagined every person was Gris, that every expectant eye was his, that every pounding heart was his, that every waiting ear was his. She looked at her papers and opened her mouth to speak. Her whole body hiccupped at the sound of the judge's voice.

Gretchen turned and looked at the judge sitting high above her. She didn't smile, but her face exuded exhausted kindness. Gretchen nodded. The judge told her how much she admired her willingness to come forward and share her thoughts and feelings. She used words like "courageous" and "strong" and "powerful." She went on from there, but Gretchen no longer heard what she was saying. The judge leaned back in her dark leather chair. The courtroom was quiet, the air pensive. "You may speak now, Mrs. Hennefer."

Gretchen grabbed the lectern and cleared her throat. She looked down at her papers and up again, this time seeing Edith from the corner of her eye. She studied the orange striped man at the table in front of her. He didn't look up.

Gretchen lifted the lectern and stepped down from the podium, duct tape ripping from the floor. She placed the lectern directly in front of Edgar Stinson-Golding.

"There, that's better," she said. "I wanted to make sure you could see me."

Edgar raised his eyes.

"You probably don't remember me. My husband, Griswald, and I lived down the street from you when you were just a boy. I remember you. I know your mother. I think you shoveled our sidewalks a few times; maybe mowed our lawn that time when Gris broke his arm." Edgar shrugged. "Anyway, that's not why I'm here and that's not why you're there." She cleared her throat, inhaled deep then exhaled hard. "You know, I've tried not to think of this day, I've tried not to think of this, this thing I'm doing right now. And when I did think about it, I didn't know what I'd do when it came. Because there weren't any words in the beginning. I probably would have just screamed at the top of my lungs, screamed one continuous never-ending scream that would have said everything I could possibly have said in words. A scream, so shrill, so anguished, so furious, so hateful that it might have killed you dead on the spot.

"As time passed, and I thought about standing here, I figured I'd cry and cry and cry, filling this room and the city below this building with my tears, so many tears that people way out in the county would think a flood was coming, that the world was ending, and they would be right.

"And then, I thought maybe I wouldn't say a thing. I would just be silent, you know? But my silence wouldn't be quiet. No, my silence would thunder in your ears, and you would hear them, the victims, my Gris, even though they were gone, you would hear their screams, not outside somewhere, but inside your head, filling you with the horror, the horror they felt, the horror of your evil.

"In recent months, though, I've found my words. I've found things I want to say. But I am of two voices, that's what's confusing to me. The first voice, the first voice covers about ninety-five percent of what I have to say to you. And what that part of me has to say is simple.

"On the day you killed my Griswald, your mother and I stood outside the Busy Beaver together, not knowing, frightened at what might be going on. We leaned on each other. I think it helped both of us. But then we both saw you, how they were taking you away to a cop car, how blank your face was, like you didn't have an idea what was happening. I can still see your mother, the horror, the love. She went to you. I watched. I felt bad for her, I did. You can't help but feel bad for a mother when a child has gone wrong. When they are in trouble of their own making.

"But you know, when I found out Griswald was one of the ones you murdered, I lost all feeling for everyone, including your mother. I did. And seeing you at the arraignment, seeing your dead eyes, like you were some kind of shark or something, seeing those dead eyes and that, well it looked like a smirk on your face, I have to be honest, I wanted to shoot you dead right there. I could have done it, easy, and walked away feeling good about myself. You were just a rabid animal that needed to be put down.

"You killed eight people, you erased them, and you ruined the lives of countless others. I wanted to ask you why. But then I realized it didn't matter to me. It didn't matter if you had some twisted reason, it didn't matter if you were abused or neglected or if you were some kind of bad seed, there wasn't a reason in this world that would have mattered to me, nothing that would have made me think, even for a minute: Oh, well, now I understand. You didn't deserve my understanding; you didn't deserve to have your story heard by me.

"I had more important things to do. I had to figure out how I was going to live without the only person I ever loved. How does a puzzle piece live without the rest of the puzzle? I had to figure out how to remember his voice, his laugh, the way he pinched the corners of his mouth before he smiled, the way he smelled, the way he was there, always there...all the little things that were so big. I had to learn how to be one half of something that used to be whole. I had to learn how to grab hold of him and never let go, even though I could feel him disappearing each and every day. I had to get used to crying in line at the grocery store or in the car on the parkway. I had to learn how to keep going when there was nowhere to go and no reason to go there.

"It would have been easy to give up. It would have. Except for Gris. When I didn't want to keep going for my own sake, I kept going for his. It took a very long time, but I'm starting to live for my own sake now. I'm starting to live as if there are tomorrows that are worth staying around for. I am happy that you will never have any tomorrows. You will have day after day after day for the rest of your life, but you'll never have all the promise that one single tomorrow brings.

"I could easily say the same things that others have said before me. That I wish you were dead. That I hate you. That I wish I could get my hands on you. That Gris's life is worth ten of yours. That you are nothing and nobody. You are spit on the sidewalk."

Edgar pulled his arms off the table and buried his hands in his lap. His chest moved in and out quickly. There was a sheen to his face.

"Like I said, there's another voice in me, too. It is a tiny voice, a voice that I try to ignore, a voice I try to erase. It's my five percent voice. And, against my better judgement, I've decided to let it talk because it has something to give you. It wants to give you a burden, it wants to give you the burden of my forgiveness." A murmur rose in the courtroom. Edgar looked away, staring at the side exit. "Look at me!" He looked at her from the corners of his eyes. "No one will ever forget what you have done. Not even justice can erase the memory of what you have done. Nevertheless, justice is good. Life upon life upon life in prison is good. But I don't want to go to prison with you. I don't want to live my life in a cell of hatred, no matter how much you deserve it. I want to be free of that hatred and free of you. So, I am releasing it all; I am letting go of you and all the anger and hatred I have shouldered because of you. I forgive you for being a murderer, for being the one who took my husband's life, who wronged me beyond measure."

Gretchen's arms locked, she gripped the lectern like the room was spinning round her and she might fall. She held her breath briefly. "And now it's up to you, you've got to figure out what you will do with my forgiveness. Because, believe me, you won't be able to ignore it. It will hang like a heavy yoke across your shoulders for the rest of your life. And every day it will say: She's right, you are a murderer, you don't deserve a quiet thought, a restful sleep, a comforting sigh, until you decide what to do with her forgiveness. That is what my five percent has to say. It is calling out to you: Hear my forgiveness! Hear it and respond, even if it takes the rest of your life. That is all that is left to you."

She crumpled the papers and stuffed them into her purse. She leaned forward over the lectern. "Look at me," she whispered. He raised his head and their eyes locked for a blink or two. She stood up straight again and looked at the audience, taking in the somber silence of the moment. She turned to Edith, nodded, a sad smile on her face, then stepped off the podium, walked down the aisle into the hall and out the door to her car. Reporters traipsed after her, but her stoney visage turned them away.

Once in the car, she checked her phone. "I am thinking of you," Franklin's first text said. Then, "Are you okay," and finally, "I am here for you."

She started the car and turned on the radio. "We have a special report..." Edith's son would never leave prison alive.

CHAPTER 27

Her door locked, Maggie sat yoga-style on her bed, listening to her mother pound the door repeatedly.

"We have to talk, goddamit!"

Maggie didn't say a word.

"Open this door! Open it!"

Again, not a word. Her mother tried to catch her breath. Maggie imagined her leaning against the door with both hands, calculating the cost of a new door if she broke this one in.

For as long as she could remember, her mother had urged her to grow up while, simultaneously, resisting it every step of the way. She'd push her hard and then pull her back with equal effort. Maggie yo-yoed through her youth and adolescence, never quite reaching one stage before the next one was upon her. As a result, when Maggie landed in adulthood, whatever that was, she was no more prepared for life than when she had escaped her mother's womb. Nineteen years isn't a long time unless you're the one living it. Maggie was the oldest young person she could think of. She was too old, in fact, to admit not knowing anything about life.

No more pounding. Had her mother given up? One minute, two minutes, several more. She had, so Maggie slipped back under her blanket, ruffled her pillow, and propped it behind her head.

• • •

Roz stood in the middle of the living room staring at Maggie's bedroom door, deciding whether to punch a hole through it with her fist. Almost as quickly as it had come, the fury dissipated, like a rolling thunderstorm, here one minute and gone the next. Her fists dropped to her side. Whether Maggie opened her door or not, the door that already existed between them would remain.

She'd known motherhood would be hard. What else could it be at age sixteen. Giving birth on your own. Finding a place to live on your own. Sleepless nights all alone, except for a crying baby swaddled on the bed beside her. She told herself it would get easier. The doctor said it would get easier. Everyone was convinced that things would get easier once Maggie was out of diapers, was walking, talking, feeding herself, clothing herself, and becoming more self-sufficient. Who knew it would get harder once Maggie was out of diapers, was walking, talking, feeding herself, clothing herself, and becoming more self-sufficient. More defiant. More other-than-Roz-had-expected.

Friends loved her, teachers loved her, everyone loved bright, funny, adorable Maggie. How lucky you are, customers would say. I wish I had a daughter like your Maggie. For a modest price, you can have her, Roz would joke. They would laugh. When they left the store, Roz would go to the restroom and sit for a long while, composing herself. Sometimes she wished Maggie was someone else's daughter, so she could experience how wonderful everyone thought she was.

She got a beer from the fridge, slumped onto the couch, picked at the hole in the cushion, and surfed the TV. Maybe she'll come out, she thought. Maybe she'll come out like Punxsutawney Phil, and let me know what's coming, good weather or bad.

•   •   •

It was about 4:00am when Maggie woke up suddenly, her hands across her belly. She felt jabbing pain and wave after wave of nausea. She turned on her side, and took deep breaths to relax her abdomen. It didn't work. She sat on the edge of the bed. The sheet was wet and sticky. She reached for the bedside lamp, but knocked it to the floor. "Shit." She stood, then sat down quickly, fearing she might vomit. She reached for the bedpost and stood again, then tiptoed her hands to the end of the bed and took hold of another bed post. She reached for the dresser by the door. Her thighs felt damp. She opened the door and headed across the living room floor to the bathroom, arms out so she wouldn't run into anything.

She reached the bathroom, flicked on the light, closed the door, and toppled to the floor. She hugged the toilet and vomited. "Fuck." She pressed her hand against her chest, trying to steady her heartbeat. Just when she sensed color returning to her face, she felt faint again and threw up in her lap. She lay on the floor, the cool linoleum soothing to her face. Perspiration pooled under her cheek.

She sat up and was about to call for her mother, but then thought better of it. She lay back on the floor and closed her eyes. Shortly, she got up and weaved her way back to bed.

•   •   •

The alarm screamed at Roz. It was 6:00am. Sure this was a mistake, Roz knocked the alarm clock to the floor. It didn't stop. "Shit shit." She swung her legs around and stepped onto what she assumed would be the floor. The clock crunched under her feet. "Dammit." But, at least, the alarm stopped. She sat on the edge of the bed, considering her next move. The only way to restart the day was to go back to sleep. But as she settled into bed again, Roz remembered Alicia was away, and she would have to open the store. "Christ in a bucket." Morning prayers completed, she stood, yawned, and hobbled through the living room into the bathroom, where she took a seat, eyes half closed.

She crossed her legs and examined her foot. No cuts, no bruises. She held it tight, then rubbed it until it was warm to the touch. She wiggled her toes and twisted her ankle. Good to go.

Then she noticed a stain on the floor the shape of Cape Cod. She cocked her head and squinted. "What the...?" She got up from the toilet, flushed, and stuck a toe into the Provincetown end of the stain. It wasn't a stain at all. It had the consistency of poster paint and when she looked at her toe, she saw red, deep, dark, beet red. Don't tell me she forgot her tampon, was her first thought.

Then she noticed a skid mark at the other end of the Cape, probably made by a foot, or elbow. Not good, she thought. She went to her daughter's bedroom. "Maggie!" She heard mumbling but couldn't make out what her daughter was saying. "Maggie, are you alright?" When she heard a retching sound, she pushed open the door.

Maggie sat on the edge of the bed, holding her hair, and vomiting onto the floor.

"My God, honey." Roz took her in her arms and together they shuffled back to the bathroom, where Maggie sat on the floor in front of the toilet.

"I'm okay," she whispered.

"You're not okay, honey." Roz put an arm around her daughter. "What happened?"

"I'm not drunk. I'm not hung over."

"Okay."

Maggie started rocking back and forth.

"Maggie? Honey? What's going on? Are you losing..."

"I don't know."

Roz noticed the blood-soaked sheet.

"We've got to get you to a hospital."

"No. I'll be...it's okay...I'll..."

Roz ran water into the tub. She lifted Maggie to her feet and helped her into the bath. She soaped a washcloth and washed her daughter. The water turned rose. Maggie didn't speak. She slouched forward as her mother doused her head again and again with cups of water, then washed her hair as best she could. She wrapped it in a towel, then helped her to her feet before wrapping her body in another towel.

Maggie put her arms around her mother's neck and stepped gingerly out of the tub. She was crying, her head on her mother's shoulders.

"Why do I..."

"What, honey?" Roz had reached for another towel. "What did you say?"

"Why do I have to be me?"

Roz didn't know what to say. "Here, sit here." Maggie sat on the toilet seat. Her mother rubbed her hair vigorously with the towel. "It'll be okay."

"I don't know."

"That's okay, I do."

•   •   •

Laney looked at Roz who was sitting in the back seat with Maggie's head in her lap. Roz looked out the window as she ran her fingers through Maggie's hair. Maggie closed her eyes and grabbed her mother's leg. "It's okay," whispered Roz, still looking out the window. Soon, Maggie's mouth opened slightly and her breathing became a purr.

"She okay?" said Laney.

Roz looked at her daughter's face. "Yeah. I think."

Laney adjusted the rear-view mirror and tried to fix the hornet's nest of hair that was toppling off one side of her head. She never looked directly at herself until she had her makeup on. It was a rule. Look at the eyes, look at the cheeks, look at the brows, look at the lips. Any part, just not the whole thing. That way, when she was finished, she could take it all in with a smile.

Today her face looked like someone's elbow, crinkly, cracked, dry. If she had a pen, she could have played connect the dots with the age spots on her neck. Her eyes looked like they were gazing back at her from the bottom of a pothole.

She readjusted the mirror and looked at Roz again. She tried hard to see her little girl in her daughter's face. Her cheeks, so full; her eyes, liquid, soft, alert; her skin, cottony; her mouth, a smile. But they were gone.

"Can I ask a question?"

Roz looked at her mother's face reflected in the rear-view mirror. Laney watched for a change in Roz's expression, a nod, anything. When it didn't come, she said, "Is this because of, because of the…"

"You can say it. Pregnancy."

"Yeah."

"That's where the blood's coming from, so, yes, I think it's about the pregnancy."

Laney caught Roz's eye and shook her head in sympathy.

"She seems so young to be going through this."

"Sometimes young girls get pregnant whether they want to or not," said Roz. "Sometimes they don't know better. Sometimes they don't have a mother around to help them." Laney looked at her daughter and then out the window. "Sometimes having a mother there doesn't matter. It happens, anyway."

All you had to do was call us, and your father and I would have come fast as anything. For chrissakes. Laney decided this wasn't the time to clarify and correct the past. "It must've been hard. I mean, being so young, it must have been hard having a baby, raising a kid out here in the middle of nowhere."

Hearing these words in her own voice, and knowing that Roz heard them, too, was like a fist to the face, it was so real.

Roz was surprised. Her mother had never said a thing about how hard it must have been, not in all their phone conversations, nothing. She'd ask about Maggie, but never about her. And never about what got them in this mess. Never about Jackson.

"I guess…maybe neither of us was lucky," said Roz.

"What do you mean?"

"We both got daughters that made us old before our time."

She forced a breathy laugh. Laney grinned softly in the mirror.

"I don't know. I still love the daughter I got. And I love the daughter you got, too," said Laney.

"Hm. Will wonders never cease."

"I guess not."

Maggie mumbled in her sleep, then settled again.

Laney took a deep breath, "Do you think it would have gone better if you'd had someone?"

"Had someone? You mean if Maggie had a daddy?"

Laney nodded.

"I don't know if it would have mattered. Probably. You know who I wished her daddy was, but he's been gone for, what is it, twenty-two years?"

"Twenty-three," said Laney.

"You remember?"

Laney nodded once.

"Do you ever wish you and dad had handled it differently?"

Laney pressed her lips together.

"I think...hm, how to put this..."

"Just tell the truth."

"I wish Jackson was still alive. I wish it with all my heart. But do I wish your father and I had signed off on you getting married when you were fifteen—"

"Almost sixteen."

"Almost sixteen, then. No, I don't. Do I wish I could have changed everything that happened afterwards? Yes, I do."

"But you didn't try."

They both wanted to scream, Fuck you!

"My God, Roz."

They fell silent.

Roz was right. She hadn't tried. Franklin had been adamant that giving into Roz would be disastrous, that it would topple them as parents, and destroy any authority they thought they had. Better to wait her out; she'd come to her senses. Laney wanted to say, *but*, she wanted to say, *but* we have to do something, *but* she is our daughter, not a challenge to our authority, *but* I love her, that must come first.

The thought of fighting Franklin was too much.

"I did not do enough. That's true. And I'm sorry. Very sorry."

Maggie groaned in pain.

•   •   •

When they arrived at the hospital emergency room, Maggie was sitting up and feeling little pain. She walked into the hospital without assistance. They filled out the paper work and took seats in the tiny adjacent waiting area. When Laney asked how long it would take, an attendant said, "Your guess is as good as mine."

Maggie leafed through the magazine rack, gave up, and leaned back in her chair with a sigh of frustration. The lady across from her, smiled. She held her husband's hand and whispered comforting words to him. Likely in their eighties, she sat ramrod straight; her hair was a perfect pin cushion; she wore a flowered dress and pearls. Her husband's face was haggard, tormented. He was breathing quick and shallow, mouth wide open. He rubbed his chest with his fist.

"There, there," she said. "It won't be long."

Maggie acknowledged the woman with a nod.

"It's his heart," said the lady, as if she saw question marks in Maggie's eyes.

"I'm so sorry," said Maggie and Laney.

"Have they seen him yet?" said Roz.

"No. I guess there's an emergency of some sort, ambulance came blaring, and they rushed some fella in. Car accident, I think." She shrugged.

There were tears in her husband's eyes now. The woman lifted his hand to her lips and kissed it.

"Maybe it's nothing to worry about, indigestion or something," said Roz.

"No, we know it's something, alright. Likely a heart attack."

"What? I hope not," said Laney. "I mean, if they thought it was a heart attack, they'd get him in immediately."

"They're awful busy."

"But..." Laney got up and went to the desk. She spoke forcefully, although the nurse was unmoved.

"Sometimes, you just gotta wait, no matter how bad things may seem. Someone else may be ahead of you," she said.

Laney was gob-smacked by this reasoning, but she went back to her seat as she was told.

"Thank you," said the lady. "But this isn't our first rodeo." She chuckled and nudged Joseph. "What is this Joseph, third—"

"Fourth," muttered Joseph.

"Fourth? You sure?"

"You're forgetting 2015."

She thought for a moment. "Of course, of course, 2015." She turned back to Laney. "Yes, this is Joseph's fourth heart attack."

"I'm so sorry," said Maggie. "That must be awful."

"Lots of things are awful, aren't they? We've had a drought for nearly twenty years. That's awful. But there's nothing you can do about most awful things. They come at you whether you want them to or not. At first you think, 'Oh no, the world is coming to an end!'." She threw her head back and crooned her lament, then laughed. "Same with Joseph's heart attacks. But after a while, the awful things are just things that happen, you know. They aren't things that were sent to torment you. They just come along, you know? You can't always separate the wheat from the chaff, so you accept it all as best you can. Don't get me wrong. It's not that I don't puzzle over it."

She leaned forward, taking a conspiratorial tone. "You know, when we go to prayer group and the reverend asks us to make our silent confessions and ask for God's forgiveness, I never tell him this, but sometimes I don't get to my own, because it takes so long to forgive God; he messes up just as much, or more, than I do. Look around you. That's a plain fact."

She looked at Joseph, who broke a smile and shook his head.

"We been married sixty-two years, sixty-three next month," said Joseph, his voice raspy. "She's my girl."

"Go on!" she said, love-tapping him on the arm.

"That is amazing," said Laney. "Congratulations."

Roz and Maggie applauded softly.

A nurse came through the door. "Okay, you two. Let's see what's going on."

The couple followed the nurse into an exam room. "So long," said Joseph.

"Bless you," said his wife.

More applause. The three of them exchanged glances, unintentional smiles on their faces.

"Hm," said Laney.

"Yeah," said Maggie.

Roz uncrossed her arms.

•   •   •

It was 2:00pm. When they entered the exam room, it was 6:00pm. By then, Maggie had survived two more waves of pain and nausea. She had bled once, as well.

Maggie tried to explain what was wrong, despite Roz and Laney competing to tell the story. The doctor invited them to wait in the other room so he could talk to Maggie alone, then he'd have them back. His list of questions followed. Yes, she was pregnant. No, she hadn't seen a doctor yet. Hmm, she wasn't sure how far along she was, probably eight weeks. As for other symptoms, she noticed her breasts were sore, she had no energy, and sometimes her mother was a sonofabitch. He laughed and clarified that he couldn't treat her mother's sonofabitchiness, but he hoped he could help her with everything else.

Yes, the father knew about the pregnancy. No, he wouldn't be involved. That was fine. Not sure how *he* felt about it. Yes, she could count on her mother for help; her grandmother, too, unless she left them. She explained the rift between her mother and grandmother as best she could. She explained what daily living was like.

And then she began to cry.

The doctor—thinning hair, oval shaped wire-rimmed glasses, round face, tiny eyes, white coat two sizes too large—pulled the curtain and leaned against the wall. "Yeah," he said quietly, "I think I get it. Not fun, for sure."

"And here I am with this, this person starting to grow inside of me. I mean, how unlucky is that baby gonna be?"

The doctor said that her symptoms seemed normal for someone in their first trimester.

"Is there anything you haven't told me, anything, even if it doesn't seem relevant, that maybe I should know."

"Like I said, I just bleed a lot. I mean, often and a lot."

"You said it looks pretty much like your normal menstruation, right?"

"Most of the time."

"Most of the time?"

"Up till we got here."

"What do you mean?"

She described in detail what the toilet bowl looked like the last time she bled.

"Yeah, it sounds crazy, doesn't it?" she said.

The doctor looked lost, half confused, half concerned. "No...no. It's just different."

"So, what do we do?"

"Well...I'll tell you, blood is an amazing thing. It will tell us a story about what's going on and then we'll make a plan." He urged her again to find an OB/GYN because he wouldn't be able to follow her.

Roz and Laney returned, guns blazing. What took so long? Why didn't he let them stay? Is something wrong? What's the big secret?

She's my daughter, blah, blah, blah. She's my granddaughter blah, blah, blah. We have rights!

The doctor pulled chairs from another room and asked them to have a seat. Then he sat, as well. "I can see how much you care about this young woman of yours. She's lucky to have two strong women who care so much, who will fight for her no matter what." He stopped there, looked at both women, and smiled. He looked at Maggie. "Not everyone has a mother and a grandmother like this." He winked.

Not sure what just happened, both women said, "Okay...yes...thank you?"

* * *

She left her blood and her phone number behind. The blood went to the lab where it would sit until Monday. The doctor couldn't say when the findings would be available. "Sometime between now and when you hear from me." He forced a chuckle.

The three women sat in the car after the appointment, trying to make sense of things.

"So, did he tell you to do anything?" said Roz.

"No, not really."

"Did he say whether this was normal or not?" said Laney.

"Didn't say. Blood will tell us," said Maggie.

Maggie tipped her head out the window, letting the air cool her face.

"Jesus." Roz was huffing and puffing like a locomotive.

"What?"

"I mean, did I waste a workday taking you to some damn hospital half way across Oklahoma just to have some good-for-nothing doctor I don't know from nobody tell us nothing and then send us on our way!"

"We have to wait on the blood." Maggie turned her head this way, then that, trying to untie a knot in her neck.

"You got a lot of faith in an ounce of blood, don't you."

"Wasn't an ounce, I can tell you. The tube was as long as a rope."

"'Long as a rope,' yeah, sure, right."

"I'm telling you..."

"Let's cut the bickering." Laney pushed herself up in her seat, trying to reach the moral high ground. "Think about Joseph and his wife."

"What about 'em?" Roz wagged her head at her mother.

"Wouldn't you like to be like that? At peace with life no matter what happened to you? I envy them. I envy the hell out of them." She started the car.

"You want their life? No fancy car? No fancy clothes? Yeah, right," said Roz.

"I didn't say I wanted their life. I meant, I wish I looked at my life the way they look at theirs, that's all. I mean..." There was a long pause. "I mean, I don't know if I've ever been happy. I can't remember a time. I've had fun. I've had stuff. I've been almost everywhere. But I don't know if I've ever felt the way those two people feel about their lives. And, you and I know, Joseph may never leave that hospital again. And, of course it matters whether he lives or dies, but then again, does it? They've lived their lives the way they wanted to. No regrets."

"Wow, you've been to the mountain top, haven't you; you've been to the mountain top and you've looked out over every goddamn thing and now you think you know—"

Maggie kicked the back of her mother's seat. "Stop it...just stop it!"

"Who the hell are you—"

"I'm talking! I've never known what peace is like either, and I've never been to any mountain top, all I know is that right now the only thing that matters is my blood. Everything depends on what my blood has to say. It does."

"What do you mean?" said Laney.

"What I mean is this—When I bleed, it doesn't look like any period I've ever had."

"Maggie." Roz turned in her seat.

"Listen to me. When it comes out, it comes out in bunches, like grapes."

Laney turned off the car.

CHAPTER 28

Gretchen squinted into the late afternoon glare as the sun tiptoed across the Lake Erie horizon. Franklin stood at the water's edge, his hands full of flat stones. He tried to skip one, then another, and another after that. He wobbled as he leaned over to one side. He tried again, but never got more than three skips. Finally, he tossed the remaining stones all at once, creating a modest splash.

"Jesus." Franklin, his pants rolled up to his knees, pretended not to shiver in the icy fall water.

Gretchen sat on a piece of driftwood the size of a small car. She pulled her sweater tight around her and watched the soft waves lap against the breakwater.

•   •   •

When she came back to the motel after court, Franklin was standing out front, his hair tousled, his face unshaven. She couldn't tell if he was waiting for her, or lost. She frowned and pulled slowly into a parking spot. Franklin opened the door for her. Before she could say, thank you, he threw his arms around her. After a minute, she tried to pull away, but he wouldn't let go. She rubbed his back and asked how he was doing. He loosened his hold and stepped back.

"I am sorry. Please forgive me. I should have—"

"Please, it's fine."

"I just...I don't know what..."

"Yeah, I know."

He put his arm around her again. She could feel him quivering.

"I'm glad they're putting the little bastard away for good."

She appreciated his anger. Hers was gone.

"Did you see him? I mean, when you spoke, how did it go?"

"Okay, I guess."

"Did you tear him apart."

"Yeah..."

"Good."

"Then I forgave him."

Franklin nodded one way then the other.

"What did you say? You, what?"

She shrugged.

"I forgave him."

Franklin howled with laughter.

"Wouldn't that have been something, you forgiving him! Jesus, everyone would have thought you were crazier than me."

"No, really, I told him I forgave him. Don't get me wrong, I told him I hated him and wished he was dead, too. But then, I forgave him."

Franklin's mouth hung open.

"Why'd you do that?"

"I'm not sure."

•   •   •

"Presque Isle," said Franklin, in a tone suggesting this spit of glacial residue was an underappreciated fine wine.

"Why did we stop here again?"

"Old times, I guess." He waded toward the beach, like a toddler who'd just filled his pants. "Laney and I used to come here. You know, for overnight getaways."

"Uh-huh."

"I thought it might be a nice break, you know, from everything. It's calm. Beautiful, don't you think?"

"Yes. It is beautiful."

"Yeah, it is. A good reminder."

"Of what?"

"That everything isn't shit."

She knew this was Franklin's way of lifting her spirits, no matter how far off the mark it was. "Okay."

He sat beside her. "I'm sorry that I went a little nuts the other night."

"No problem." She shaded her eyes with one hand and watched a freighter lumber across her line of sight.

"I don't understand what happened...I mean...it doesn't make any sense. I attacked that guy." He shook his head and siphoned air through his teeth. "It was dark, you know...and I could have sworn it was Dad." He laughed. "Which is ridiculous...but it was real, that's what's odd..."

Gretchen looked at her brother, then at the freighter, then her brother again. She exhaled hard through her nose.

"Franklin."

"Yeah."

"Here's the thing. Dad's dead."

Franklin's back stiffened. He stood, picked up a stone and threw it as far as he could.

"I'm not an idiot. I know he's dead."

"He's dead and he was cremated and he's gone forever. He's never coming back."

"Why are you saying this?"

"And he'll never hurt you again."

"Jesus Christ." He tossed another stone and almost lost his balance. "What are you talking about?"

"Franklin, you know what I'm talking about."

Franklin gulped and licked his dry lips. He put his hands in his pockets.

"It's Covid, that's the problem. Making me loopy." He circled one ear repeatedly with his pointer.

"It's not Covid. It's Dad. He was a fucking monster."

"Don't say that." The words dribbled out of his mouth. "He had a shitty childhood—"

"Millions upon millions of people have shitty childhoods, and they don't grow up to abuse and demean their children. They do better than that."

Franklin breathed unevenly. He took a tissue from his jacket pocket and wiped his nose. He struggled for what to say. How did she know?

"I don't know what you're talking about."

"I'm talking about your twenty-fifth birthday. I'm talking about the noises that came from your bedroom when you were just a kid. I'm talking about the crying, the begging, I'm talking about—"

"Stop. Just stop." Franklin felt his chest give way, his knees buckle, his toes curl. He looked at her, his face beckoning.

"It took me a few years to figure it out. I'd ask Mom and she would just cry. It took me a long time, too long, but then, yes, I knew. And I didn't know what to do. So, I pretended it wasn't true. I pretended it wasn't possible. I pretended that Dad couldn't...that he wasn't what he was, and, so, yeah, I knew."

Franklin bowed his head. "You shouldn't have known. It was between me and him. It shouldn't have involved you. I'm sorry."

"Franklin, Franklin, listen to me. You do not apologize to me. Understand? I apologize to you. I knew and pretended I didn't."

"You were a kid."

"So were you."

Gretchen kept talking, but he could no longer hear her. He was going back, back to that first time. He was seven. Gretchen must have been five. Yes, she had just started kindergarten. Every day was an adventure, she was so excited. It was the night of her first open house. She wore a frilly dress and black patent leather shoes and white leggings and a ribbon in her hair. Their mom beamed as they walked out the door.

Their father stayed home with Franklin. He read the paper while Franklin watched cartoons. Around 6:30pm, his dad said it was time for a bath.

Always obedient, Franklin went upstairs, ran the water, and dropped some soldiers and a boat into the tub. He got in and started playing 'war,' water splashing everywhere. He stopped when his father came into the room. Usually, his mother came in to make sure he washed thoroughly. He couldn't remember his father ever coming during bath time.

He sat on the toilet seat, lit a cigarette, and asked Franklin about school and whether he liked second grade so far. He was friendlier than usual, and Franklin was buoyed by the attention. Then his father sat on the floor beside the bathtub and, together, they played. His dad made the soldiers dive into the water from the side of the bathtub. Franklin turned on the faucet, so the boat could slide down the gushing waterfall and rescue the soldiers who were struggling in the deep blue sea.

While Franklin played, his father lathered the cloth and washed his back, then his arms and stomach. He rinsed off the washcloth and soaped it again. This time he washed Franklin's legs and feet. Then he washed between his legs. "Have to make sure this thing is clean." He rubbed Franklin slowly for a long time, first with the cloth, then with his hand. Franklin stopped playing. He looked at his father who seemed unaware of what he was doing. Franklin didn't move.

His father lifted him out of the tub, stood him on the floor, and dried him slowly, thoroughly. He dropped the towel onto the floor, then carried him naked to his bedroom. He looked at Franklin for a long time, before taking a pair of pajamas from the dresser drawer and dressing him.

Franklin's breath was rapid, uneven. His father didn't speak or make eye contact while he got Franklin ready for bed.

His mother never did any of this. She let him dry himself. She never carried him to bed. And he never walked around the house naked.

Maybe this was how things were done in his father's family. Maybe his father's father had been in charge of bathing him. Dressing him for bed. Tucking him in. Maybe all fathers did this. Maybe it was just a father thing.

"Thank you," said Franklin, trying to get his father to look at him. "Thanks." His father didn't look and didn't answer. Instead, he asked Franklin to slide his pajama bottoms down to his knees. At first Franklin didn't understand what to do, so his father yanked his pajamas down for him.

His father's gaze was cold. He stood, leaned forward slightly, his face stern, his eyes dark. "Roll over," he whispered. Franklin obeyed. It was quiet in the room. All he could see was his father's ghostly shadow against the wall in front of him. He closed his eyes tight. Then he felt his father's hands caressing his bottom. Franklin startled. His father steadied him with one hand. "Do you know when Mom will be home?" His father didn't answer.

He grabbed Franklin's shoulders and turned him over. He took Franklin's genitals in one hand and softly cupped them. Franklin's arms were pinned against his sides. He closed his eyes again.

"Don't worry. It will get bigger," was all he said. He turned off the light and left the room. Franklin waited several minutes, then pulled his pajamas up and yanked the covers over his head.

"What?" said Franklin. "What did you say?"

"I said, 'He's dead.' He's dead and gone except in there." Gretchen pointed at his head. She was breathing hard, her face was red.

CHAPTER 29

When they returned home, Maggie, exhausted, went to bed without a word, while Laney sat on the front porch and Roz brewed coffee.

Laney searched "blood like grapes" on Google. Roz stared out the kitchen window at Horace Turner mowing his lawn with an old-timey push mower. Turners did the same things every day. Mow the lawn on Fridays. Hang out the wash on Mondays. Sit on the porch Saturdays, Sundays, and Tuesdays. Shop on Wednesdays. Roz wished her life was simpler.

The coffee maker stopped gurgling. Roz took two mugs from the cupboard, emptied the coffee grounds into the wastebasket, poured coffee, and put the rest into a carafe she'd bought at a yard sale. She added two spoons of sugar and sipped her cup, exhaling coffee breath. She added a spoonful and some cream to her mother's mug. I am pouring coffee for my mother, she thought.

At the door, she watched Laney's thumbs tapping away. The woman is always at that phone, she thought. She opened the door and went out on the porch.

"Here," she said, handing Laney a mug. "You know, you still got that mask on. Probably don't need it. Turners are a mile away. If you'd like, I'll sit on the steps so—"

"There, I took it off. Okay?" Laney folded her rainbow mask and tucked it in her pocket.

Roz took off her sweater, slid her chair into the sunlight and both women nursed their coffee.

Laney sat up and leaned over her phone, her lips moving.

"Hey, I think I found something."

"What?"

"Maggie's thing."

Roz often grew weary of Laney's Google discoveries. It seemed every time she went on Google, she discovered Roz was wrong about something. Everyone with half a brain knew the election was stolen, but not Google.

"Oh." Roz leaned back in her chair and put her feet on the railing.

"Roz. Come'ere. Really."

Roz took a minute, slowly lowered her legs, sipped her coffee, put her mug on the floor, then went to see Laney's most recent discovery.

"Here, read this."

Roz scrolled slowly through the Cleveland Clinic posting. Laney watched her daughter's crimped face go blank, then darken.

"Not good," said Roz.

"Not at all."

• • •

Maggie clenched her whole body, hoping the pain would pass. She pulled her knees up to her chest and closed her eyes. She took deep breaths, slowly, slowly. Then again. In through the nose out through—The pain came too fast for her to keep up. Nausea followed in waves. She reached for the wastebasket and threw up. She did her breathing again, stretched out her legs, and waited until the pain was gone.

She opened her bedroom door slowly and peeked into the living room to see if anyone was there. She heard voices from the porch. She dashed quickly to the bathroom, locked the door, and sat down just in time. It felt like a release valve had opened and everything inside her was escaping. She felt light headed and clammy. Breathe, breathe, breathe. Maggie spread her legs and looked. The blood was brown with tiny clusters of...things. She wiped, flushed, and got up as fast as she could. She slammed the toilet seat closed.

She doused her face with cold water and looked at herself in the mirror. What's happening? she wondered. Why won't this stop? She put both hands on her belly and caressed it. There, there, everything will be...everything will be... She shook her head, sat down again on the toilet seat, and pulled a line of toilet paper off the roll. She dabbed her eyes and wiped her neck. Give yourself a moment. Pull it together, pull it together, pull it together, you're okay, you're okay. She could feel color seeping back into her face. Okay, good. Okay, that's good.

She stood. The pain was gone. The nausea, as well. She was herself again. She tossed the toilet paper into the wastebasket and reached for the doorknob. When she opened the door, her mother and grandmother were standing within inches of her, their faces stiff as mannequins.

She stepped back. "Jesus Christ."

•   •   •

"Not good at all." Roz sat back down in her chair and picked up her coffee but didn't drink it. Laney got up and leaned against the porch post beside her daughter.

Roz covered her mouth with one hand. She blinked rapidly and sniffed once. Her eyes went soft and moist. She pinched her lips tight until they disappeared.

Laney sat down on the top step. She patted her daughter's foot, then reached for her hand. Roz was inclined to pull it away, but didn't. She let it hang limp as her mother held it, caressing the palm with her thumb. Her mother smelled like clean wash just pulled from the dryer. She smelled real.

"We'll figure this out," said Laney. "It'll be okay."

"How long did you hate me?"

Laney's thumb stopped moving and her eyebrows shot to the top of her forehead. "I never hated you. I was angry at you. I didn't understand you. But I never hated you. Never."

"I'm sorry that I hated you for so long. Even after I adjusted to everything that happened, I didn't have any other feeling for you, so I kept hating you. It was the only thing I had."

Laney sat on the porch floor and hugged Roz's leg. "It's hard being a daughter. And it's hard having a daughter."

"This is true."

Their ears perked when they heard the bathroom door close. They looked at each other, then walked quietly into the house, making sure the screen door didn't slam behind them. They parked in front of the bathroom, waiting, and listening.

"She's sick again," said Laney.

Roz's head was bowed, her ear was against the door.

"Should we go in?"

"No," said Roz. "Let's give it a moment. She needs her space."

Roz *knew* her daughter, thought Laney. This was comforting, comforting to know that with no help from anyone, Roz had learned enough about her daughter to respect her needs even if, as a parent, she couldn't meet them.

They could hear her vomiting. Roz placed her open palm on the door. Soon it was quiet.

"Do you think she's okay?" said Laney.

"I don't know." She exhaled hard and shifted her weight from one leg to the other.

There were two heads and two ears pressed against the door when Maggie opened it.

"Jesus Christ."

"Jesus Christ, for sure," said Roz. "Are you okay?" Maggie's face was lily white.

"No."

"You're not?"

"No, I'm not," said Maggie, her voice agitated. "Why would you think I was okay? I'm bleeding God knows what out of my...and..." Maggie covered her face and broke into tears. Roz watched at first, then gently put her arms around her daughter. Maggie laid her head on her mother's shoulder. Roz rocked slowly side to side.

"I got you, honey."

While Roz tended to her daughter, Laney called the clinic and spoke to a nurse. After Laney described Maggie's bleeding, there was a long silence on the other end of the line.

"Are you there?"

"Thinking," said the nurse.

"Thinking what?"

"Lemme put you on hold."

"But..." She stopped as raspy music blared in her ear.

Roz helped Maggie back into the bathroom.

"C'mon, c'mon," said Laney to no one.

When the music stopped, there was a new voice on the line. She asked Laney how she could help. Laney told her story again. There was another long silence.

"Tell you what," said the voice. "You know the hospital over in Guymon?"

"Maybe."

"Well, I think your daughter..."

"Granddaughter."

"Okay. I think she needs an ultrasound to see what's going on with the pregnancy. We don't have one, but Guymon does."

Laney's whole body went on alert. "Do you think, I mean, is this necessary? I mean, I don't want to scare her. It's her first—"

"Yes, it's necessary."

The voice said she would call the emergency room in Guymon to alert them.

"Is your granddaughter able to come to the phone?"

"I'm afraid not. She's in the bathroom."

"Well then, as soon as she can, get her into a car and go. You'll get her there long before I can get an ambulance to you."

Laney went to the bathroom, tapped twice, and opened the door. Roz sat on the floor, Maggie curled in her lap. Laney used her best matter-of-fact voice to say she'd spoken with the clinic, and they thought it would be a good idea to get an ultrasound, just to confirm that everything was okay, but they'd have to go to Guymon. Roz and Laney's eyes met.

"Okay, okay, that makes sense. Just to ease our minds, okay," said Roz.

Maggie didn't say a word but started to get up. Laney took her by the arms. Maggie gestured that she didn't need help. She went to the sink, doused her face with cold water again, then leaned over to drink from the faucet.

Roz grabbed a banana, some saltines, and three bottles of water. In a matter of minutes, they were on the road.

•   •   •

Guymon was an hour drive through oil fields and pig farms. The hospital was the hub of the panhandle's sorely strained wheel of healthcare. There was a half-dozen in the emergency waiting room, lively conversations in Spanish filling the air. Roz and Maggie waited in the women's rest room, while Laney, mask tight on her face ("Saving Lives, One Breath at a Time"), checked and rechecked the wait list at the nurses' station. Mostly farm injuries that day, broken bones, lacerations. Patients came, they went, more arrived.

Soon they were escorted behind the curtain where Maggie fell asleep on a gurney. Roz and Laney sat in silence, gathering their thoughts and worries. Maggie's crisis brought all the old battles between them into stark focus. If they could go back, what would they have done differently? How would they have salvaged their relationship?

Roz thought her teeth-grinding battle with her parents over their unwillingness to let her become a teen bride had been foolish, selfish, immature, all the words you can apply to such adolescent hubris. But for a long time, it all seemed simple. If you had given me permission to marry Jackson, he would be alive now, and we would have lived happily ever after. But Jackson, sweet as he was, would never have kept any vow, he was so committed to his burgeoning drug habit.

She knew this even as she stood in numb silence over his casket. But what do you do when your future not only falls apart but is revealed for the empty fairy tale it was from the beginning? Blaming herself was too much to bear, but blaming her parents seemed justified. Blaming her parents had given her the adrenaline she needed to go it alone for all these years.

Roz looked at her mother sitting on the other side of the gurney. Her mask under her chin, her face sagging, age lines from her inner cheek to the corners of her mouth. Her mother's skin had always been smooth as linoleum, not a crease, not a fold, not a hint of life's battering ram.

And yet, looking at her now, she seemed more beautiful than she had in Roz's memory.

Laney's left leg felt numb. She rolled her ankle and then crossed her legs. Her eyes were glued to Maggie, who slept on her side, mouth open, drooling like a baby. She reached out with a tissue and dabbed the tiny pool that was gathering on the gurney.

She smiled at Maggie, her granddaughter... their granddaughter. She hadn't let herself think about Franklin. She'd blocked his phone so she could have the distance she needed. But she wished she could share this grandparent time with him. He would love Maggie, she was sure of it. There was something about her willfulness that he would appreciate. Maggie would make him smile, maybe even make him listen, something he had seldom done with her.

Two hours later, a tech took Maggie for her ultrasound. When Roz and Laney asked if they could go with her, the tech paused, then said, "I don't know. I don't think so." She helped Maggie into a wheelchair and drove her away. Roz and Laney leaned back in their chairs and stared at the walls.

"You know," said Laney, "I'd like to tell your father what's going on?"

"Why?" Roz's upper body twisted in her chair.

Laney thought for a minute. "I'm not sure. It just seems like he should know. I mean a grandparent should know if their grandchild, you know, if something's going on." She pulled her mouth up to one side. "Right?"

Roz hadn't thought about her father much in years, let alone contacted him. He was always so busy when she was growing up, that they seldom spent time together, unless it was on vacation or a holiday. Even then he'd seem preoccupied with work, sometimes even taking a few hours on Christmas Day to "go in" as he called it.

She had admired him, but couldn't remember if she loved him. She assumed he loved her. He had told her more than once that he did, sometimes calling "I love you" over his shoulder as he went out the door.

"I don't know."

"Okay, well, think about it."

"Yeah."

When Maggie returned, she was accompanied by the tech and a doctor with braids and yellow crocs. Maggie got out of the wheelchair and sat on the gurney, her eyes cast down. The doctor introduced herself, then leaned against the wall, crossed her legs at the ankle, and puckered her lips tight, thinking.

"I read the results of the ultrasound. And this is the story. Maggie is pregnant, but not really."

CHAPTER 30

At first, Gretchen had refused his offer. But he was insistent so she relented. Franklin hadn't driven a car on the interstate in months. When the first semi passed him, he almost hit the brakes, it frightened him so. But after an hour of attentive driving, he felt more focused than he had in a long while. Even Gretchen noticed. She felt comfortable enough to crawl over the front seat and fall asleep in the back.

Behind the wheel, Franklin felt exhilarated, like he was his own pilot and navigator, captain of the road. He remembered feeling the same way when he'd passed his driver's test at sixteen and had taken the car out by himself for the first time. He drove around town, through every neighborhood, and even on some country roads, ones he'd never driven before. There were no cell phones in those days, no way to check on someone once they were behind the wheel. When it dawned on him that nobody knew where he was, he understood for the first time what it meant to be free.

He drove down Breakneck Rd., aptly named for its snake-like curves and steep embankments. He pulled to the side of the road, got out, and stood on the precipice looking down at a crooked creek he'd never noticed before. He sat on the berm and listened to the faint babble far below. He lay back, closed his eyes, and imagined soaring with the crows that were cawing high above him.

Had he ever felt like that since?

Time just goes, he thought. It goes and there's no accounting for it. All that's left is what you can store in the file cabinet between your ears. Age and Covid made it hard to access those files, to leaf through them, hoping whatever you were looking for would still be there. So much was lost, lost forever, while other things stayed no matter how much you hoped they would disappear. His father, for one.

It had been forty years since his father's death. Franklin was old enough today to be his father's father. At the end, his father was so feeble that Franklin could have thrown him across the room, if he'd wanted to. How he wished he could have done just that when he was too small, too young, to protect himself. He is dead, thought Franklin, and I have to make sure he stays dead.

Franklin put on the turn signal, hit the gas, and passed his first semi. He felt power in his foot. His back sunk into the seat as he pressed the gas pedal ever closer to the floor. He opened the window and thrust his arm into the wind. He looked in the rear-view mirror. The semi was far behind him, and there was nothing in front of him. He straddled the center lane, the white stripes whipping by.

"Franklin, really?" called Gretchen. "Can you close the window? I'm freezing."

Without a word, Franklin pulled in his arm, closed the window, turned on his signal, and slipped back into the other lane. But he'd felt the speed, the power.

Gretchen rolled onto her back and thought of Griswald. She thought of Edge and Edith. She thought of the home she'd left behind. So many leave-takings. She thought of her mother and father. She thought of Franklin. Her big Brother, seeming so small. She thought of Laney and Roz and the granddaughter Franklin and she hadn't met.

When I'm gone, that will be the end of the line, she thought. That branch of the family tree will be no more. She'd tried for years to adjust to childlessness, but the regret was in the marrow of her bones. To be a mother, she thought. When it was clear she would never conceive, she clung to the hope that she and Griswald would become "old coots" together, sitting side by side on the sofa forever, like one might see in a Norman Rockwell painting. She felt foolish.

Franklin had a wife who'd left him, a daughter who'd left him, and a granddaughter he'd never met. How ridiculous. What Gretchen wouldn't give to face that dilemma, knowing she had the energy, the drive, the desperation to change it, to make it right. It didn't matter what she thought of Laney. It mattered that things had come apart, molecule by molecule, and that nothing was being done about it. Maybe Franklin's clutching hope that Laney would return wasn't so stupid. Maybe acts of apparent stupidity were called for.

She sat up again. "You still wondering where she's at?"

"Laney?"

"Yeah."

"Wondering, yeah, but beyond that, I don't know."

"Never liked her."

"I am so shocked."

She watched and gulped as Franklin pulled into the passing lane again and took the measure of six cars. Back safely in the right lane, she took a breath.

"How'd I do?"

"Good. You did good."

"I pulled back over because I could see a twitch developing in your left eye."

They both laughed.

"Still trying to figure out where her car is?"

Franklin shook his head and shifted his weight to his right hip.

"Why are you bringing this up?"

"It feels like things are too scattered, too fragmented."

He glanced at his sister through the rear-view mirror.

"Is something wrong?"

She shrugged.

"Nothing's wrong, I just wish things hadn't fallen apart."

"Sometimes things fall apart, Sister. You know that better than anyone."

"Doesn't keep me from wishing it wasn't so."

He turned and looked over his shoulder at her.

"Something's bugging you, isn't there?"

"My husband was murdered. Knowing I would face his murderer one day, so I could shake my fist and give him hell, that's what's kept me going these last few years. Made it possible to get up and face another day. *My* day in court, you know what I mean. And I finally got the chance and what did I do? I forgave the fucker. And now it's over. And I've got nothing."

"What do you mean, you got nothing? You've got me and you always will."

"Take no offence, Brother, but you're not exactly a winning lottery ticket. I love you, don't get me wrong. But I'm talking about something different. I feel like I'm finishing my lap of this race and there's no one to give my baton to."

"Baton? What baton?"

"When I die, that's it. There's no one to keep the line going. When you die, you've got a daughter and after that, a granddaughter to carry on. When all is said and done, that's it. That is the *it* we live for."

Franklin hit the rumble strips on the berm of the highway and the car shook like the devil. He veered back onto the road, a big ass SUV's horn screaming at him. It took a mile or two for them to settle down.

"That's not true. Lots of people don't have kids or grandkids. That's a fact. And it's not the end of the world."

Gretchen wasn't having it. "Look, you've got family. You have to make things right."

Franklin got huffy. Laney had left him after all. And for no good reason. He'd tried to reach her, but she'd made herself unreachable. He'd done what he could do. As for Roz, the walls were now too high to climb over, break through, or go around. And if he couldn't reach her, there was no way he could reach Maggie. Both his palms went up in the air.

"I can't do anything about this."

"I'm calling bullshit."

"What?"

"That's bullshit. If you wanted to, if your life depended on it, you could, I mean, you *would*. Plain and simple."

"Jesus God, nothing you're saying makes sense."

Franklin turned on the radio and cranked up Sixties Forever as loud as he could. Gretchen, her arms folded tight across her chest, her chin jutting, unwrapped her arms, leaned over the seat, and turned off the radio.

"What I'm saying makes all kinds of sense. And you know it."

It was dark on the final stretch from Buffalo to Rochester. Franklin tilted his rear-view mirror and peeked at Gretchen. Thankfully, she had fallen back to sleep.

At night, the semis owned the thruway. He settled into the slow lane and opened the window a few inches. His hands resting in his lap, he steered with his fingers.

Gretchen's rant was on his mind. It had been Laney and him for so long that he didn't think about family. He could barely remember what his daughter looked like. As for his granddaughter, he hadn't a clue.

He waded through the pool of molasses that had become his memory trying to conjure up Roz and the conflict that led her to flee. There had been a boyfriend. Something terrible happened to him. Roz blamed them. Then she left. Sometime after that, she had a daughter.

Franklin looked out the side window at the muck land near Batavia, a frown on his face. Could this be all he remembered about his daughter? There had to be more, but, for him, trying hard to remember was like trying hard to walk on water.

His eyes welled. With every lost memory, he lost part of himself. Fingers, toes, limbs of his life. His head throbbed.

He pulled into a rest stop, tilted his seat back and closed his eyes for several minutes. Unable to sleep, he went into the plaza to use the bathroom. He returned with two cups of Starbuck's coffee and two cinnamon raisin bagels. Gretchen was outside, leaning against the car.

"What's the deal?"

"Needed a break."

"You could have woken me up."

"So you could walk me to the potty?"

He handed her a cup of coffee, and raised the paper bag. "Bagel, too."

"Cream cheese?"

"Nothing but the best for you, Sister."

Gretchen grabbed the bag and took a peek.

"G'boy."

A crescent moon skittered between two angry clouds. Gretchen yawned and stretched. They got back into the car, got out the plastic knives, added cream cheese to the bagels, and drank their coffee.

"Okay, so where are we?"

"Close to home. About a half hour."

"And you had to stop?"

"Yes, I forgot my catheter."

"Jesus." She sniffed the coffee, then took a sip. Her brother's face and eyes were puffy. "Sure you're okay? You look like shit."

"No, I'm not okay. Did you mean everything you said back there?"

Gretchen chomped her bagel.

"You mean about family?"

"Yeah."

"Yes, I did. I meant it all. You know I loved Mom and I hated Dad and there was all this, well, this stuff going on and, in the end, I never felt like we were a family. I had you and you had me, but that didn't make a family. Gris came along and filled my world, and then he was gone and..." She shrugged and raised her eyebrows. "I don't think it has to go that way for you."

"You always hated Dad?"

"Most always, yeah."

"But he treated you like a queen. You were everything to him. He played with you, praised you, told you how proud he was of you. You, you, you. I don't think he even liked Mom as much as he liked you."

"And that was great. Until I was about seven. Then I started getting suspicious. Things didn't feel right. All the stuff he did to you, I started to get the drift. The bastard. And he used me to abuse Mom."

"Whadaya mean?"

"He used me to make her feel like nothing. It was all about hurting Mom. He gave me everything he should have given her. The attention, the affection, the love. Or what he pretended was love. He wiped her nose in it. And I, well, I was oblivious. I can't believe she didn't hate me. In the end, I didn't mean a thing to him." Gretchen's face was red.

"I don't think that's the whole thing. I mean, I think he loved you, I do. Maybe only you, who knows."

"I remember when Mom got the call. She could hardly make sense of what he was saying. He was gasping and coughing. All she knew was it was bad. She called me and, at first, I thought, 'Yeah, this is the same old Dad thing,' you know, trying to get attention. But Mom's speech was so slow, so tentative, like it got when you knew something was up. So, I met her outside his apartment. She didn't want to go in alone. Remember, I called you? You didn't pick up, so I left you a message?"

"Uh-huh."

"Well before you got there, he was a total mess, but he was alive. He was lying in his bed, covers all disheveled, pillows thrown across the floor. It smelled something awful. Pee and sweat and filthy clothes piled everywhere. There were flies all over the place. He hadn't shaved in God knows how long. His hair was stringy, greasy. He was paper thin. And there were empty bottles everywhere."

Gretchen put her bagel back in the bag and her cup in the holder.

"And he was scared as shit. I mean, he cried and begged us to stay with him, and folded his hands as if he were praying. They shook like leaves in a wind storm. And he kept saying 'I'm sorry, I'm sorry, I'm sorry' in this squeaky little voice, and he'd reach out to Mom, and when she wouldn't go near him, he'd reach out to me and, I didn't know what to do, he was so pathetic, so I went toward him, but Mom stuck her arm out blocking me. And she was like 'Don't.' I could almost feel a burst of cold, like when you open the freezer, but it was coming from her."

"That doesn't sound like her."

"I know. It was like, 'Is this Mom?' But it was."

"So, how long before he died?"

"I never saw Dad desperate before. I never saw him afraid, or anxious, none of that. But there it was all over his face like a bad rash. I mean, I started crying, it was so frightening to see him like that. But, Mom, she didn't flinch. He cried out, 'Please, you gotta forgive me, I'm so sorry, forgive me, please!'"

Franklin's mouth went dry. "What did she say?"

"I couldn't believe it, but she looked at him all calm like and said, 'No,' just like that— 'No'."

"She said, no?"

"Yeah."

"I'll bet he wanted to kill her."

"I don't know about that. He stopped crying, his face was aghast. He opened his mouth to say something and she said, 'Don't.' But he kept going. 'Please,' he said again. 'Please forgive me. I don't want to die like this'."

"And what did she say?"

"She said, 'I'm sure you don't. No one does. But you'll have to.'"

"My God."

"Yeah."

"She was right, though, but Jesus..."

"Yeah."

It was quiet in the car. Thruway traffic sped by. Cars parked and left. They sat.

"So...did he just...die, I mean, did he have a heart attack or something? I never knew."

"He kept crying until nothing came out of his eyes. He fell back in the bed, breathing hard, just exhausted. He didn't have anything left. Mom asked me to leave the room so she could have time alone with him. So that's what I did. I was out there for what felt like forever. I leaned my ear against the door, but I couldn't hear a thing. So, I knocked and called for Mom. She came to the door and let me in without a word. And I looked at him. His arms were spread out like wings and his eyes and mouth were still open."

"Yeah, I remember now."

"But did you notice?"

"Notice what?"

"The pillow. There was a pillow lying at the top of the bed, right beside him."

"Don't remember. So?"

"There weren't any pillows on the bed before I left the room. In fact, they weren't even near the bed."

"So...what are you saying?"

Gretchen met his eyes and held the look.

"Are you saying that Mom...?"

"Yeah, pretty sure."

Franklin laid his head on the steering wheel.

"Did she ever tell you?"

"She never talked to me about Dad again. You?"

"I don't remember."

"I wish I'd been there when Mom died. She shouldn't have been alone. No one should be alone, you know."

"Yeah."

"She just slipped away."

Franklin sat up and turned in his seat.

"Why didn't you ever tell me about this?"

"Well, for a long time, I didn't believe that two plus two actually equaled four, that she'd actually done it, and when I finally believed it, well, we were living our lives, you know. And, I guess, I didn't want your last thoughts of Dad to make you feel sympathetic."

Franklin winced, a quizzical look on his face.

"He'd hurt you too much, Brother."

Emotional exhaustion won the day. They both fell asleep in the front seat of the car. It was morning when Franklin's phone woke them up.

CHAPTER 31

If you watched closely, it looked like plumes of smoke were gushing from Roz's ears. She had dispensed with the first doctor and was working on the second.

"How can my daughter be pregnant and not pregnant at the same time. I am sick and tired of this medical bullshit. Just tell us what's going on. Please!"

The young doctor ("What grade are you in, anyway?" said Roz.), sat on her rollie stool, legs crossed. She pushed her glasses back up her nose, looked at her feet, and sighed.

Laney, herself flushed, watched Maggie, who was pale as a sheet hanging in the midday sun.

"You okay?"

Maggie looked at her grandmother, smiled, and shook her head. In which direction was hard to tell. She felt like she was walking through someone else's nightmare, making a guest appearance without understanding her role, or what the outcome might be. Once the test results came back, she had little to say.

"What do you mean the ultrasound didn't show a baby? Where did it go?" Listening to Roz, one might have thought there had been a kidnapping, that the baby had been snatched from Maggie's womb when no one was looking. If she bellowed loud enough, maybe they'd bring the baby back.

Maggie, in shock, listened to bits and pieces of the conversation. No placenta...several bags full of fluid in her uterus...like a collection of tiny water balloons...but no fetus.

She looked at her grandmother who was blowing air in such rapid spurts that, for an instant, Maggie thought she had gotten everything wrong, not only had she never been pregnant, but it was her grandmother who was going into labor.

In the meantime, Roz pounded away on the doctor.

"You've gotta be kidding me! A molar! What do you mean, her molar?"

"No, not a molar, like a tooth, a molar pregnancy."

Roz shook her head and scowled at the doctor.

"Here's what happened. Things didn't go right from the beginning. Usually, the sperm fertilizes the egg and an embryo is formed. The placenta develops to nourish the growing embryo. And so on."

She stopped and looked at each of them, seeing if this was making sense.

"With a molar pregnancy, none of these things happen. Because there is no fertilized egg, the whole natural process stops."

She waited again. Maggie shifted in her chair. Roz and Laney leaned forward. No one spoke.

"This is the hard part. Even though all systems aren't 'go,' the body doesn't give up. The placenta has nothing to nurture, but still creates these, well, like I said, fluid filled cysts, that look like little sacs. This tissue creates the hormone that tells us incorrectly that the woman is pregnant. The body is confused. It is making a wish that isn't going to come true."

Maggie wept. She covered her face and tears trickled between her fingers. Roz slid her chair across the tile floor and pulled her daughter toward her. "Okay," she said. "Okay, now."

The doctor explained that molar pregnancies often resolve on their own. But sometimes they don't. Sometimes, for the sake of the woman, the tissue had to be removed before it spread outside the uterus, causing more problems.

"Jesus Christ," said Roz. Irate when she found out Maggie was pregnant, Roz was irater when she found out there had never been a pregnancy to begin with. She felt a deep sorrow, like a fist in the bottom of her belly. She looked at her daughter, such a child, she thought. Why did she have to go through this?

"So, what needs to happen?" said Laney.

"Surgery. A D&C to remove it."

"Okay, so when can you do that?"

The doctor leaned back in her chair and took off her glasses. She straddled them on her thigh. She swallowed and pursed her lips.

"Here's where it gets...complicated."

"What do you mean?" said Maggie. "Complicated, how?"

"It is still considered a pregnancy and the procedure to remove it is still, technically, an abortion."

"So?"

"Remember, you're in Oklahoma."

"But there's no baby." said Laney.

"And the courts are still deciding what that means exactly."

"What?" Laney tossed up her hands. "You've got to be kidding."

Roz pushed up the sleeves on her sweatshirt. "What you're saying is—there's no baby, right? There's just a bunch of stuff. And the stuff has to come out, right?"

"Right."

"And the only way to do that is surgery."

"Uh-huh."

"And if it doesn't come out or go away or whatever, something bad could happen, is that what you're saying?"

"There is a risk of cancer, yes."

"What?" Maggie was standing now.

"And the court can't decide if this is okay to do?"

The doctor shook her head.

"Wait a minute, wait a minute," said Laney. "In the meantime, since the court hasn't made up its mind, can doctors still—"

"No. No one's doing abortions of any kind in the state. No one wants to lose their license. No one wants to go to jail." She put her glasses on, her face blank. "I'm sorry." She handed them a box of tissue.

Maggie walked away. She stood by the window watching cars come and go in the parking lot.

"Maggie? You okay?" Roz stood behind her, unsure what to do.

Maggie didn't answer. Roz put her arm around her daughter's waist. "Come'ere, let's sit down."

"What am I going to do?" said Maggie.

Roz didn't have an answer. She pulled her daughter closer. "Don't worry, we'll figure it out. You'll see, it'll be okay."

• • •

The three women sat on the porch, Laney bent over her phone scrolling and searching, while Roz held Maggie's limp hand.

A car cruised down the highway and pulled into the driveway. Sandman got out, a sheepish smile on his face. It had been a few weeks since the last time Maggie and Sandman had talked. He'd called her over and over, with no reply. At first, he understood her reticence, but when the days dragged on, he worried that something bad had happened. Nevertheless, he waited, gave her space, and counted the days.

Finally, he went to Save-a-Lot under the guise of needing cleaning supplies for the motel. He wasn't planning on asking Roz about Maggie. He figured he'd be able to read the situation by talking with her about mundane things, how you doing, how about this weather, that sort of thing. Roz was not one to hide her feelings. If she didn't make eye contact or only replied in monosyllables, or got a pinched look on her face, then he'd know something was up.

What he hadn't planned on was Roz not being there. He went back a few times over the next several days, then asked Christy-May, who was behind the counter, where she was. "Don't know. She hasn't been in for, I don't know, a while. Leaves us texts about what we need to do." Christy-May shrugged hard and put a piece of Juicy Fruit in her mouth. "Don't tell anyone, but for sure something's up. I mean, Roz, she's never missed a day of work as far as any of us can remember. Maybe she got sick or run off or something. Maybe that daughter of hers is in some kind of mess." She raised her eyebrows and smiled, impressed with her hypotheses.

In the meantime, he'd hired Juanita to pick up Maggie's slack. He'd posted a "part-time help needed" sign in front of the motel. She showed up within the hour and started work that night. Sandman was ashamed to admit it, but Juanita worked rings around Maggie. She was committed to her job. Maggie wasn't committed to washing floors, cleaning toilets, none of it.

When Juanita came into work on Monday, Sandman told her the job was hers for good if she wanted it.

"Hi," he said, waving half-heartedly. He stood beside his car, waiting for a sign he could join them on the porch. When it didn't come, he took several steps forward and said, "Nice weather, we're having, isn't it?" Roz and Laney nodded.

Maggie stood and pressed a smile onto her face. She went down the porch steps to meet him. Together, they walked back to his car and sat on the back fender.

"Look at that." Sandman pointed across the road at a mule deer doe and her two fawns. The fawns sniffed in their direction. Mother watched, steely-eyed and suspicious. She snorted and the fawns fell in behind her.

Maggie shaded her eyes and caught them as their tails went up and they bounded off.

"Something, huh? See them all the time, but it never gets old. Just a simple thing."

"Yeah," she said. She looked at him, while he watched, wide-eyed, until they disappeared over a fold in the field.

"I always watch until they're gone, you know."

"Why's that?" The only time Maggie had spent with Sandman had been at the motel or the bar. He was different when he wasn't plunging toilets or getting drunk. He seemed younger than her.

"I don't know. It's always been a special thing, seeing the deer; they're so sleek and graceful, and those dark, dark eyes. My old man was the same way. We watched them together when I was a kid. 'Watch 'em, don't kill 'em' he'd say. 'They belong to the wind'."

"They belong to the wind. What does that mean?"

"I never asked. When he said it, though, I always felt I understood. The wind does what the wind does. It's free, you know. A little like you, I think."

Maggie leaned away. "I don't know about that. I don't know that I've ever felt free. I feel more like a deer in the headlights than a deer on the hoof."

They both exhaled a laugh. Sandman looked across the open field again. "Keep looking, you'll find it, I'm sure."

Maggie looked away. Her mother and grandmother had retreated to the kitchen. She could see them through the window, heads bent over her grandmother's phone, mouths moving rapidly.

"Hey, I'm sorry about, you know, not coming back."

"Not a problem."

"Good. I figured you'd find someone."

Sandman picked up a stone, threw it across the road, and watched for the tiny puff of dust when it hit the ground. He picked up another stone and rolled it over and over in his hand.

"How's everything going? I mean, there." He gestured toward her belly. "Looks like things are moving along."

Maggie swatted tears from her cheek, not wanting him to see, not wanting him to comfort her.

"Just not in the right direction."

"What?" He dropped the stone.

"Turns out, it's kind of a fake pregnancy. Things didn't click the right way. There's something in there, but it's not a baby."

"No."

"Yes."

"What—"

"Long story. I don't want to get into it."

"I am so sorry, Maggie, I am. This is just...this is my fault. I should never have...goddammit...goddammit to hell...is there anything..."

"Look, really, this isn't your fault. I was there, remember? I wanted to as much as you did. I guess I didn't think about what could happen. I didn't think I'd get pregnant. I didn't think everything would fall apart, basically. But it did."

He touched her arm softly with the palm of his hand, then quickly pulled it away. They'd had one night, nothing more. They fell into each other's arms, sloppy drunk. He got up the next morning and went to work. She got up and went away. That's all it was, he thought.

"Do you have to...I mean, what's going to happen next? You said, there's still something there. Will it just go away or something?"

"No. I have to have surgery."

"No. No, really?"

"That's what the doctor told us. Not sure when, where, anything."

"Can I help some way?"

"No, really, but thanks. You've...I appreciate you coming. I've stayed away and I shouldn't have and I'm sorry and I wish it hadn't gone this way and, I don't know..." She took him in her arms and held him tight. "You are a good guy. Please know that."

Maggie waved as he drove off, then rushed to the bathroom. She sat on the toilet and vomited into the bathtub. Elbows on her knees, she closed her eyes, not wanting to see what was in the toilet bowl. The clear water quickly turned dirty brown. She wiped, flushed, and leaned against the back of the toilet. Pain gouged her belly again. She bent forward and held her breath until it passed. She breathed slowly for several minutes, then took a water glass from the sink and doused the bathtub clean. She felt captive to a body she no longer knew or understood. It did what it did randomly and without forgiveness.

She ran cold water onto a wash cloth, then pressed it to her face. She refreshed the cloth several times until her skin was cool and tight. She stroked both arms, wrists to shoulders, letting drops of water fall to the floor. Then she pulled up her sweatshirt and laid the cool cloth on her belly trying to sooth what was no longer there.

When she opened the bathroom door, the sound of her mother and grandmother, so often edgy and crackling, rose from the kitchen, harmonious, if pressured. It stopped abruptly as she entered. Their faces seemed frozen, their eyes buggy.

"What?"

CHAPTER 32

"Hello," said Franklin, his cell phone upside down in his hand. The voice on the other end sounded like it was coming from the bottom of a trash barrel. "Hello?" He held onto the steering wheel as he adjusted his seat and turned the phone around. "Who is this?"

Gretchen rolled off her side and sat up. She rubbed her eyes and stretched. She tapped Franklin's shoulder and pointed with her thumb at the rest stop, then left for the bathroom.

"I can't hear you."

He started the car and turned the heat up to the max. The hair on his arms rose to attention.

"Who—" Then he recognized the voice. Even from afar, it sounded like velvet. At first, he was too shocked to listen to her words. He could only feel them. "Laney? Is that you?"

Laney put her thumb over the microphone. "I think I woke him up."

Roz poured Maggie a cup of tea, then topped off Laney's coffee and poured herself another cup. Both women sat with elbows on the table, hands wrapped around their cups.

"Yes, Franklin, it's me."

Franklin's back straightened and a triumphant smile crossed his face.

"Long time."

"Look I've got to talk to you about something."

Here it comes, he thought. He would try to be gracious when she said she wanted to come back. He wouldn't rub her face in how foolish and hurtful their last night together had been, him being humiliated at the restaurant, then being blocked from contacting her, as if he were a stalker. He wouldn't tell her how sick he'd been, how he'd almost lost his mind. He wouldn't tell her that his life had become a shambles.

Laney held the phone away from her ear while Franklin hacked several times, trying to clear his throat.

"I've been pretty sick," he said. Had to start somewhere.

If she hadn't been sure she'd called the right number, she wouldn't have recognized Franklin's voice. Gone, the near baritone, replaced with a whispery alto rasp. He sounded old, old and tired and off-kilter, she thought.

"I'm sorry to hear that. Look, Franklin, I've got to talk to you about something.

"That's what I assumed."

"Can I put you on speaker?"

"Speaker? Are you in the car? Where are you?"

"Oklahoma."

Maggie's stomach pain was getting worse. Goddammit. She went to the bathroom, pressed her hands against her swollen abdomen and sat on the toilet again, and again the water turned sewer brown with tiny sacs. Like the tail end of a tornado, the pain lifted and was gone, wreckage left behind. This time, though, she'd had it. What the hell? Looking at her pallid, ghostly face in the mirror, Maggie felt pissed. She was tired of feeling like a yo-yo dangling on the end of string. This is fucking ridiculous, she thought. She'd hit bottom. And rather than splatting on the concrete, she bounced. Enough, enough, enough. She opened the bathroom door and strode into the kitchen. She took the phone from her grandmother.

"But—" said Laney.

"Is this him? My grandfather?"

"Yes."

She put the cell to her ear.

"Hi, this is Maggie, your granddaughter. I don't know you and you don't know me and this may be too much to ask, but I need help, and I need it fast. They can't help me here, they won't or can't, I don't know. So that's what this call is about. I want you to do whatever you can to get me the help I need, okay? I mean, I'm your granddaughter, right? So, I'm counting on you, okay?"

"Yes, yes, I'll get on it right away," said Franklin, unsure what he was being asked to do.

"Okay, then. Good. Thank you. I have to go. Here's Mom." She handed the phone to Roz, then took it back. "I look forward to meeting you."

"Okay," said Franklin.

With that, Maggie went to her bedroom, closed and locked the door, crawled into her bed, and went to sleep.

Roz held the phone in front of her. Laney gestured for her to say something.

"That was your granddaughter."

Franklin held his breath on the other end. "I'll say."

Roz didn't know what else to say. She gave the phone to her mother and left the room. She pushed the front door open, stepped onto the porch, and began to cry. For years she'd kept a speech fresh in her mind, a speech she would give her father the first time she had the chance. Sometimes, when she was doing laundry, or cleaning the house, or stocking shelves at the store, she'd give that speech. Her father would be plaintive and beseeching in response. She would ignore everything he said, so she could reign her vengeance down upon him with all the self-righteous fury she could muster. He would crumble in pieces to the ground. And she would simply walk away. Sometimes there was a crowd watching that would cheer her as she waved to them triumphantly.

He was the one who slammed the door on her teenage dreams. He was the one who screamed, "Over my dead body!" She was horrified by his—What had she called it? — "stupidness." Who was he to decide if she and Jackson could be together? What was the big deal, anyway? Just sign the goddam paper and let her marry the man she loved!

"Man!" he'd said, "Ha!"

She remembered that after his pronouncement, he went back to his newspaper and sipped a cocktail that her mother had made. She was shocked how easy it was for him. She stood in front of his newspaper-covered-face and pled her case again, and again, as calmly as she could.

Roz then appealed to her mother, hoping to leverage her by showcasing her father's "ridiculous meanness." She knew her mother understood what she meant. She'd seen her mother's face when her father ignored her or crushed her ideas. For a moment, her mother seemed to soften, her eyes coiled at what her husband had said to Roz. But then it was gone and her answer was, "No." The way she said it, her eyebrows raised, her chin out, her head tipped slightly forward, told Roz the game was over. So, she warned her mother: "You'll see."

Then she was stuck.

She went to Jackson, eyes swollen, voice hiccupping, tear stains on her jersey, but he didn't seem to care. He said, "That's too bad," as if she'd told him, "I lost my favorite necklace." Instead of consoling her, instead of being outraged, he showed her a letter from a friend in Brooklyn who said a friend of a friend's cousin might be interested in him auditioning for their band. And then he said, "Can you believe that? I'm gonna be in a freekin' band in, like, Brooklyn, which is pretty much the same as New York, right?"

"You're fucking crazy!"

Jackson laughed. "You're joking, right? I mean, this is everything. You get it, don't you?"

She reminded him he'd been taking guitar lessons for less than a year, and that his instructor had urged him to practice between lessons, but Jackson felt that was an unnecessary burden. He listened, mouth open, eyes half-mast.

Then she reminded him they were planning to get married, as soon as possible. That they were going to the JP to have it done. And that when she asked her parents to sign, they almost lost their minds. And that she was devastated. And he should be, too. "Remember?" she'd said. "That's the real Big Deal, not some fantasy about bands and Brooklyn."

"Of course, I remember, babe," he said. He took a half-smoked joint from his pocket. "You wanna?"

She walked out.

Once home, she realized her dream had been a Disney-sized fantasy, nothing more.

Her parents weren't speaking to her. Her boyfriend was an asshole. And her future was gone.

Over the years, when she thought of her fifteen, almost sixteen, year old self, she tried to be understanding, but every time she reviewed the facts, she shook her head and thought, Just plain stupid.

A week later, when he found out Brooklyn was a no go, he got drunk, took all the pills he could find in his mother's medicine chest and died. No warning. No note. Much as Roz pretended it was all about her, it wasn't. He'd already been seeing someone else on the sly for a few months. She was fourteen.

When she told her parents Jackson was dead, they were shocked and sympathetic. Her mother even cried. But Roz wouldn't have it. She told them it was their fault, that he'd crashed after learning they wouldn't permit her to marry him, and then, in despair, killed himself.

She remembered how quiet the living room became, how powerful she felt, how impotent her parents were. She had regained the advantage like an underdog turning the tide at match point.

Then she walked away, slamming the door to her bedroom.

What next? Study for that biology test? Do her French homework? Go to bed? Get up and go to school like nothing had happened? Impossible. She packed a suitcase and her school duffel bag, then announced she was leaving. Her mother cried again. Her father demanded to know where she was going. Even though she hadn't a clue where she was going, she said, None of your business.

Once she landed in a friend's house, she felt a deep sense of relief. She'd won. *What* she'd won wasn't clear, but *that* she won, was. Soon, though, she found herself in an Afghanistan War-ish dilemma: she couldn't figure out how to leave and go home.

And here she was, mid-thirties, a nineteen-year-old daughter in crisis, and lo and behold, her parents were back. Life is a goddam circle, she thought.

•   •   •

"What's going on?" said Gretchen, once her brother had clicked off the call. "What was that?"

"It was Laney...and Roz...and Maggie. They don't call her Margaret."

"Really? All of them? Wow."

"Yeah."

Franklin explained what was going on in Oklahoma and how it was up to him to find a doctor, because they were coming back to Rochester.

"When?"

"Soon."

"That's good."

"Good?"

"Uh-huh."

"Were you listening when I told you what's going on?"

"Yeah."

"So, what's good about it?"

"Everything."

•   •   •

Laney poured herself another cup of coffee. She leaned against the sink and looked out the window at the clouds, like smoked marshmallows, hanging over the plains. He didn't ask, she thought. She had prepared herself in case Franklin asked if she was coming back to him. She rushed into the story about Maggie, hoping he wouldn't have a chance to pop the question. But he never tried. There were long pauses as she repeatedly explained what was going on. Plenty of opportunities to change the subject, Franklin's forte. But he didn't. Then Maggie burst into the room, snatched the conversation away, and, just like that, it was over.

She'd gotten back on to say goodbye, but he'd already hung up.

She felt guilty she hadn't thought of him for so many weeks. She never considered maybe he hadn't been thinking of her either. Perhaps, after all the years of being the sun around which he'd revolved, she had fallen out of his universe all together. Thinking this made her feel alone. Without realizing it, she'd been tethered to him all this while, even though she'd thought of herself as freely roaming, delightfully unattached.

Franklin stood in the foyer, arms folded, studying the gash in the wall and the broken window beside the front door that for weeks had been covered with a poorly fitting piece of plywood. A battle had been waged there in the recent past, and these were the markers left behind. Franklin imagined a plaque that read: "On their forty-second wedding anniversary, the marriage of Franklin and Laney Stafford came to an abrupt and shocking end, eviscerated by the ravages of time and indifference."

On the phone, Laney was as *Laney* as ever. She was polite, even warmish. Her greeting, sincere; her voice, melodic. If he hadn't known better, it could have been the day after that memorable dinner. Her next sentence could have been, "Just checking in. How's your day going?" And he would have answered with a list of mundanities to which she would have responded, "Great!" His mood would have improved tenfold from hearing her voice. There would have been no hint of something going awry.

Recently, as his Covid fog began to clear, a light had come on, a light that revealed the gaping holes in his understanding of their marriage. Their marriage, from the very beginning, had been built on a fault line invisible to him but crystal clear to Laney. He'd never understood that her periodic leave-takings had not been isolated episodes, easily explained away, but they'd been linked tremors warning of the inevitable earthquake that would change the landscape of their lives forever.

He saw that she'd always wanted to love him, and the security and safety he could provide. And to get it she'd closed her eyes and taken a leap. But instead of landing safe and sound, she'd fallen and fallen and fallen ever since.

He ached thinking of this.

Franklin measured the broken window and ordered a new pane. He then rummaged around the basement for a bucket of plaster mix so he could fix what he could fix.

CHAPTER 33

Sandman woke with a start. His head thumped and his stomach gurgled and his eyes refused to open. From behind his lids, he could tell it was daylight. He sat up, rubbed his eyes, and tried to find a reason to get out of bed. He looked at the clock on the bedside table. It was 1:00pm. Early for him. Usually, he stayed in his room until evening and only left long enough to check the number of cars in the lot. Juanita took care of the rest. Before the stores closed for the night, he would drive to Earl's Liquor, buy a case of Prairie Bomb!, and hurry back to his room. He'd lie back in his unmade bed, swat the flies, and drink.

Juanita left tacos and burritos, rice and beans, sometimes mole, at his door, whatever she had left over from home. She'd tap lightly, then walk away. When she found the food untouched, she would cup her hands against the door and yell, "Eat!"

Today a sheet of paper, folded awkwardly, had been slipped under the door. When he got up at 2:00pm, he unfolded the paper and found a crayon drawing of a little girl with big dark eyes, braided hair, and a half-moon smile on her face. She was standing on top of a rainbow. The bubble over her head said, "Happy Day!"

Sandman pulled back the curtain a few inches and took a peek. Juanita Ortega was leaning on a mop watching her six-year-old daughter, Sofia, dig in the dirt with a plastic shovel. Sofia's dark eyes flitted as she talked to Baby, her stuffed kitten. She pulled up her flowered jeans and tossed her hair back over one shoulder, then knelt again and kept digging.

"What are you doing?" her mother called.

Without stopping, Sofia looked over her shoulder. "Digging, Mama."

"I can see that. What are you digging for?"

This time, Sofia stood, dropped her shovel, and raised her hands over her head. "Gold!" She said this as if anyone with a brain would have known.

"That is very good. We could use some gold."

Sofia smiled, pleased that her mother understood.

"What will you do with this gold when you find it?"

The little girl cuddled Baby to her chest. "I will weave it into a necklace for Baby."

"Oh my," her mother said. "Could you weave one for me, too?"

Sofia put one finger in her mouth and closed one eye. "We'll have to see if there is any left."

Juanita laughed and flicked her wrist at her daughter, as if to say, then get back to work.

When she turned, she glimpsed the curtain moving in 24. She dropped her mop, marched to the door, and knocked. Sandman stood in the middle of his room.

"I know you're in there, Mr. Sandman."

He'd told her there was no need to use mister, but she insisted it was a show of "respect."

She knocked again.

"What is it, Juanita?"

No answer. Sandman went to the door, put his hand on the knob, but hesitated to open it.

"Juanita?" When she didn't answer, he knew she was trying to force him out of his "cave," as she called it.

When he opened the door, Juanita's fists were on her hips and her left foot was tapping.

Sandman's mustache curled into his mouth and his hair stood on end. His breath smelled sour and his body smelled worse. His eyes were puffy slits and his belly filled his nightshirt. He took a deep breath. "I'm sorry...What do you need Juanita?"

"I have to tell you something, mister."

"What's that?"

Sofia waved wildly. Sandman smiled and waved back. "Thank you for the picture! She is quite the artist."

"Yes, she is, but that is not why I knocked on your door."

"Okay, so—"

"This is my last day."

"What?"

"This is my last day."

"Why?"

She looked him up and down. "I like you, Mr. Sandman, but I cannot come here anymore. This is your place, and you can live however you want, drink as often as you want, get up whenever you want, do whatever you want, whatever you want, whatever you want, whatever you want! But I cannot have my daughter see this. I cannot have her watch a grown man give up on his life just because he cannot have some woman, I mean girl, who is too young for him, anyway. It is not how I want her to grow up, to witness this waste." With that, Juanita turned and walked away.

"Wait a minute, wait a minute..."

She stopped, her back to him.

"Look...you are...You are the best worker...I mean, you look after things that don't even cross my mind...I could never find—"

"That is right, you could never find someone like me again. I am the best. And I deserve a boss that is the best, too."

He could tell by the angle of her head that her chin was up. He imagined that her narrow-set eyes were steeled.

"Look—"

"Please don't 'look' me, Mr. Sandman."

"I don't want you to leave."

Juanita turned around. "Then things must change, mister. I've seen this before. I've left this before. My daughter can't be around this. Neither can I." She cocked her head to one side for emphasis.

"Okay. Yeah, okay, I get it." He shook his head like a bobblehead doll. "Will you stay?"

"One more thing."

"What's that?"

"Two dollars more an hour."

Juanita grabbed her mop and headed down the walkway.

Long ago, when his father had died and he'd left college to run the business, he'd convinced himself that it was a worthwhile challenge, not what he'd wanted to do, but it would be okay. He'd learn how to run a business, maybe expand, or even buy other properties. Become a member of the Righteous Chamber of Commerce. No, it wasn't photography, but he could still shoot in his spare time, maybe sell some photos, maybe do weddings, anything was possible.

By year's end, he was spending his days alone, feet on his office desk, eating Doritos and trying to stay awake. By evening he'd be so stir crazy he'd turn off the vacant sign, lock the office, then go to Cooney's to drink and play darts. On the way back from the bar, he'd put a box outside the office so customers could drop their keys off in the morning, and he wouldn't have to deal with them.

Somehow the Sunrise crept along, like a wounded animal, bringing in enough money for Sandman to eke out a living, even hire occasional help. His dreams, though, disappeared, like marbles falling off a table top.

Then Maggie happened into his life, someone as lost as him. His spirits soared and then returned to earth when she made it clear she wasn't interested. But as long as she was there, he had a pleasing view of what could be, which, no matter how false, was better than nothing.

Then the *Big It* happened. She was at loose ends when she came into the bar that night. And with a few beers' worth of encouragement, she let her defenses down, her mood brightened, her sense of humor emerged, and her face, often grim, was light, playful, mischievous. She pressed herself against him and kissed his cheeks. He was a drink or two ahead of her and feeling carefree, even reckless. In this haze of inebriation, everything seemed to be in play.

And it was.

When he got into bed beside her, she was in tears. She cuddled against him and said, "Hold me, please." He pulled her in close and told her not to worry. Then he kissed her, and she kissed him back. He remembered little after that.

In the morning, life fell back into its normal orbit and Maggie, embarrassed, moved so far away from him it was as if they'd never met.

When they finally talked about the pregnancy, it felt like they were talking about two other people, like he'd never been a part of it. And never would be. That's how she wanted it, and he didn't fight her. He was sad, and relieved, and disappointed in himself.

Sandman stood in the shower for a half hour, hoping he'd come out clean, renewed. He took a shirt off the floor and jeans from the corner and ironed them.

When he left his room, the sun smacked him in the face and the dust from a car careening into the parking lot filled his lungs. When the dust cleared, there was a lavender Mercedes sitting in front of him.

"Who is that?" said Juanita, holding Sofia in her arms.

Sandman didn't answer.

Laney got out of the car.

"What do you think you are doing, missus whoever you are? You could have killed someone driving like that."

By then, Sofia was running her hand along the side of the car, saying repeatedly, "Purple is my favorite color."

"Hello," said Sandman.

"You must be the grandmother. I have heard of you and your fancy car." Juanita's back became ramrod straight. "And your granddaughter."

Laney looked at Juanita, a spare smile on her face.

"I'm sorry to—"

"What is it?" said Sandman.

"We need your help."

Juanita bit her bottom lip.

CHAPTER 34

Sandman had packed the Mercedes the night before. Laney was standing in the Sunrise parking lot at 4:30am. It was cold and the air was dead still. The horizon was yellow and pencil point thin. Sandman came out of the office with Styrofoam cups of coffee, and a Ziploc baggie full of Sweet 'n Low and creamer. Neither spoke on the short drive to Roz's. They waited for fifteen minutes, then Laney went in the house.

Ten minutes later, all three women returned, pulling suitcases, and carrying backpacks.

Sandman got out of the car. "Good morning," he said to mumbled replies. He put everything in the trunk while they arranged themselves, Laney in the front, Roz and Maggie in the back, Maggie with a pillow and blanket. Coffee was dispersed.

Back in the driver's seat, Sandman tried again, this time using his best 'welcome to the Sunrise Motel' voice. "Good morning!" Startled by his buoyant tone, they looked at him, blank-eyed.

"Let's get going," said Roz.

As he pulled onto the highway, Maggie leaned forward and placed a hand on his shoulder. "I really appreciate this, Sandman. I mean, really."

It was eighty miles from Righteous to the regional airport in Liberal, Kansas. It boasted direct service to Denver and beyond. The first leg of their flight east was scheduled to leave at 7:00am.

It was 6:00am in Rochester, NY. Franklin lay on his back, covers up to his chin, eyes wide open since 3:00am which was also when he went to bed. He could hear Gretchen tiptoeing down the hall to the bathroom.

He felt tingling in both legs, and his wrists and elbows ached. He rubbed a strained muscle on his leg. He shut his eyes and massaged his lids, hoping to relieve his headache. He had the distinct impression of sinking slowly through the mattress, his body felt so leaden. The doctor said these were the last vestiges of Covid, the final tug and pull that his body would have to endure before emerging, like a chick from an egg, into a "relatively normal life." He had emphasized relatively.

Franklin counted backwards from one hundred and said the alphabet in reverse as well. His phone on the table beside him, he would tackle Wordle as soon as he felt able.

He pulled his knees up to his chest and stretched his arms out to the side. He grabbed his knees and pulled them to his chin, forming a seventy-year-old fetus. He extended his legs and let them rest on the mattress, his arms outstretched again. He did this five times. He massaged the sore muscle in his leg briefly, then rolled on his side and sat up, his feet dangling to the cold, oak floor.

The day was coming into focus. He reached for his phone to check the time. No need to hurry. He reviewed the weather in Denver, Chicago, and Rochester. Clear sailing, although O'Hare was always a wild card. A gusty day could ruin everyone's hope of reaching their far-flung destinations. He filled his lungs with air and then let it out by inches. He did this five times as well.

He massaged his thighs again, then his calves, reducing the tingling from a buzz to a hum. "Do this a few times every day, it helps with circulation. Circulation is your friend." His doctor said things like this— "Circulation is your friend." "Sloth is your enemy." "Healthy living is simple—everything in moderation."

Franklin was trying hard to, in effect, turn his life into a "bowl of Wheaties, the breakfast of champions." His doctor smiled at this.

Gretchen would shake her head. "What's up with this guy? Nothing is that simple. Nothing. Don't kid yourself, life is oatmeal."

Franklin rubbed his hands together, warming them, then took five more deep breaths. He was sure that breathing was his friend, too. So was showering, the water coursing down his back, his legs, the steam heat making his body supple again. He felt almost new. It had been weeks since he'd seen Laney, years since he'd seen Roz, and never since he'd seen Maggie. He had to make the most of this day.

Gretchen, still in her fuzzy pink slippers and black terry cloth robe, stared at the coffee maker, as it gagged and coughed to life. Sweat formed on the pot, and dark brown droplets began to fill the bottom. She took a deep breath, the smell so thick she could taste it. Gris used to say, "Want me to get the IV?" "Hook me up!" she'd reply.

She filled her mug, took several sips before it cooled, then filled it again. She poured the rest in a carafe and closed it tight. She took another sip, then warmed it again, this time in the microwave, before going out front to fetch the morning paper.

The maple tree in the front yard, its leaves gold with red tips, glistened in the morning sun. It had rained during the night, and everything smelled like potting soil. The sky was painted with gray, and pink, and purple brush strokes. She picked up the soggy plastic bag, shook off the water, and removed the newspaper. She opened it to the national weather and checked Denver and Chicago. She tucked the paper under her arm and went back to the kitchen.

"Good morning," said Franklin. He poured his coffee and then added three packets of Splenda and what seemed like a half cup of cream. Gretchen shook her head at this peach colored, lukewarm concoction masquerading as coffee.

Franklin was fully dressed and ready to go. He wore black jeans, his New Balance sneaks, and a pale-yellow collared pullover. His bomber jacket was draped over a kitchen chair.

"We don't have to be there until this afternoon."

She worried that Franklin's expectations for this reunion might be overblown, overwrought, over-the-top…any or all of these. She thought he'd made peace with Laney being gone, never to return. But since the phone call, framed photos of Laney had emerged from drawers about the house and reappeared on table tops and mantles. She didn't want him to get hurt again, so she gently reminded him not to be "stupid about the whole thing."

"Your granddaughter is sick, very sick. We're here to help her. That's the focus. Not Laney. Remember that, okay?"

"I know that. I just wanted the place to look homey."

He had spent two days calling OB/GYNs, finally finding one that was taking new patients. The soonest appointment he could schedule was a telemed visit in two days. It would have to do.

•　•　•

Maggie studied the checkerboard world thirty-five-thousand feet below. Everything in tiny gold, yellow and tan blocks, perfectly symmetrical. Glassy ponds and lakes. Winding rivers with occasional bulges like a python's belly after a meal. Or a pregnant woman.

Even her X-large American Eagle sweatshirt and baggie pants couldn't keep the suspicious from looking and wondering. And asking.

"Excuse me." She took off her sunglasses and looked around, as if she were going to share a secret. She was one of seven people waiting at the Glenn Martin Air Terminal in Liberal when they arrived that morning.

Maggie pretended not to hear her.

"I don't mean to bother you." Maggie smiled but didn't speak. "Oh darn, just let me come over and sit beside you." Maggie looked over her shoulder, hoping her mother and grandmother were returning from the ladies' room. "My God, you are so skinny. I bet you can wear any old thing you want. Zero, right?"

"What?"

"Zero, size zero. You are, aren't you? I can tell these things because I used to be a zero back in the day. Like before three kids popped out of my v'jayjay." She liked this so much she burst into laughter, then tried to rein it in, so no one would look. "Anyway, you are gorgeous and your body is perfect, but I can tell something's going on there." She pointed at Maggie's abdomen.

"Well, not really."

The woman zipped her lips with two fingers and pretended to throw away the key, then whispered, "I get it, still too early to blab about it." Then she quickly patted Maggie's stomach and said, "You'll be a great you-know-what." She grabbed her carry-on and her lunch bag and headed to her gate.

It happened again in Denver, but before Maggie could speak, her mother stepped in gracefully: "Why don't you mind your own fucking business?"

Maggie watched two small towns drift into view, several miles apart, both hugging the same river. They looked perfect, like intricate jigsaw puzzles, every piece in place. Maggie imagined they were buzzing with life, abundant with opportunities, teeming with people, most of whom were happy. Most of whom knew what they were doing.

But on the ground, it wasn't like that. It was hard. It was jumbled. The pieces didn't fit together exactly, and it was even cloudier than being in a plane at thirty-five thousand feet. Difficult as this realization was for Maggie, there was consolation: Everyone's life was like this. Not just hers. Life was a grinding proposition and sharing it with fellow travelers was the chief reward. If there was any *happy* in life, that's where it came from. If you thought the struggle had to stop before you could be happy, you'd be unhappy all the time.

She glanced at her mother, arms crossed, head back, mouth wide open as she snored, and her grandmother, elbow on the armrest, head on her hand, eyes open, mask on. She thought of her grandfather, someone she'd never met, someone who had always been a shadow figure, not a person at all. And her aunt. What was her name again?

Shattered marriage, bitter conflict, malignant estrangement, catastrophic loss. If you asked for volunteers to go on a life and death mission, were these the people you'd want to raise their hands? Probably not. And yet, they had. Despite their personal muck, they found their footing, stood up, hands high, and said, "Yes!"

Was it perfect? Not at all. Was it good enough? Yes. Was 'good enough' good enough? Had to be, that's all there was.

Maggie pressed her palms into her belly to keep the pain at bay. She looked out her window again, then closed her eyes and fell asleep.

Laney stood in the aisle, stretched her arms, and did ten squats. She looked all around before lowering her mask below her nose and doing ten more. A quick count showed that almost everyone was masked. Except her traveling companions.

Since she was a child, Roz had always slept with her mouth wide open, her jaw drawn to the left. Maggie's neck was twisted awkwardly, and her cheek was pressed against the window. Her hands lay limp in her lap, her nails bitten off.

Three generations, still strangers. Looking at them in repose, though, without the yelling or the door slamming or the glowering expressions, she felt something she hadn't expected, love, like a tiny votive candle, burning modestly, yet steadily. A winsome smile crossed her face. Then faded as she thought about the uncertainty ahead.

Maggie had been bleeding continuously. It was manageable, at first, but troubling in its volume with each passing day. She'd been to the restroom three times already and the final leg of the flight was still ahead.

In the ladies' room before they boarded in Liberal, Roz had broken into tears. She hadn't slept in two days. She was so bone-weary that she could think of nothing except losing her child. "What have I done?" Roz kept saying. "Nothing. You have done nothing," said Laney. She took her daughter into her arms. Roz went limp as a glove. Gone the tension, the resistance, the push-back that had defined them. Laney breathed deep the scent of her daughter, damp and earthy.

Laney pulled up her mask and sat. She checked the time. They would be in Chicago soon, then it would be two and a half hours before they landed in Rochester. What was awaiting them? They had laid a heavy weight on Franklin's shoulders. Could he find an OB/GYN who was available right away? Could surgery be scheduled soon enough?

And—Gretchen? What was she doing there?

There hadn't been a shred of connective emotional tissue between them since the day they met at Franklin's first shoe store. Laney had been a "sweet young *thing*" in Gretchen's eyes, a "gold digger," a "manipulative little bitch." Was she right? Perhaps. It was clear when Franklin fawned over Laney, giving her the grand tour of the store, treating her like a princess, she had felt swept away by the attention and wanted as much of it as she could get.

Her own father had berated her beauty, as if it were a foul odor that only attracted boys who wanted one thing, "a piece of that," he'd say, pointing at her. Her mother would scream at him, but in her next breath warn Laney that her father was right, she'd better be careful because all she had were her looks, and "boys don't care for much else."

In a whisper, she confessed that was how she'd met Laney's father. He came around "looking for something." And he found it, she said, red streaks of guilt on her face. At least, when she found out she was in the "family way," he did the right thing. That was the saving grace, the thin gauze of dignity covering the whole shameful affair.

Franklin had been honorable, generous, and kind. She felt comfortable, protected, safe with him. That had to be love, she thought.

Franklin's adoration meant she didn't have to care at all what Gretchen thought. So, she didn't. And she made sure Gretchen knew it. She flaunted her designer clothes and her beautiful home in the most exclusive neighborhood.

Gretchen's preoccupation with her brother waned when she and Griswald got serious. Then they moved to Pennsylvania. Distance suited Laney and Gretchen's relationship perfectly.

She was stunned when Griswald was killed, but her feelings hardened again when Gretchen made it clear Laney wasn't welcome at the memorial service. She even raised Franklin's ire with this sleight.

But she was back, living with Franklin, it appeared. It was unclear why, although Franklin had made a point of saying he'd been sick. It was not unusual for him to claim 'sickness' when it suited him. He was often sick when she made plans to go shopping for the day. In the early years, she'd jettison her plans so she could stay by his side. In later years, though, his claims of infirmity would hasten her departure.

There were question marks punctuating every aspect of this trip, chief among them, the health and well-being of her granddaughter. Next in line were Franklin's expectations, Gretchen's animus, and Roz's long delayed homecoming. Would they all be sucked into a black hole or would they, by some miracle, achieve harmonic convergence?

She looked at Roz and Maggie again, then reached into her bag, pulled out two colorful N95s, assessed the cost/benefit of slipping them onto their sleeping faces, then put them back in her bag and closed her eyes.

CHAPTER 35

Sandman sat in Liberal Airport's empty parking lot watching a lone plane taxi onto the runway. There was nothing to stop it.

In the moments before she'd gone through security, Maggie had taken his hand and squeezed it. She smiled and tried to speak, but her voice got lost before the words came out. "That's okay," he said. "Thanks," she said. Neither of them knew what she was thanking him for, but it seemed like the right word.

The plane sat on the runway for a long time, engines roaring. He opened the glove box of Laney's car, took out packs of tissues, a pile of masks, three tubes of lipstick. He got out of the car and put them in a trash receptacle. He opened the trunk, as well. There were assorted bungees, a gallon of windshield wash, and a case of Fiji water. He opened a bottle and took a drink. Always wondered what was special about it. Turned out there was nothing special about it.

He slammed the trunk shut and got back into the car just as the plane lifted off, veered slightly, and soared into the deep blue. In less than a minute it was a speck.

He took the envelope from his pocket.

He never got to know Laney, not really. She was a rich lady from back east. Well heeled. Particular about what she wore, what she said, what she believed about Covid. Her masks seemed to cover more than her mouth and nose.

She'd blustered into the Sunrise Motel parking lot driving a dazzling, lavender Mercedes. He assumed she was only stopping to ask for directions. He was surprised and embarrassed when he gave her a key to one of the rooms, but she never commented on how sad, how worn it was, or how sad and how worn he was.

There was a connection between her and Maggie, although, at first, it was unidirectional. Maggie didn't seem to care.

But Laney was like water, drip, drip, dripping all the time. She drip, drip dripped until she had made a mark that Maggie couldn't ignore. Maggie opened up to her and that's when he saw another side of Laney, her tenderness, her caring. She loved that girl with a furious kind of love. Sandman understood how that could happen.

He felt honored when Laney came to him for help. They needed to get to the Liberal Airport first thing in the morning, and she didn't want to leave her car in the parking lot for someone to steal. She wanted him to park it at the motel and keep watch over it. He shook his head, "Sure."

She handed him her keys and a credit card. Sandman drove into town and filled her up at the Conoco. He leaned against the car as he pumped, acting like it belonged to him. More than a few people honked or gave him a thumbs up as they drove by. He nodded nonchalantly, casually lifting one hand, and tipping two fingers at them. He steered with one limp wrist and took the long way through town while returning to the Sunrise.

Laney was outside her room, bags beside her when he drove up. He packed her luggage in the trunk, and asked if there was anything else he could do. She thanked him and said she'd be ready in the morning, 4:30am.

Once on their way the next morning, Maggie slept in the back seat, her head in her mother's lap. Roz nodded off, too, leaning against the window. Laney sat in the front beside Sandman. It was quiet for the first ten miles or so, then Laney took a deep breath, curled up, her head resting on her travel bag, and went to sleep. He watched the sunrise and listened to the cadence of their breathing.

Laney hung back from the other two as they went through security. She thanked Sandman again, then opened her travel bag and pulled out an envelope and gave it to him. He assumed it was a tip. When he hesitated to accept it, she told him not to argue, that she wanted him to have it.

Later, back in the lot, he held the envelope up to the light. He saw a small slip of paper inside. Sandman tore open the envelope and fished it out. A purple post-it was stuck to the paper. "Don't think of this as a car. Think of it as your future," it said.

He studied the pink slip of paper and shook his head. "What...?" Then he read it slowly. "You gotta be..." And then a third time. He laughed and smacked his leg. "You've gotta be shittin' me." He held it at arm's length in front of his face. "I'll be damned."

Sandman found New Country 98.5 on the dial, cranked it up, and laid rubber tearing out of the Liberal Regional Airport lot. He started blaring the horn a mile before he reached the Sunrise. Juanita came running, Sofia close behind. Sandman stepped out of the car and into a cloud of dust.

"What is wrong with you?" said Juanita.

"Look at this." He held up the pink slip. "You know what this is? It's the title to this car. I am now the proud owner of a lavender Mercedes Benz automobile."

Seeing how excited Sandman was, Sofia hooted and hollered, then jumped into his arms as he swung her round and round.

"This is good?" said Juanita, cautiously.

The next morning, Sandman drove fifteen miles to the nearest Walmart. There he bought a tiny plexiglass frame. When he got back to the motel, he put the post-it-note inside. He stood the framed note on his bedside table so he would see the message first thing every morning and the last thing every night.

CHAPTER 36

Franklin perused the Hudson News near baggage claim. He bought a *Sports Illustrated*, a Snickers, Reese's Peanut Butter Cups and a Bag of Lay's. Gretchen yawned and checked the time. The plane would land in two hours.

"Hungry, are you?" said Gretchen.

"I'm a growing boy."

"You know we could have eaten a seven-course meal and still gotten here early."

"But I would have missed out on all this," he said, holding up his bag of junk food.

Neither of them had slept. When Gretchen gave up and came downstairs for a glass of milk, she found Franklin standing outside on the front steps in his bare feet. Uh oh, she thought, is it happening all over again? The 'New Castle Episode' as she thought of it, had rattled her confidence in Franklin's emotional state.

Once they got home from Pennsylvania, Franklin seemed almost normal. His sense of humor, his memory, the yardsticks she used to measure his well-being, were much better.

They didn't talk about their father. She didn't ask if Franklin had had any more visitations. But when he couldn't sleep, when she'd find him awake and wandering at night, she'd feel a jolt of panic.

"I'll get us some coffee before the sugar coma sets in."

Franklin watched his sister walk away. When she'd first arrived at the house, he was apprehensive. When they were kids, he once called her "persnickety." Since she didn't know what the word meant, she didn't know how to respond. Later, she looked it up. When she saw "fussy...difficult," she tracked him down and took a roundhouse swing at him, landing a punch on his shoulder. "I figured you'd be back," Franklin had said with a laugh.

Griswald concurred with Franklin, although he never used the word "persnickety." "She irons my T-shirts and underwear. She arranges my socks from least worn to most worn. My eggs and bacon and toast are arranged on the plate the exact same way every day."

Franklin howled at this, but also thought, If it weren't for Gretchen, Gris would never get out of bed in the morning, he'd eat nothing but Frosted Flakes, he'd never go to work.

Two weeks into her stay with him, Franklin realized she affected him the same way. If it weren't for Gretchen, every day he'd sit in his recliner, wearing only underwear and his ragged terrycloth robe, eating caramel corn, sugar coated nuts, and drinking Mountain Dew.

Although Gretchen understood he was ill, how he dealt with it pissed her off. In her view, he was wasting his life, which had nothing to do with Covid and everything to do with Laney. She decided that had to change, whether he wanted it to or not. Whatever her motivation, there was no doubt Gretchen's fussiness made a difference. He had thanked her multiple times. Once, she said, "Sorry for being so difficult." He laughed. "If you weren't 'difficult,' I wouldn't know who you were."

Gretchen watched her brother as he added creamer and Splenda to his coffee. Recently, she'd seen a documentary about rock balancing, the art of stacking different shaped stones into pieces of art. Some of them were not to be believed. She wondered if they were super glued together. How else could their balance be explained?

That's what she thought of when she looked at her brother. All his parts were connected. But the balance was delicate. And there wasn't any super glue to hold things in place. An outsider might not notice. But she did. She knew that life's gravitational pull could bring him down at any moment. A single stone, a snippet of his heart, a splinter of his mind could slip and fall, and he would be gone. Could the plane coming from Chicago be his undoing?

"Okay, yeah, thanks," said Franklin, sticking his cell into his pocket as Gretchen approached.

She put both coffees down on the table beside him. There were stir sticks and several additional packets of sweetener in a pile of napkins.

"What was that?" she said.

"Nothing. Just confirming tomorrow."

"What time?"

"One."

•   •   •

Maggie nibbled Saltine crackers her mother had brought from the Save-a-Lot. Roz opened a bottle of water. "Drink," she said, worried her daughter was getting dehydrated. Maggie had been to the restroom a half dozen times at Roz's last count. She opened her shopping bag to see how many sanitary napkins were left.

Her mother was finally asleep. Laney had paced the aisle so often and for so long that she could have made better time walking to Rochester than flying.

Despite Maggie's episodes of pain and nausea, when moments of panic arose, Roz was surprised how well her daughter was handling everything, how strong she was.

When Roz was pregnant with Maggie, she had morning sickness throughout the pregnancy. The nurse at the clinic said it wasn't common, but it also wasn't uncommon. "Can't you stop this?" she'd said. The nurse took Roz's hand and squeezed it gently; she cocked her head to one side and looked at Roz with eyes that said, You're so young, aren't you? "Fuck you then, if you can't do anything," said Roz. The nurse let go of her hand and left the room.

All the other pregnant teens had their pimple-faced boyfriends or still-very-young mothers with them. Roz could tell she was getting extra attention because she was alone. A social worker came in next to offer her some services, including food stamps. "Get lost."

The social worker had long graying hair, a triple chin, and piercing blue eyes. Her face said, I give a shit, but only up to a point. "You're making this impossibly hard for yourself, aren't you? Good luck with that."

Roz was a kid, but her outer shell had grown so thick, so hard by then, that she didn't know how to be a kid in need, how to touch or be touched. The shell had softened over the years, but not much. She still projected a snapping turtle aura.

She reached into her bag for more Saltines and balanced a stack of them on Maggie's armrest.

Maggie drank several sips of water. "Thanks, Mom," she said, as she nibbled another Saltine.

Roz wished they weren't on a plane heading east. She wished her daughter wasn't going through this ordeal. But she also wished this tiny moment could last forever. That she could sit beside her daughter, stacking Saltine after Saltine on her armrest, her daughter saying over and over again, "Thanks, Mom," in a tone so easy, so matter-of-factly appreciative, that Roz would know what heaven was like.

•   •   •

Gretchen pulled an envelope from her purse.

"What's that?" said Franklin.

Gretchen held it up so Franklin could read the return address.

"Came yesterday."

"Jesus, how many is this?"

"Three."

Since her appearance in court during the Edgar Stinson-Golding sentencing, Gretchen had received two, now three, letters from his mother, Edith. The first one read like a letter from a childhood friend, full of newsy items about what was going on in Ellwood, the proposed railroad museum, the new Sheetz Plaza, the hospital bankruptcy. Reading it, you would never have known that Edith had a son, a son who had murdered her Gris.

She read the first letter several times, shaking her head. She put it back in the envelope and took it to the recycling bin, but didn't deposit it. Instead, she tucked it in the kitchen junk drawer.

When the second letter came, she put it in the kitchen drawer without opening it. Two days later, though, she read it. Edith talked at length about the fall festival in Ewing Park. In the last paragraph, she abruptly changed topics. She apologized for writing to Gretchen, but said she felt compelled because of what they'd shared. She often thought of how they had clung to each other in the Busy Beaver parking lot, anguished at the thought of what was happening inside.

Then everything changed and would never change back.

Edgar refused her visits. Her letters to him were returned unopened. Her friends turned their backs on her. She received hate mail daily and vicious graffiti stained her house. She thought coming back to Ellwood was the right thing to do, but it wasn't. She had found an apartment several towns away and would move soon. She hoped it would be far enough.

Instead of "Sincerely," she closed with, "I hope someday you won't hate me." Gretchen cried tears of rage. How dare she? How could she ask anything of me? she thought.

She opened the third letter. In the first line, Edith apologized for asking Gretchen not to hate her. She'd felt foolish as soon as she had dropped the letter into the mailbox.

Her big news was that Edgar had written to her. He'd been in and out of the infirmary a lot. Cracked ribs. Broken nose. Concussion. But they'd taken him out of population again, so he'd be safer.

"I can't believe she thinks you care about this bullshit," said Franklin, reading over her shoulder. "Nobody is sent to solitary confinement as a safety measure. I'm sure he earned his transfer."

What must it be like to love someone who is evil? Gretchen and Gris had seen Edgar's dark heart even as a young boy. They worried about how many people he'd hurt before he was killed or went to prison. They saw it in Edith's eyes, she knew, she understood her son was "different," as his teachers would say. He didn't feel things, he didn't care. Something was missing. No matter how closely she looked, there was no silver lining to the dark cloud of her son. Somehow, she found a way to love that dark cloud. He was her son, after all. You love your child no matter what. And blame yourself.

Edith included her new mailing address.

What Gretchen didn't show Franklin was Edith's P.S. which was on the back of the letter: "Edgar told me to tell you he hasn't forgotten what you said."

Gretchen looked at the passengers arriving from Charlotte as they converged on baggage claim. A skycap bumped her leg. "So sorry," he said. Gretchen's gaze returned to the letter crumpled in her lap. She opened it, then smoothed it on her thigh, folded it, and put it back in her purse.

"You okay?" said Franklin.

"Okay enough."

He rubbed her back briskly with the palm of his hand.

"Why do things go the way they go?" he said.

"Because."

Franklin checked the arrivals. The plane was on time. They would fly over Niagara Falls soon, then begin their approach to Rochester.

•   •   •

"This is your Captain speaking. Those of you on the right side of the plane, if you look out your windows, you'll see beautiful Niagara Falls."

Laney didn't open her eyes. She'd been there a dozen or more times with Franklin, three times to celebrate anniversaries. They'd ridden the Maid of the Mist on their twentieth. Even their hooded slickers couldn't protect them from the dense mist, like pins and needles, pelting them as the ship ground its way into the vortex of Horseshoe Falls. The deafening roar was intoxicating. Afterwards, they had crossed to the Canadian side for dinner under the awnings at Queen Victoria Place. They lingered at the bar well into the night, watching massive colored spotlights turn the falls into a cascading rainbow. She smiled, thinking of it.

Roz stood and leaned over her daughter so she could get a better view.

"Wow," said Maggie. "Something, isn't it." In fifth grade, Mrs. Fisterbaum had shown the class a video about the Falls. Living in Oklahoma, it was hard to imagine such a torrent, such a wonder. Mrs. Fisterbaum had the students close their eyes. She turned up the volume and then sprayed mist into each student's face. Some of the kids yelped when the water hit them. Others laughed. It had a calming effect on Maggie, as if she were being washed clean.

"I guess," said Roz. "Looks like a toilet bowl flushing forever."

Maggie side-eyed her mother.

Minutes later, they were fastening lap straps, returning seats to their upright and locked position, and dumping any refuse they'd collected during the flight.

Maggie's stomach turned over as they started the steep descent. She perspired and her hands tingled. When they hit dense cloud cover over Lake Ontario, it was like disappearing into a suffocating blanket of soiled cotton. Her equilibrium was deserting her. She tilted forward, about to faint, but there was no place to fall.

"Mom," she said.

"You're okay, you're okay." Roz reached for a bottle of water. "Here, here, drink this."

Laney hit the call button and leaned into the aisle, waving to a flight attendant.

Franklin nudged Gretchen and pointed at the arrivals. "Just landed."

They jumped up from their seats and rushed to the waiting area on the floor above them, where they watched anxiously.

"Here they come," said Franklin.

"Where?"

"There," he said pointing to a cluster of people heading their way. Upon closer examination it was a contingent of Disney Worlders garbed in the finest rodent-wear.

The security guard, masked and sitting at his post, looked up from his phone.

"Chicago flight?"

Brother and Sister nodded.

"They're waiting for their gate to open up. Be a few more minutes."

Ten minutes passed, then fifteen. First there was a trickle of travelers, then a steady flow, and finally, the stragglers.

"Where are they?" said Franklin.

"Ladies' room?"

Several more minutes passed before EMTs arrived on the scene, their soft soles screeching on the floor as they rushed a gurney through the checkpoint and sped down the concourse.

"What's going on?" said Franklin.

"I don't know...something," shrugged the security guard.

"Shit," said Gretchen.

CHAPTER 37

Franklin's eyes were glued to the ambulance ahead of him, tailgating it through as many redlights as possible.

"Poor girl, I mean, she got lightheaded and then threw up and just when she thought she was okay to walk, she fell in the aisle and hit her head. I mean, really." Laney turned and looked at Roz sitting in the backseat beside Gretchen. "You okay?"

Roz nodded and then opened the window a few inches.

"You can put it the whole way down, if that'll help," said Gretchen. "Franklin, could you turn the heat down? It's roasting back here."

This wasn't how Franklin expected the reunion to go. He imagined a cordial welcome, an exchange of hugs and smiles. He would load the luggage. Maybe they would stop for dinner on the way home. All of this would create the right atmosphere for, well, whatever. But this, this high-speed chase through the streets of Rochester desperately trying to keep pace with the ambulance as it slashed its way through traffic, his only granddaughter inside, a granddaughter he hadn't yet met, speeding, speeding to save her life, or at least make sure nothing was broken, it was too much.

It was hard to believe that Laney was right there beside him, looking radiant as ever despite the situation that had brought them together again. She explained in rapid fire how Maggie had been pregnant, but not in a traditional way, and how Oklahoma's laws meant they couldn't help her, despite the danger she was in, and how scared and frustrated they all had been, and how much she appreciated Franklin's help bringing Maggie to Rochester. He felt foolish, all he wanted was for her to smile at him.

He looked in the rear-view mirror at Roz, a middle-aged version of the frightened, angry girl who had left so long ago. The three of them were back together, not because they had chosen to, but because his granddaughter, once a child and now a woman, was in crisis.

"Jesus Christ," he whispered, then wondered if he had said this out loud.

Laney looked at Franklin, surprised at his empathic response to his granddaughter's catastrophic arrival at the Frederick Douglass International Airport.

"Exactly," she said.

Franklin was surprised that Laney understood how crazy it was, everyone being thrown together like this. "You, too, huh? You're feeling it? I thought it was just me."

Jesus Christ, she thought, does he think we're getting back together? Shit.

•   •   •

The ambulance hit every pot hole on every street. Maggie gripped the side of the gurney and listened to the EMTs talk about their favorite craft beers. She could see a ledge slowly protruding over her right eye.

Passengers on the plane had balanced on tiptoes to reach their luggage and then step over her to get out. Most were understanding— "So sorry." "I hope you feel better." —but some were not— "Jesus Christ, I'm gonna miss my connection." "Why do they let people drink so much on these goddam flights." Her grandmother snorted back tears and her mother yelled at the offending passengers. "Hey you, go fuck yourself." Maggie decided that closing her eyes and pretending to be unconscious was best.

•   •   •

Roz and Laney snuck into the emergency room, while Franklin and Gretchen got coffee, then paced the hallways. Eventually, Franklin found a seat in the waiting room, amidst the moaning throng. Did everyone in Rochester have an accident...or get shot? he wondered. He stretched his left leg several times and massaged his thigh. Gretchen put her coffee on the window sill behind Franklin and watched.

"What's wrong?"

"Nothing."

He stretched his leg a few more times, then stood, then sat again.

"Something's wrong," she said.

"Nothing. Pulled muscle." He took a tiny bottle from his jacket pocket and dropped two pills into the palm of his hand, then tucked them under his tongue. "Leg cramp pills."

Franklin stood, shook his leg, walked several paces, and turned around.

"Voila."

She clapped three times, then took his seat.

•   •   •

The emergency room doctor took one look at Maggie's Frankenstein-ish forehead and said, "We better scan this."

"I feel fine, really."

"That's good, but I wouldn't want you to leave without checking for a bleed." Then he was gone.

The three women looked at each other.

"This is best," said Laney.

. . .

Laney walked past a half dozen gurneys in the hallway, makeshift curtains separating them, loved ones crowded into corners, patients staring blankly at the ceiling. There must have been fifty in the waiting room, many sprawled on the floor, some crying, one couple playing cards.

Gretchen sat with legs crossed, a Styrofoam cup in her hands, Franklin leaning against the wall beside her. Laney had been surprised to hear Gretchen's voice in the background when she called Franklin about their granddaughter. She was surprised again to see her at the airport. Had she left Pennsylvania behind and moved in with Franklin? It made sense. Laney couldn't imagine living in the town where her husband had been murdered. People looking at you all the time, pitying you, reminding you that you were wounded, even broken.

Gretchen looked up and caught Laney's eye. Laney took her mask off. Neither one knew what to do, so they stood still for a few seconds, the noise and activity in the waiting room buffering them. They both were at the far end of middle age. The long, slow, final lap lay ahead. Life had been hard on them in such different ways. Neither could have anticipated any of it. And yet, despite their clashes, their mutual distaste, here they were, still trying to make something of this disordered, awkward fitting conglomerate, this family.

Gretchen nodded and Laney smiled and walked toward her, tired expressions on their faces. Laney reached out with a hand, but Gretchen ignored it and took Laney in her arms. She didn't say a word but held her tight. Laney could feel her breath on her neck, deep exhausted sighs.

Gretchen couldn't remember ever embracing her. It wasn't that all the old grudges and suspicions had faded away, it was more that they seemed foolish now. We only have so much time, she thought.

"I'm glad you're here," said Gretchen.

"You, too."

Franklin held his breath. He could see melancholy expressions on their faces, like two long-separated enemies who couldn't remember what the fight had been about.

They leaned back from each other, smiles on their faces. Laney wiped her eyes. He watched her closely, how she held her hands and tilted her head as she spoke. How she smiled at the end of every phrase and nodded affirmatively as she listened. How she clapped when she laughed. She seemed different.

For the first time in over forty years, he wasn't seeing her as an extension of himself, someone defined entirely by his love. He approached them, then stood a step or two away, waiting for permission to enter the conversation. Laney turned, a tired grin on her face, her eyebrows raised.

"Everything has been so rush, rush, I haven't had a chance to say a proper hello, so... hello." She laughed at this, then hugged him. Laney was startled by how brittle Franklin seemed, how weary, his body so delicate. People had always joked about Franklin being older than her but never about him being old. For the first time, that was the right word. She'd gone away, and he'd gotten sick and old.

"Hello, Laney." Not hello, honey, or sweetheart, or darling.

"Gretchen tells me you've been very sick." She shook her head and frowned. "Covid is so awful. Sounds like you had the worst of it. Sorry I didn't know. I would have, I don't know..."

"Yeah, he was in bad shape. Worried we'd lose him." Gretchen swatted his arm.

Franklin looked at his sister quizzically, unsure if she was being serious. "Really?"

"But he's getting better inch by inch," said Gretchen.

"Must have scared you two half to death." She reached for Franklin's arm. "You're lucky you have this sister of yours."

Both Gretchen and Laney were as tight as guitar strings. Breaking the ice felt good, but now what? Their relationship had been built on mutual disdain. They had looked at each other through the prism of Franklin. And what they'd always seen was so distorted, that standing face to face now, they barely recognized each other. Where was the acrimony that had been the lifeblood of their bond? Not knowing what to do, they settled on civility and pleasantness as satisfactory alternatives. It helped them *see* each other better, if not with 20/20 vision, at least 20/40.

As the three of them stood together, trying to get their bearings, Roz returned from the emergency room. Franklin had stolen glimpses of her while driving to the hospital, but they hadn't spoken to each other yet.

"The scan came back and looks like she's okay. No bleeding. Maybe a slight concussion but nothing bad. She doesn't have to stay," said Roz. Laney put her arms around her. Franklin drew close.

"Gonna get her stuff together, then we'll meet you." Roz turned to leave.

"Roz?" said Franklin. She looked at him over her shoulder. "That's good, that's good news. And, you know, it's good news that you're here."

She turned, facing him, shifting her weight back and forth. "Thanks, yeah." She looked at the floor. "It is for me, too. Yeah. So, thanks...Dad."

Franklin had forgotten what the word sounded like.

CHAPTER 38

Franklin awoke and sat up slowly. The leg cramp pills he'd taken the night before had done the trick. But while the cramps had subsided, the throbbing pain in his thigh had worsened. He was sure he'd pulled a muscle getting out of the car a week prior. He'd put ice on it regularly since then, but it wasn't getting better.

It was early and quiet, yet the house felt like it was humming, like it was filled with life in a way it hadn't been for a long time. He thought he heard Gretchen in the bedroom next door, but when her bed stopped creaking, he assumed she'd fallen back to sleep.

Maggie and her mom slept in Roz's old room. It had become a junk room in recent years, with boxes of old linens and stacks of books and piles of clothing intended for the Salvation Army. In the flurry of activity before everyone arrived, Franklin had cleaned and emptied the room as best he could.

Laney was in the downstairs guest room.

He got a whiff of coffee and assumed it was her, probably reading the news on her phone and enjoying her first cup. Having her in the house again felt like a minor victory. Back together, kind of. He told himself that it was over, but there was a faint voice inside that still whimpered, "Really?"

Maggie felt the lump on her forehead and the pain in her belly. She rubbed her bulge gently. "C'mon now, you're okay," she said. She went to the adjoining bathroom to change her pad. It was dark brown and more was coming. At the clinic they'd given her an iron supplement and encouraged her to take ibuprofen to offset the blood loss. The ibuprofen added to her nausea and the iron made her constipated.

She sat on the toilet, closed her eyes, relaxed her body, and did ten slow, deep breaths. "In, out, in, out..." In her darker moments, she had found this comforting. It took her away from her belly, her bleeding, her panic, and brought her back to the simplest of things, her breath.

When she stopped and opened her eyes, she picked five things to look at and to name. Washcloth, shower curtain, toothbrush, floor tile...Little One.

This took less than five minutes, but when she was done, she felt like all her free-floating parts had coalesced into a whole, a whole with cracks, a whole that could come apart in little more than an hour, but a whole nonetheless. That was enough to help her get up, dress, smile at herself in the mirror, and meet the day.

This morning, she pulled the curtain back from the bathroom window and admired a maple tree, nearly bare, surrounded by a yard covered in yellow and orange leaves. Then she threw up. "It will be okay," she said to her belly.

•   •   •

It was a slow start to a fast day. By 11:00am everyone had had ample coffee or tea. Franklin had made waffles, scrambled eggs, and bacon. He ate most of them. No one talked about the looming doctor's appointment.

Roz dug through her closet, pulling out memorabilia from the few years she'd spent in high school. Maggie unfurled a poster of Eminem, dark hat shading his squinting eyes, full beard, and a "fuck you" look on his face. Then she pulled out another poster, this one of Britney Spears, bright-eyed, bubbly blonde with a plunging sequins neckline. She held them up side-by-side.

"How do you explain this? I didn't know you were schizophrenic."

Roz laughed. "Hey, what did I know?" She unraveled a poster of 50 Cent. "This was my go-to, though."

"Alright, I get it," said Maggie, nodding her head in approval.

Maggie looked gray as a shadow, her skin, her eyes, everything. Her mood, though, was better than it had been since they left Righteous. She had stopped updating Roz about how she was feeling, how much blood she was losing, how much pain she was suffering. She was making it her own baggage to carry.

"So, honey, how are you doing, you know, with all this?"

She sat on the student desk beside the bed. "This has been going on for so long it almost seems normal. I wake up and the pain is there, the bleeding. Sometimes it feels like I've been possessed or something, and other times, it's just the way it is, you know."

"I'd gladly take your place—"

"I know. The pain is bad and all, but it's not the worst thing."

"Really?"

"No."

"So?"

"When I thought I was pregnant, I mean for real pregnant, I didn't know what to think. I was in shock, really. It didn't seem possible. I remembered almost nothing, you know, about me and Sandman. So, for a while, I kind of ignored it."

Roz nodded and sat on the bed.

"You remember at the clinic when that nurse asked me how I felt about it? And I couldn't answer?"

"Uh-huh."

"I wasn't being a little shit. I just didn't know. And then the pregnancy wasn't a pregnancy. Or it was and it wasn't. And I thought, what the... But I was so sick, so scared, that pregnancy or not, I just wanted to be done with it." Maggie swallowed hard. "But after a while, this thought, way back in my mind, this thought kept, like, speaking to me. And it said, 'You could have had a baby.' And even though I never had a baby growing inside of me, it was like I started feeling sad way down deep, because, you know, I could have…I mean, it was one of those 'might-have-been' things that you look back on with all this sadness and regret. Even though nothing was ever there, I started calling it Little One, not out loud, but in my mind, in my heart. Is that okay? I mean, is it okay for me to name something that's really nothing? I mean, I'll always remember."

Roz licked her lips and sighed. "Yes, it is very okay for you to do that, for you to love something, even if it was gone before it got here."

•   •   •

Maggie sat on the exam table, a roll of white paper crinkling under her. Roz moved her chair closer to her daughter. The others, Franklin, Laney, and Gretchen, stood against the wall. The florescent light buzzed like a dying hornet, and after twenty-minutes, the room was getting as warm and humid as an Oklahoma summer day. With each passing moment, the room got smaller and smaller. Maggie's mouth was parched. Laney searched through a cabinet for paper cups.

"This will have to do," she said as she filled a specimen container with water.

"What color is the water?" said Maggie. Everyone forced a laugh. Laney filled it a second time.

The most memorable thing the doctor said was "Whoa" when she opened the door. In her experience having so many family members in the exam room at the same time was unusual. "Lots of support, I see."

She was prepared. They all watched her computer screen as she walked through the scan results she'd received from Oklahoma. She pulled the curtain briefly and examined Maggie. It had been approximately twenty-one weeks since Maggie's positive pregnancy test. She explained molar pregnancy and gave Maggie a pamphlet on what to expect.

"So sorry. Must be very hard on you...all of you, actually."

Maggie stared at the wall while everyone nodded in agreement. They scheduled her D&C on the way out the door.

In the parking lot, Maggie vomited again. She drank two more specimen containers of water, while everyone waited by the car to see if she was okay. Once she gave them the high sign, Roz said, "There must be a Starbuck's around here somewhere?"

CHAPTER 39

The waffle mix, closed tight with a rubber band, sat on the shelf. Eggs lay nestled in their carton. Cheerios, Bran Flakes, and Life perched on the top shelf of the pantry. An open package of bacon was hidden in the refrigerator cheese drawer. White, rye, wheat, and sourdough breads lay on their sides, twist tied closed.

Maggie was fasting for the surgery so no one ate.

"You can eat, you know," she said.

"Full from last night," "Not hungry," "I'm fine," lied everyone.

The smell of coffee, though, was in the air. Franklin filled the carafe, while Laney placed sugar, Splenda, and cream on the table. Gretchen pulled mugs from the cupboard and arranged them in a cluster on the table.

"To each his own," she said.

In recent days, Franklin would boil water in the kettle for Maggie when she woke up. He would bring her a china cup and saucer from the dining room hutch, gold rimmed with a hand painted English Garden motif of peonies, hollyhocks, and lavender. He'd drop a tea ball of Earl Grey into the cup and place a honey bowl beside it. She would blush and say, "Thank you Grandpa."

Not today, though. She sat at the head of the table, arms folded, hair pulled back in a pony tail, no makeup. She wore yoga pants and a Lululemon T-shirt her grandmother had bought her. And white Crocs.

She had the option of a spinal or general anesthetic. "I don't think you want to be awake for this," her mother had said. She agreed. "I wish they could have given it to me a few days ago," she quipped. The procedure itself would be quick, fifteen to thirty minutes. She'd be in recovery five hours. Then home.

The doctor had been matter-of-fact when Maggie asked what to expect afterwards. "Not much, really. Light bleeding, maybe some cramping, but after a week, you should be good." The doctor nodded and smiled. "Pretty routine."

As she sat in the waiting room, Maggie thought how drunk she'd been that night, how she and Sandman had ended up together. She thought about the tests, the news she was pregnant, then that she wasn't. She thought about how trapped she felt when the doctor explained nothing could be done for her. She thought about her mother and grandmother fighting for her. She thought about the pain, all the times she spent on her knees over a toilet. She thought about the old couple they'd met at the hospital and Sandman driving them to the airport. She thought about her grandfather and her aunt, both at the ready when they arrived. She thought about all of them clustered around her, forming a nest to hold her.

When the nurse called her name, Maggie stood, looked at them all, then took a moment to give them each a hug. Amoeba-like they followed her to the door, where the nurse explained that only one family member could enter. "C'mon, Mom," said Maggie.

"I'm going to get some air," said Franklin. He walked gingerly around the parking lot several times while Laney and Gretchen pretended to read magazines. He tapped on the window and raised his eyebrows as if to say, 'Anything?' and they shook their heads.

He sat on the bench by the door. He zipped his jacket and watched dry leaves swirl in the wind. He rubbed his leg slowly, scrolled through Facebook, then email, and finally the most recent Instagram reels. He looked at the time repeatedly. He went back into the waiting room. Laney and Gretchen were leaning on their elbows.

"Shouldn't be long," he said. Neither one looked up.

CHAPTER 40

Three Months Later

Although some trees still clung to their leaves, the first snow had come during the night. Everything looked like it had been spray painted by a fastidious elf. The sky glowed like a silver bowl. And the sidewalk had yet to be cleared.

Maggie stood in front of the mirror, her palms against her flat belly. Although the bleeding had continued for almost ten days, the procedure had gone smoothly. The pain, so long her companion, had disappeared. No more nausea. No more vomiting. No more Little One. She and her mother had gone to the mall where she bought a small silver box with velvet lining. She kept her hospital bracelet inside.

At her grandfather's behest, she had taken a job at his inaugural shoe store, still called Stafford's, a name that promised quality. He and her grandmother had also opened a tuition account in her name, available for whenever the time was right to start community college.

In their house she felt at home. Oklahoma seemed a distant memory.

Her mother had been less convinced about where home was until recent days, when she decided to remain in Rochester. Farewell Save-a-Lot. Farewell flatlands and whistling winds and long horizons. She had come home to stay.

"You be ready soon, Maggie?"

"Yes, I will...where's the dress?"

"In your closet. Need help?"

"No."

Roz had collapsed once Maggie disappeared into the procedure room. It was like her daughter was being torn from her womb prematurely. Laney tried to comfort her. Anything could happen, she thought.

Franklin had gone outside again, finding a bench to rest his leg. At the forty-five-minute mark, Gretchen went out to see her brother.

"You okay, Brother?"

"Yeah."

"For real?"

"Yeah, I'm okay, it's just…the waiting, it makes me crazy. It's not exactly the same, but do you remember when Mom was dying and we'd go to the hospital day in, day out, and just sit all day, waiting. What was it, like a week? But it seemed like forever. It felt like she would always be dying but never die. And we would always be waiting, but nothing would happen."

"It'll be okay, Brother."

"I don't like waiting. Never have."

When they turned back to the family waiting room, Laney was at the door.

"It's done. She's okay. She's okay." She began to sob and fell into Franklin's arms.

Maggie came home the next day to a sheet pizza from Salvatore's and a double chocolate cake from Wegman's bakery. Her grandfather had hung a banner that said, "Welcome Home."

•   •   •

At Sephora's Laney perused row upon row of lipsticks, all the shiny luscious tubes, like Rockettes at attention. She picked up a tube of Rouge Dior, Paris satin finish. Franklin had bought her the first tube just before they went to Paris for the first time. They'd been married eight years. He knew nothing about lipstick or Dior, except that it was French and it was expensive. He included airline tickets in the box. When she put on the lipstick for the first time, he said she could go directly from the runway at de Gaulle to the fashion runway at Dior or Chanel. She didn't know who they were, but she loved how the slender tube felt in her hand.

He bought her a tube every year for Christmas. For a time, she stopped wearing any makeup and when age urged her to try some again, she used a lighter touch and seldom wore the Dior. Her collection of unused tubes was stashed in a box underneath her makeup table.

The girl behind the counter was dressed in a black jump suit with a wide pink belt, pastel pink lipstick, smokey eyeshadow, mink strip lashes, and purple fashion contacts. When she saw the tube of Dior, she said, "Good choice. That should make a difference."

"Thank you?"

In the jittery excitement after Maggie's surgery, Franklin and Laney found themselves awake at midnight in the kitchen. Laney got the Orville Redenbacher's out and popped a couple of bags in the microwave. Franklin poured two Genny Cream Ales and they settled into their usual places at the table.

They reviewed the events of recent months, Maggie's pregnancy, Franklin's surprise at how Roz had changed, his bout with Covid, her stay in Oklahoma, and how delicious the popcorn was. Then they were silent. After a moment, Laney couldn't help but laugh.

"We ran out of gas pretty quickly, didn't we?"

"Forty years isn't bad."

"No, I mean here, now, talking to each other." Franklin laughed.

He went to the refrigerator for another beer while Laney nursed hers.

"You're right, though. Forty years. It's something," she said.

"Went fast."

Laney sipped her beer.

"You know, when you got off the plane and were coming down the concourse, I thought, 'My God, she's pretty as ever.' I did. And you are."

Laney smiled and reached for another handful of popcorn.

"But you were different, too."

"How?"

"On the way to the hospital from the airport, listening to you, it was like I was meeting you for the first time." He looked down. "No, that's not exactly it. It was like I was getting to know you for the first time."

"What do you mean? You probably know me better than anyone."

Franklin chuckled. "I don't know if I can explain it. It's like...the other day I got one of those Facebook messages where the person asks you to checkmark how many states you've visited? You know, like ten or thirty-five, whatever. Before all this happened, if someone had asked me about you, I would have said fifty out of fifty, I was well acquainted with all of you. But I don't think that was ever true. Since you've been back, I probably know less than half of who you are."

There wasn't any complaint in his tone.

"I don't know what to say. I don't think I tried to hide—"

"I didn't look close enough," he said, his eyes downcast. "I'm sorry."

At first, when Laney exited the mall, she looked for her Mercedes, then remembered it was long gone. She got into Franklin's Lexus and opened her Sephora bag. She took out the lipstick, adjusted the rear-view mirror, and drew it gently across her lips, then puckered and kissed a tissue. She looked in the mirror again, surprised how much she liked what she saw.

•   •   •

Roz opened the manila envelope she'd found in a box of CDs in the family room closet. It was taped shut. The envelope was crinkled, one corner was dogeared, the edges of the masking tape were dry and curled. She would have put it back in the box and forgotten about it, except for how tightly it had been sealed. She became curious. It hadn't been opened in years and perhaps was never meant to be. And yet, here it was. Why hadn't it been thrown away?

When she tore it open and tipped it over, the first thing that fell out was a birthday card with a baby elephant on the front holding a cluster of pink balloons. She opened it. "Happy first birthday, my little peanut! Daddy loves you!" Each birthday card was there. A gigantic "Yay!!!" on her double-digit birthday. An "I can't believe you're a teenager!" when she turned thirteen.

She'd forgotten that he sent her his own birthday cards, even though he also signed the ones her mother got from both of them.

The card he gave her on her fifteenth birthday didn't reflect the gathering storm that would explode a few months later. "Wishing you all the happiness that life can offer!" There were more cards, sixteen through twenty-one, each bought after she'd left home. There was nowhere to send them, so he put them in this envelope. Each one signed, "Love you always."

Roz put the cards back in the envelope and hugged them to her chest. She tried to take a deep breath, but stuttered and began to cry.

She came downstairs, hoping to show the envelope to her mother, wanting to ask if she'd known all along, but she wasn't back from the mall yet. She turned to go upstairs again and noticed her Aunt Gretchen sitting in her father's chair, a crackling fire in the fireplace. Roz could see the back of her aunt's head, her curly graying hair. The reading lamp beside the chair wasn't on. Her elbow was on the armrest and her head was in her hand. A cup of coffee sat untouched beside her.

Roz took a step toward the study, then stopped. She called to her aunt in a whisper, but Gretchen didn't move. Roz watched for a few more minutes, then went up to her room again.

•   •   •

In the six weeks after his granddaughter's surgery, Franklin had felt contentment he'd never experienced before. He slept soundly and woke up early, feeling ready and expectant about each new day. He made hefty breakfasts for his family, drank beer with his daughter, told stories to his granddaughter, and realized he didn't have to hold his breath any longer when he saw Laney and Gretchen in the same room together.

Of course, there were slammed doors and disagreements, mostly over Covid and politics, but it was superficial, at least in Franklin's mind, never something that threatened the invisible silken strands that were slowly weaving the five of them together.

Though he wouldn't admit it to anyone, he found Laney's return, and the clarity it brought about the end of their marriage, to be a relief. He'd harbored unreasonable hopes that everything would work out. It had been a saving fantasy.

It was Laney's idea to go out for dinner at Grayson's.

"Grayson's?"

"Yeah."

"Why there?"

"Well...it was always our place, right?"

"Yeah, well, the last time we went I got indigestion and it never went away."

She laughed. "I was thinking it would complete the circle. We celebrate beginnings and dread endings. But the endings, endings are just as important. And deserve champagne."

They sipped Dom Perignon over eggplant parm and salmon. They talked about their daughter and granddaughter and said goodbye to their past. For Franklin, like most things, it was good and bad, but right.

·   ·   ·

Gretchen stared at the dancing flames and listened to the crackle and pop of the fire. She got up and jostled the logs, then added two more. She sat down again, curling her legs underneath her. She raised a cup of cold coffee to her lips.

She had found him in this chair, the fireplace quiet, the ashes cold. "Franklin?" she had said. His arm hung over the side. His head rested on his shoulder. His lips were pursed, his eyes half-mast. She was startled by his stillness. She took his hand in hers, his fingers as limp as a newborn's. "No," she whispered, then sat on the floor beside him and nestled her head in his lap.

They had been fooled by his clarity of mind and the absence of his cough. They had laughed about the hallucinations and the bumbling. It was merely a story of what had been and was no more. He had beaten Covid.

And yet. His leg. The tightness and cramping, at first. The soreness and swelling that wouldn't go away. A blood clot after all, loosed from its mooring, racing headlong to the man's heart, silencing his life. Yes, it was a remnant of Covid, said the coroner in his report.

•   •   •

There were four women standing in the kitchen, each dressed in black. "Are we ready?" said Gretchen, a stiff smile on her face. She would drive them to the municipal building auditorium where several hundred old friends and former customers would be waiting. They would give him a sendoff that would have made him blush.

CHAPTER 41

One Year Later

"How was work today?" said Roz.

"Good. I hired that girl, the one that stopped by the store the other day," said Maggie.

"*You* did the hiring?" said Laney.

"Yeah. He said 'You're the assistant manager now, earn your keep'."

"Really?" said Gretchen, a frown on her face.

"It was fine. He's okay, just a little rough-edged."

Roz looked at her phone. "You better get going."

"It's accounting, instructor's never on time." Maggie slipped her backpack over one shoulder. She took two granola bars from the cupboard and a cherry Celsius from the fridge. "Hey, look at this." She unzipped a side pocket, took out an envelope, and tossed it onto the kitchen table. "Read this. Pretty amazing. Don't wait up. I'll be late."

Laney opened the envelope. She looked at Roz. "My God, it's from Sandman."

It had been well over a year since Laney had given Sandman her Mercedes. Turned out he'd sold it.

A guy passing through from Oklahoma City had stopped, not for a room but to look at the car. He'd never seen such a thing. "A goddam lavender Mercedes! For sale? I'll pay whatever." Sandman

said he'd think about it. The man laughed and shook his head—
"That's good news, son!"—and tore off down the highway in his '67
GTO.

Two days later, he showed up again. This time, Sandman took
Juanita's advice— "Don't be stupid!"—and sold it, making a hefty
profit. He had enough money to buy a new sign for the motel and
upgrade some of the rooms. Again, Juanita said, "Don't be stupid."
Instead, he put a for sale sign by the highway.

Ten months later, the Sunrise Motel was gone, replaced by an
OnCue gas station and convenience store. For the first time in his
life, Sandman was solvent. He and Juanita bought a little house on
the edge of Righteous, where Sofia put in a small veggie garden.

"Says he bought some photography equipment and started
taking classes in wedding photography at the community center."
Laney held up a picture of a bridal party. "'This was my first job,' he
says."

There was also a wedding invitation in the envelope. Sandman
and Juanita were getting married.

Roz chuckled. "I wonder if she got down on one knee and said,
'Don't be stupid'."

CHAPTER 42

Two Years Later

The house was much quieter than it had been two years before. Maggie was the first to leave the nest. Once she became store manager, she got her own apartment on the other side of the city. She came for dinner on Sundays as often as she could, even bringing Ellen, the young woman who'd become the center of her life.

Roz moved out recently, after being promoted to produce manager at the Wegman's store in Gates. From time to time, when the liberal leanings of New Yorkers got to her, she'd threaten to go back to Oklahoma. But no one believed her, including herself.

As for Laney, no sooner had Franklin's death become public than men started calling, texting, and DMing her. She had to admit she loved the attention. She started dating and even fell in love briefly, but never fell hard enough to make a lasting match.

She told Gretchen that she was proud that, in the end, she and Franklin had never divorced.

"Hm."

"What?"

"Who knew his passing would save the marriage," said Gretchen, a glint in her eye.

Laney choked on her scone, she laughed so hard.

"My God, Sister-in-law," she said.

ABOUT THE AUTHOR

Until It Was Gone, is David B. Seaburn's tenth novel. His work has received numerous honors. He started his professional life as a Presbyterian minister before switching to mental health and academics. When not writing, he collects old baseball cards and Lincoln head pennies. Seaburn and his wife live near Rochester, NY. They have two married daughters and five wonderful grandchildren, and he loves to spend time doing just about anything with them. An avid reader, David has been keeping a journal for over fifty years.

BROKEN PIECES
OF GOD

DAVID B.
SEABURN

NOTE FROM DAVID B. SEABURN

Word-of-mouth is crucial for any author to succeed. If you enjoyed *Until It Was Gone*, please leave a review online—anywhere you are able. Even if it's just a sentence or two. It would make all the difference and would be very much appreciated.

Thanks!
David B. Seaburn

www.ingramcontent.com/pod-product-compliance
Lightning Source LLC
Chambersburg PA
CBHW060700190726
48289CB00002B/491